I0618718

For my family.

Table of Contents

Chapter 1

The Mover twirled the stick above his head, spinning it between his fingers as the bark flaked off and floated down into his hair. He didn't seem to notice as it nestled into his tight curls and stuck to his skin. Instead, he continued to dance, moving almost gracefully around the stage that he'd created for himself. Though Rohan knew he shouldn't, he couldn't help but be drawn in. He wasn't the only one. The crowd edged closer as their curiosity got the better of them. The children couldn't hide their excitement and pushed their way through to get a better view. Rohan grinned, when he'd been their age, he'd done the same. That was the thing, they'd all seen it before. Movers had been around for years performing the same tricks and telling the same stories, but for some reason there was still something magical about what they did.

Rohan watched as the man knelt down and handed the stick to the unwanted of the city. Like Rohan, these children had been abandoned by their families, surviving only on what they could beg, steal, or borrow. Even so, the most callous of merchants watching couldn't help but smile as they took the branch from the Mover and smacked it on the ground searching for answers. Unable to find anything unusual, they handed it back to the Mover, faces scrunched in confusion and frustration. He smiled consolingly before leaping to his feet and throwing the branch into the air like a circus performer. He caught it easily and twirled it behind his back as the disappointment on the children's faces was replaced once more with wonder. Rohan watched, not the Mover, but the crowd as they stared in awe. Rohan smiled once more, then went to work.

He slipped through the watching audience, bumping into merchants and townspeople, dipping his nimble hands into the purses of the distracted. Into his pockets went nails, food, wire, and anything else he could wrap his fingers around. The merchants scowled and gripped their bags tightly as he pushed past. They recognized him as one of the unwanted, and their natural suspicion prevented him from stealing more. Rohan rewarded their distrust with a knowing wink. This did nothing to endear him to them and they lashed out with swift kicks or knees to the leg. Rohan laughed and skipped out of reach. He knew they wouldn't do anything more. As much as the merchants hated him, they were pragmatic to a fault. Rohan's victims were their best customers, and following the show, those customers would return to the market to replace what had been stolen. So, while the merchants publicly rebuked the thefts, they quietly purchased their own goods back from him and resold them for a tidy profit. So, Rohan continued working his way through the crowd. By the time he reached the other side, his pockets were bulging. For a small crowd, it was a good return. He was about to make his escape when he saw the Mover raise the long branch to eye level and begin to move his hands across its splintered surface. Rohan paused surprised. This was something he hadn't seen before. A stillness fell over the crowd, and only the shuffling of feet broke the silence. The Mover's hands began to flash over the wood. At first, it seemed like nothing was happening, the long branch doing nothing more than spinning furiously between his fingers. Then with a small squeak, one of the children pointed at the end of the stick, directing the eyes of the audience. The stick had changed so slightly that many were still questioning whether anything had happened at all. That doubt evaporated as the branch began to grow, lengthening until the Mover could barely reach each end. The rough bark that covered its surface spread like butter on bread and morphed into the grain below. The crowd began to murmur in astonishment. Even Rohan's eyes bulged. This Mover was different from the others. Most of the time they entertained the crowds by levitating small stones or fusing together broken branches.

The Mover began to move his hands faster, flashing his calloused fingers over the wood. The bumps and knots that had covered the stick began to disappear, evening out the surface until it was as smooth as polished metal. It flashed in the sun, completely transformed into a long narrow staff, as perfect as if it had been tooled by a machine.

Then, in an instant, the stick exploded into a shower of splinters.

The audience, so intent on the transformation, leapt back in shock. One moment, the Mover had seemed in complete control, the next, he was staring at a pile of kindling.

As the last splinters fell to the ground, the crowd clapped politely before turning back to their day. Rohan watched as the Mover recovered from his own shock to beg the retreating audience for a token of their appreciation. Most brushed him off, but eventually some of the children convinced their parents to part with a few small coins. The Mover nodded in appreciation before making his way to the nearest alley and collapsing. It seemed that the explosion had sapped all the energy from him, and he lay motionless, his eyes vacant and defeated.

That was the problem with Movers.

As amazing as their powers seemed, they were practically useless. Anything more than lifting a few rocks completely drained them. At any moment they could snap, their eyes going blank, and their bodies retreating into shells. That was why most of them ended up as beggars. Not an easy life in a region with nothing to spare.

Rohan, like the rest of his audience, turned back to the market, keen to relieve his pockets of their burden. He had no intention of being caught with stolen goods and quickly unloaded his takings to the same merchants that lashed out at him only moments before.

Chapter 2

Rohan's current home was a communal structure known as Shackle St., a decomposing rat hole composed of crumbling concrete and rust. Once upon a time it had been a school for the unwanted of the city, but those ideas had died long before he moved in. Now Shackle St. was an incubator for crime, drawing the filth of the city into a single building.

While Rohan appreciated the education and shelter Shackle St. provided, he was also bound to its only rule. The rule was simple. Once you turned sixteen, you could no longer call it home. It ensured the building wasn't overrun with bodies and provided space for the unwanted that would inevitably make their way through its doors. For Rohan, that time was approaching quickly, and it left him with only two options.

The first was to join one of the gangs. It was an option that provided safety, in numbers and shelter. Its disadvantage was having to pass a brutal initiation. If unsuccessful, you usually ended up dead or sold to the North. That was the second problem. Most of the gangs were aligned with the North, and their main job was to find people to work in their mines. Rohan had seen too many of Central's citizens taken this way, and he had no desire to be part of that life.

His other option was to find a place of his own. This gave him independence and meant he didn't have to work for the North. Unfortunately, it also left him vulnerable, both to the gangs and the elements. Central was unforgiving and so were its people. Any mistake could cost him his life. Still, as Rohan made his way between the abandoned cars and rubble that littered the city streets, he felt confident in his choice.

Tonight, Rohan was headed towards the financial district, a scarcely populated section of the city. He'd tried to find something in a nicer area, but the choices were limited. So far, he had found several temporary shelters, exposed holes in buildings, covered eaves and even a few abandoned vehicles, but nothing permanent. There was a problem with all of them. Either they were too visible, too small, or encroached on gang land. His destination tonight was a disused kitchen on the fourth floor of a decrepit office building, and as he entered the space, he wondered if he'd finally found a home.

The floor was made of spotted linoleum, the type designed to hide stains, blending them into the pattern that crossed the floor. The walls were a uniform and inoffensive beige, and the cabinets, which now stood open, were a darker shade of the same colour.

Overall, it gave the room an impression of compromise. Nothing that would cheer a person or seek to brighten their day, but nothing to complain about either. In the corner stood a white topped plastic table and a couple of old steel chairs. The stuffing of the chairs had been torn out, most likely by rats, and the table wobbled as Rohan leant on it. It was perfect.

The space was fully enclosed, there was plenty of room for storage, and most importantly, it was close enough to the market to make daily outings. As he explored the room, he found loose tiles that could be pried up to hide food, and a small vent that would help cool the room at night.

Rohan sat back against one of cupboards and smiled. This was by far the best place he'd scouted. It was so good that he wondered why it wasn't already taken. As he took a moment to look around, it dawned on him. The room wasn't good at all. There were rat droppings on the floor, no electricity, and a weird smell that had leached into the paint. If anybody else had discovered it, they would have dismissed it as dirty, grimy, and lacking in basic facilities. Rohan allowed himself a wry smile, compared to Shackle St., it was a palace.

If it hadn't been dark outside, he would have headed back to Shackle St. to sleep, however, it was only the stupid that wandered the city at night. The threat of gangs and snuff addicts was real. The gangs would be looking for anyone wandering alone, whilst the addicts were filling their noses with a random concoction of tobacco and chemicals. This made them irrational and dangerous. Rohan shuddered. Snuff was tobacco mixed with anything from dishwashing detergent to paint, anything that could alter their state of mind. Sometimes it made them happy, sometimes it made them angry, and sometimes it killed. It was as scary as it was random. Instead, he settled in for the night trying his best to drift off.

It felt like his eyes had only been closed for a minute when his dreams were interrupted by a blood-curdling scream.

Rohan bolted upright, his heart pounding as the sound filled the room. It seemed to invade every crack and crevice, growing in pain even as it faded to silence. Rohan sat perfectly still, too scared to move. Screams in the night weren't uncommon in Central, but it was rare they sounded as close as this one did. Rohan waited in the darkness, his imagination ensuring that his eyes remained open.

The sound rang through the room once more.

This time, Rohan knew he wasn't mistaken. It was close, it was coming from the room next door.

Instinct told him to run, to flee from the danger that was only steps away, and he was only too keen to listen. Moving as quietly as he could, he slowly untangled himself from his bed and began to gather his things.

He was about to make his escape when he heard it again. Only this time it ended in a whimper.

"Please... I... I'm sorry."

Rohan stopped. The voice sounded familiar. Not friendly, but a voice Rohan recognised. He stepped back from the window ledge, driven by an invisible force to investigate. He edged towards the door that led to the adjacent room. Before he could let reason reassert itself, he found himself reaching for the cool metal door handle. With a delicate touch, honed from years of thieving, he turned the knob and peered into the room beyond. He withdrew almost immediately as the light from a burning fire stung his eyes. Once his vision cleared, he looked back, this time noticing the dark shapes moving purposefully in the flickering light. His stomach dropped almost immediately. This was not an unwanted neighbour; this was a gang interrogation. As he looked closer, he could see a group of gang members standing in a circle, crowding around a snivelling figure.

Rohan could tell that they were gang members by the softly clanking weapons that hung from their belts. Whilst not overly sophisticated, the weapons were none the less deadly. The most common was a sheared piece of metal, usually stripped from an old car or electricity box, shaped into a jagged blade with strips of fabric covering one end to form a handle.

One of the members, a skinny man with a mohawk, stood over the huddled figure, waving his blade angrily.

The huddled figure spoke, revealing herself to be the source of the whimpering Rohan had heard.

"I'm sorry, I tried, I couldn't get it."

The desperate voice belonged to a girl called Asha.

Asha was another of the unwanted, and like Rohan was coming to the end of her time at Shackle St. Rohan guessed that like many before her, she had chosen to join one of the gangs.

"Trying is not succeeding, nor is it rewarded," sneered the man hovering over Asha. "If we let failures join the Sun Bringers, we wouldn't be known as the strength of Central, would we?"

Rohan hissed silently at the mention of the Sun Bringers. Of all the gangs to join, they were the most ruthless. There were other gangs that were bigger, but none that struck fear into the hearts of the people like they did. The Sun Bringers took their name from the way they reinforced their threats. Whilst most gangs responded with simple violence, a broken arm, kicked in teeth, or in extreme cases, a side-street amputation, the Sun Bringers went big. If you displeased them or failed to respond to their threats, they would burn you down. They would set fire to your home, your family's home, and all your possessions. One of their punishments was to heat a serrated knife so much that it glowed, and then use this to cut the fingers from their victim. This elongated the pain and torture whilst simultaneously cauterising the wound. This was not a sympathy but a business decision. Dead people don't pay debts.

Sure enough, Rohan saw a black-haired woman heating a large, jagged blade over the fire that burned in the middle of the room. Rohan guessed that they weren't angry enough with Asha to hurt her permanently but felt she needed a reminder of the type of family she was joining.

The ringleader was now pacing the room, his feet scuffing the floor as he listened to the panicked breathing of his new initiate.

"If you wish to join the Sun Bringers, you must know the consequences for failure. If it was up to me..." He shrugged as though the decision was out of his control.

He took the blade from the black-haired woman and walked behind Asha's chair, he casually placed the white-hot steel on her exposed shoulder.

Asha let out a piercing shriek as the knife blackened the skin beneath it. Even from a distance, Rohan could hear the skin popping and cracking. Moments later, the nauseating smell filled his nostrils, forcing him to turn from the door and retch.

Rohan's mind was swimming as he wondered how anybody believed that joining a gang was a good option. Sure, it stopped you from being sold to the North to work in the mines, but at what cost?

As Rohan had no wish to join the gang and even less desire to be caught, he decided to take his leave. There was nothing he could do for Asha.

As he turned to make his escape, he bumped one of the chairs that remained abandoned in the room.

He watched in horror as it fell, its steel frame ringing loudly as it crashed to the floor.

He grimaced, holding his breath, hoping the sound hadn't travelled. For one brief moment he thought he'd gotten away with it. Then he heard a rush of movement in the next room.

He didn't need to wait for an introduction.

He hurled himself towards the exit, catching a glimpse of his pursuers as he escaped through the door and down the staircase.

"Get him," he heard a voice scream.

Rohan glanced back to see the leader of the gang brandishing the still glowing blade. His underlings didn't need to be told. They were already on their way, hollering in feverish excitement as they charged after him.

Rohan sprinted down the stairs, taking them three at a time, swinging around the worn bannisters as he turned each corner. His shoulder slammed into the wall as he made his way down. He grimaced in pain but didn't slow down. He knew that if he were caught, he would never see the sun again.

As Rohan reached the bottom of the stairs and broke into the night, he looked around. It was not an area he was familiar with. He didn't know the streets, the layout of the buildings, or any of the escape routes. He cursed himself. He should have scouted the area better. It was a rookie mistake to enter any area without knowing how to get out quickly. The only thing he knew for certain was how to get back to the market.

"That's it," he thought. The market. Nobody knew it as well as he did. If he could make it that far, he could lose them.

He didn't wait for the gang to arrive, and instead, turned on his heels, sprinting down the street. Moments later, the gang exploded from the building, their knives brandished in the same way as their leader. Spotting Rohan moving away, they ran after him, screaming in excitement as the bloodlust filled their ears.

As Rohan ran, he could hear the doors around him slamming closed. The people of Central had heard the hollering and followed basic protocol. Don't get involved and don't get in the way. As a result, they simply ignored what was happening on their doorstep.

If Rohan had used the same logic, he would have been back at Shackle St., lying safely on his patch of the floor. He cursed himself again as he dodged between the abandoned cars and trash that littered the road.

As he ran, he hoped that the gang would grow disinterested in the chase. That hope was quickly extinguished as their screams bounced off the buildings nearby. Rohan could tell that they were gaining on him as the yelling grew louder. He kept running, moving closer and closer to the market. Then, out of the corner of his eye, he saw the black-haired woman appear. She was carrying a large knife in her hand and grinning as she moved towards his right side.

"No, no, no," thought Rohan as he dodged a pile of debris. They weren't giving up, rather they were hunting him like a rat in the sewer.

As he turned back, he heard a loud bang and two large boots slammed down on the hood of a car next to him. He turned to see another gang member running beside him, laughing psychotically as he dashed between cars and over the fallen walls and uprooted asphalt.

Rohan's mind was screaming, drowning out the sound of his blood pumping. All he knew was that he had to escape.

They had surrounded him now. Two of them had overtaken him and were now running in front, blocking his escape. The others moved in closer as they began to close their trap. Rohan started to panic, glancing left and right as he tried to find a way out.

They were drawing closer and closer to the market and Rohan began to recognise the surrounding streets. He could see the stalls, the flags, and the containers that had been left behind from the day's trading. It felt alien to see it late at night, without the hustle and bustle that made it so captivating. That should have been the least of his concerns. His legs were growing heavy, and each breath felt like fire in his chest. It didn't appear that the gang members were having the same problems. They were stronger and faster than him and were accustomed to hunting the unwanted.

In that split second, Rohan decided that instead of trying to outrun the leaders, he needed to even the odds. So, he pushed harder, forcing himself to catch up to the gang members that had overtaken him. He leapt across the hood of a car, crashing through the weeds and thorns without stopping. In doing so, he edged sideways, drawing closer to the black-haired woman.

She had been running in front to prevent Rohan from rushing down any of the side streets. Unlike him, she ran above the debris, jumping from car to car to avoid the rubble.

Rohan waited, biding his time until finally he saw his opportunity, and as the woman leapt from atop a green station wagon, he charged.

Rohan catapulted into her, pushing the full weight of his body through her legs as she travelled through the air.

She yelped in surprise as her feet disappeared from beneath her. As though in slow motion her body spun and instead of landing easily on the car in front, she slammed into the back of the trunk. Rohan heard a sharp crack as her head collided with the fender and her eyes went blank.

He looked back, feeling guilty about the damage he'd inflicted. That was until he remembered that she'd been the one chasing him.

In the moment Rohan had taken to look back, the other members of the gang caught up. They didn't even stop to check on the woman. Instead, they hurdled her body, raging after their elusive prey.

Rohan zigzagged through the streets, trying to lose his pursuers, but they remained close behind. With his legs about to give way, he turned for what he thought might be the last time and immediately tripped, falling over a soft lump that lay strewn across the ground. It was the Mover from earlier in the day. Rohan had forgotten that the market was never truly abandoned. It was always populated by snuff addicts and beggars.

He fell forward, his palms ripping on the stones that littered the hard ground. Bleeding and exhausted he scrambled forward, jamming himself between a stack of broken crates. Seconds later the gang arrived.

"Where'd he go?" the leader demanded, his voice rasping as he struggled to regain his breath. His eyes scanned the alley, "find him."

Rohan held his breath, not an easy feat for someone who had just run the longest distance of their life. He could hear them working their way down the alley, searching for any signs of life.

They were almost upon him when he heard one of them yell out.

"Look what we have here!"

Rohan heard a deep thud as one of them kicked the Mover in the stomach. The Mover groaned and flopped onto his back.

"Pathetic," Rohan heard a voice say.

"Anything down there?"

The one closest to Rohan must have shaken his head because a moment later he heard the sound of feet shuffling away.

"Spread out. Find him."

Rohan dared not move. He was still catching his breath and his nerves were on edge. If it hadn't been for the Mover, he would definitely have been caught.

Slowly his wits returned, and he could take a moment to think. There was no way that he could go home to Shackle St. They had seen him and would have immediately recognised him as one of the unwanted. They would come looking for him, and no one would dare try and stop them, regardless of the rules. He racked his brain, searching in vain for a solution. There was nowhere he could go that he would be safe.

As Rohan sat in the dark alley, he lowered his head into his hands. Not only had he interrupted a Sun Bringer interrogation, but he'd hurt one of them. They would search all of Central looking for him. They couldn't let him escape, it would make them look weak and that was not something they could tolerate.

He let the enormity of his actions overwhelm him. He hadn't felt this alone since the day his parents were taken.

He remembered the feeling of his mother's hand slipping away from his, and how helpless he felt watching his father get knocked to the ground by the Northern soldiers. He felt the same now. Completely alone, and completely helpless. All he wanted to do was go home.

Instead, he waited, listening as the gang combed the stalls around him. They were angry, focused, and determined to find him. Rohan knew that the longer he stayed where he was, the more likely they were to find him.

He waited until he heard the footsteps move towards the furthest stalls, then ducked out of the alley. He kept his head down, trying to stay out of sight. He ran in a half crouch, weaving in and out of the wooden crates, desperate to avoid detection. He didn't have far to go, if he could make it down the next street he could escape into the safety of the city beyond.

As Rohan peered over the top of the crate, he could see two of the gang members casually knocking over stands and boxes in their search. It was now or never. He moved forward, preparing to sprint down the street.

He didn't know what it was, but in that moment, Rohan knew he was in danger. He spun, coming face to face with the mohawked leader. The knife he carried had long since cooled, but its razor-sharp edge remained. He swung it hard at Rohan who dove to the ground, barely avoiding the blade. The knife sliced into a wooden crate, throwing dust and splinters into the air. If Rohan had any doubts as to the deadliness of the blade, it was gone now.

The mohawked man pulled the knife out and strode towards Rohan. Rohan scrambled backwards, his feet sliding beneath him. The man walked purposefully forward, brandishing his blade in front of his victim. Across the market, the remaining members of the gang whooped in excitement as they noticed the commotion.

The gang's leader swung again, this time catching Rohan on the arm. It was a glancing blow, but enough to draw blood. The mohawked man grinned. Rohan realised that he wasn't trying to kill him; he was toying with him. He continued to prod at Rohan, drawing his blade in and out of reach, threatening, but not striking.

Rohan backed away until he found himself pressed against a stall covered in a sticky concoction of dust and blood. Rohan reached over his head, scratching at the top of the crate, too scared to take his eyes off the knife. Finally, his fingers found what he was looking for. It was a long wooden board, marked with a thousand cuts. It was one of the chopping boards used by the butcher. Rohan had recognised the stall the moment he'd smelt the distinctive steely musk. The board was stained a deep brown and was worn at the edges from years of use. Rohan grasped it in both hands as the mohawked man laughed at his pitiful attempt to protect himself.

"You think that will save you? You are nothing more than a bug."

He swung his blade harder this time, expecting Rohan to use the board as a shield.

Instead, his eyes widened as Rohan rolled to the side.

Rohan had predicted his move perfectly, and instead of backing down, he moved to attack. With a hand on each side, Rohan gripped the board tightly and with all his strength slammed the board, not into the face of the man, but directly into his shins.

Rohan heard the sharp crack of wood colliding with bone and winced at the scream that followed. In attacking the man's legs, he'd made a tactical decision. He knew he didn't have the physical strength to overpower the man, so hobbling him was the next best option.

Rohan leapt to his feet, running for the side street, knowing that if he could just make it that far, he could escape. He could see the other gang members still making their way towards him, but they were too far away, he was going to make it.

He looked back one last time to make sure the mohawked man was still down.

The leader of the gang hadn't given up easily. As Rohan had scrambled to his feet, the hobbled man took the only option available to him. He drew his arm back and hurtled his knife at Rohan's back.

As Rohan turned, he stumbled and as much as he wanted to dodge the blade, his feet wouldn't cooperate.

So, he waited. He waited for the knife to plunge into his chest, he waited for the fear to overcome him, and he waited for the panic to take control.

Instead, he felt a calmness wash over him, like still water in a teacup. He could see every vivid detail of the blade rushing towards his chest. He could see the nicks in the steel, the dimples on the metal, and the threads that formed the grip of the handle. Time hadn't slowed, but Rohan's awareness of the moment intensified like the sun under a looking glass.

As the blade cut through the night, he could hear it ringing. That sound was music, but not just music that he could hear and feel. It was music that he could touch and shape. He raised his hands, barely in control of his own actions and as though capturing the sound, directed the blade away from his body. Rohan watched as the knife curled like a swooping crane and crashed into the stalls nearest the incoming gang members.

They dived for cover as the blade ricocheted off the wooden benches.

Rohan fell to the ground once more, stunned and a little frightened.

The mohawked man stared at him, unable to move or speak.

Rohan looked down at his hands, then back at his tormentor. He had no explanation for what had happened. Finally, after what seemed like an eternity, he came to his senses. He scrambled to his feet and sprinted down the alley nearby, leaving the gang members staring at the knife that lay bent and twisted on the ground.

Chapter 3

Rohan hid in the darkness, shivering in fight and shock. He had barely made it down the alley before his legs crumbled beneath him. He wasn't used to running so far, and the enormity of the last few moments exhausted his reserves.

He was close enough that he could still hear the gang members talking.

"He can't be."

"How else do you explain it? Have you ever seen a person catch a knife mid-air and redirect it at somebody else?"

If only they knew the truth thought Rohan. He hadn't gotten anywhere near the blade.

The silence hung in the air until a voice proclaimed triumphantly, "see, there's no other explanation. He had to be one of the Faithful."

Rohan ears pricked up at this.

The "Faithful" were a bedtime story; one of those tall tales that parents told their children. They were both fearsome and fearless. They were bogeymen, snatching children off the street on one hand and protecting them from the North on the other. They were an enigma, both praised and cursed, but ultimately, they were nothing more than a fairy tale.

Rohan heard the shuffling of feet moving closer.

"What are you two blabbering about?" he heard a voice demand. It was the voice of the mohawked leader and from the sound of it, he was none too pleased.

"We was saying…" one of them started before abruptly stopping, realising how foolish he sounded.

"Saying what?" snarled the leader.

Rohan could only imagine that the man was looking at his feet awkwardly now.

"…that he was one of the Faithful," he heard the voice mumble, clearly embarrassed.

"What? The Faithful?" snapped the mohawked man incredulously. "Have you lost all your brains? You're a stupid Northerner you are. He was just some little unwanted that got lucky."

Rohan heard the man continuing to berate his underlings as they moved away from his hiding spot.

He'd never been more relieved than he was now. He leaned forward, resting his head in his hands. The pressure he'd been feeling in his chest released in a single breath. This moment of calm was immediately followed by a sharp pain as something hit him in the back of the head. He didn't even get the chance to open his eyes before passing out.

Chapter 4

Something hard was poking into Rohan's ribs. It was sitting uncomfortably and no matter how much he tried to ignore it, it demanded attention. He groaned as he rolled over, instantly relieved from the pain in his side.

His entire body ached as if he'd been scrunched up like a piece of paper and then hastily flattened.

"How did I get here?" he moaned as he slowly gathered his bearings.

He was lying on a cold damp floor, the moisture leaking through the thin cloth of his shirt and pants. There was an overpowering aroma of mould and mildew and as his vision cleared, he could see a steel gate blocking the only exit. In the distance, or perhaps they were standing right next to him, Rohan could hear voices. In his present state of mind it was hard to tell, but as his mind began to clear he was able to focus on the words being spoken.

"He's not much. I know Edith said to chase every lead, but this one's a bit thin."

"What on earth were they talking about?" wondered Rohan. They were the ones that brought him here, they must know what he'd done. His mind was too fuzzy to fully understand what was happening.

"Wha!!! WHAT ARE YOU DOING?!!" screamed Rohan as a bucket of water hit him directly in the face.

"Wake up," he heard a voice growl.

Standing above him was the most terrifying man Rohan had ever seen. The man wasn't overly tall but had arms like tree trunks and a neck that pulsed with every heartbeat. With his very being, he radiated strength, control, and an intangible force. For a few moments, Rohan sat blinking in the details of his captor. Yes, he was a physical specimen, but beyond that first glance, Rohan saw more.

The man was strangely tattooless, something exceedingly rare in today's society. It was as though he had no connections, no permanent holds placed upon him. His eyes were a steel grey, revealing nothing about the man, except intelligence. Even his age was nearly impossible to determine. His head was completely bald, and his ears crumbled like paper thrown in the wastebasket. He wore a short beard, cut square on the edge of his chin. If Rohan looked closely, he could see that it was flecked with silver, but barely so. All these features combined only strengthened the appearance of the man, who was the physical embodiment of a rock.

"Com'on then, I don't have all day to wait on your sorry arse," said the man as he swung open the door of Rohan's cell. He reached and using a single hand hoisted Rohan to his feet.

"Follow me," said the man and stalked off without waiting for Rohan to respond.

Given the alternative was to stay sitting in that dank cell, Rohan followed the hulking specimen down a long narrow hallway. They were obviously underground somewhere as the walls of the walkway were composed of jagged rock. They were moist to the touch and every twenty paces or so Rohan spotted moss growing up the sides. The floor was slippery, and Rohan had to walk very carefully to avoid falling. This was almost impossible as his captor moved with unexpected speed.

Finally, they reached a long staircase with the sun radiating through the opening. The rocks in the hallway sparkled as the sun hit the droplets that clung to its jagged edges. Rohan shielded his eyes to avoid the glare and followed the man upwards.

Moments later, he found himself in the courtyard of a long-abandoned housing complex.

Filling the courtyard were people from every background, creed, and station. It was the most diverse group of people Rohan had ever seen. Rohan had noticed that people tended to stick with others like themselves, yet in this single courtyard in Central, these people had come together. Rohan immediately questioned this line of thinking. Was he even in Central anymore? In reality, he had no idea where he was.

The people in the courtyard all seemed to be deeply involved in one thing or another. Some were lifting heavy stone blocks and hurling them from corner to corner, some crowded over chess sets, and others were simply sweeping the compound. The rest seemed to be involved in some sort of physical combat training, but it was nothing like anything Rohan had ever seen. Every motion was smooth, deliberate, and beautiful. Rohan found himself staring at the group, trying to take in every moment.

The courtyard itself was a dull grey colour, obviously not designed to house the upper echelons of society. It was crumbling in certain areas and almost everything in sight was cracked, chipped, or in the process of falling down. There were bright flashes of colour where the steel supports had rusted into the surrounding concrete. These glinted with bright red and browns, contrasting the dull grey of the buildings.

A rough hand shoved him in the back. "No lingering," gnarled the human rock. "I was halfway across the courtyard before I realised you weren't following."

Rohan reluctantly tore his eyes away from the courtyard and trailed after the man.

Eventually they reached a small building that separated the courtyard from what appeared to be a second compound beyond. The man marched up the stairs towards a large steel door, pounded upon it and waited impatiently for it to open. After what seemed an eternity, Rohan heard a voice yell hoarsely from the other side, "who's there? Identify yourself."

"Takash," the human rock responded. "Now open this blasted door or I'll knock it down."

"All right, all right, keep your hair on," laughed the man through the door. The man Rohan now knew as Takash growled in response.

The man was still laughing to himself as the door swung open.

"Shut up," snapped Takash at the grinning man.

"Oh, come now, don't be such a sour puss," smiled the stranger as he winked at Rohan.

Rohan looked at him in surprise. Not only had he been expecting everybody to be as serious as his captor, but for some reason, the smiling man seemed familiar. Before he could think further, Takash interrupted his thought.

"Galvor, the only reason I'm sour is because I have to put up with you." He pushed past the smaller man impatiently and entered the room beyond.

The room had a slightly musty smell, as though the structure of the building was rotting away. The floor beneath their feet groaned with every step as though its very existence caused it pain. Even the rugs lying atop looked as though they were fighting for their life.

"Who the hell are we meeting here?" thought Rohan.

"Edith, Edith!!!" bellowed Takash. "Where are you?"

"That blasted woman is always hiding," he grumbled to Rohan.

After what seemed an eternity, a huddled figure emerged from a dark passage at the end of the room.

"Who is that?" whispered Rohan to Takash.

"She's the one that determines whether or not you go back to that rat hole I just pulled you out of."

The huddled woman was not what Rohan expected from the leader of a cult. It had to be a cult, right? Dungeons, weird fighting, and rundown housing. Rohan didn't know much about cults, but it fit into everything he imagined.

The lady was tiny. So small that Rohan imagined she was shrinking in front of him. She wore a pale blue nightgown that looked like it had seen better days. It was frayed at the bottom with the bare threads dancing upon the dust of the floor. There were moth holes covering the dress that made it almost appear translucent, as though she were some sort of incorporeal being. As she shuffled towards him, he feared she might break.

"Hello dear, it's so nice that you could come," smiled the woman called Edith.

"What can you tell me about him?" she asked, seemingly directing the question at Takash but never turning her face away from Rohan.

"We found him in the city. No family to speak of, been living at Shackle St. for the past few years. Calls himself… um… oy, boy, what's your name?"

Rohan blinked, almost failing to comprehend that someone was talking to him. "Uh, Rohan, Rohan," he stammered in response. Takash grunted.

"Well, let's have a look then," said the woman in a slow soothing tone. She walked in front of him slowly, staring him up and down.

Rohan felt like a chunk of meat in a butcher's window.

Rohan imagined she could see everything he was. All his faults, his flaws, the tiny cracks in his spirit. She could see the pain that shaped him, the agony of losing his family, of scraping through every day to survive, of just being him.

After what seemed an eternity, she spoke again.

"Well, it's definitely there," murmured Edith. "It's buried deep, like a splinter after a hard day's work. It won't just come out naturally, you'll have to poke it and prod it, and try to squeeze it out of him. You may even have to cut it out. Even then, you may not get it all."

Rohan looked at her, his face revealing his confusion. "What the hell was she on about?" he thought.

Edith moved across the room, distancing herself from the others, as though contemplating her words. "Hmmmm, it won't be easy, but with hard work... well, you never know."

Chapter 5

It had been two years since Rohan first come to the "Grey". That's what they called the compound they all lived. Not a hugely original name, but appropriate none the less.

If Rohan's first impression had been one of urban dilapidation, then it had only been reinforced by living there.

The Grey was in every aspect grey. The inhabitants wore grey, the blankets they used at night were grey and every question was answered in grey. What Rohan meant by this was that no answer was ever clear, it was always a compromised answer.

He once asked Takash what colour the sky was. Takash responded, "well, it's different to everybody. To you it may be blue, but right now its pink." He waved his hand at the setting sun. "In a few hours' time it's black. Why don't you tell me? What colour is the sky?"

"Blue," thought Rohan in frustration.

Even so, as he woke in the early hours of the morning, he counted himself lucky to be a part of the Grey. He had seen what happened to the others that left Shackle St. and he didn't envy them.

As he rolled out of his cot, he peered into darkness and saw the other recruits starting to stir. All he could hear was the sound of softly shuffling feet and the occasional cracking of bones. Nobody dared to break the silence with idle chatter. Like the others, Rohan dressed silently and then turned to make up his cot. It was one of the absolute rules of the Grey. Every recruit was required to keep their personal space pristine. The leaders of the Grey maintained that starting the day with order, brought order to your day. Rohan wasn't sure this was true but didn't see a reason to argue.

Rohan waited in the darkness for the leaders to inspect the barracks. They walked in together, none speaking, each holding onto the still of the morning. As they inspected the room, they nodded satisfied allowing the recruits to relax. Eventually Takash signalled that they should follow him out the door. Rohan breathed deeply as they escaped the musty air of their sleeping quarters. As much as life had changed, the joy of leaving his sleeping quarters remained the same.

As they entered the central courtyard, they spread out into perfect rows, leaving an arms breadth between each other. This had become automatic, and even as Rohan wiped the sleep from his eyes, he found his position in line. He waited in silence as Takash patrolled the lines, reminding the recruits to use the time to prepare themselves for the day ahead. Rohan stood with his eyes closed, wondering if he could actually fall asleep again. He'd almost managed it when he felt the first warm rays of the sun peek over building walls.

As the sun enveloped them, it signalled that it was time to start the day. They quickly broke into small groups composed of recruits of similar ages. It made sense, Rohan supposed. He didn't have the same knowledge as some of the older recruits, nor could they cope with the physical demands made of him. As one of the youngest, Rohan was placed into a group commonly referred to as the "Pups." He hated it. He'd lived harder and rougher than most and in his mind that demanded some level of respect. But nobody else cared. In fact, nobody else complained at all, they just did as they were told.

Rohan knew exactly what was coming next, and he looked forward to it. They were about to set out for a run. Most envision a run as a leisurely trundle along level streets, sometimes with beautiful scenery to look at, a sunset in the background, and maybe a hint of perspiration upon your brow. That was not running, that was jogging.

These runs were a physical and mental challenge that Takash had turned into a game, one with gut wrenching, bile ensuing punishment for losing. The premise was incredibly simple. On "Run", you had to keep up with him. He would disappear into the city with the goal of losing his pursuers, and for every minute it took to find him, you had to run a lap of the Grey. The first time it took Rohan almost two hours.

This morning, Rohan waited in anticipation; his heels raised in expectation. He was the only one of the recruits that stood any chance of catching their elusive teacher, and he longed to close the gap. Takash sprung from the compound like a rabbit scared out of a briar patch, leaving the recruits in his wake. For a man built like a mountain, he could move like a feather in a hurricane. Rohan sprinted after him, desperate to maintain contact. He had learnt from experience how easy it was to lose Takash in the maze of buildings that surrounded the Grey. He was inhumanly wily and seemed to disappear with ease.

On these runs, they explored abandoned sewers, scrambled up drainpipes, cross crumbling buildings, and sprinted down narrow alleyways. Today was no different. Takash scrambled and shimmied across buildings as though they were on a flat running track, often leaping across huge divides to escape his pursuers.

Rohan trailed behind him easily at first, content to warm up his muscles before the real chase began. His fitness had increased significantly since that night running from the Sun Bringers. He'd physically changed as well. No longer was he the malnourished unwanted that stalked the markets each day. Instead, he could be described as an above-average height, if slightly, gangly-looking youth. His hair, once a tangled mess of weeds, was now cropped short with two lines shaved into his scalp. The lines ran from his left eyebrow to the nape of his neck. He had done this himself. It was standard practice for recruits to shave their head. Too much hair got in the way. It got hot when you ran, required more maintenance, and overall, wasn't worth the hassle.

Takash pushed on, glancing behind to see if Rohan was still on his tail. When he saw Rohan grinning back, he scowled and began to speed up. Rohan smiled. His extra height allowed him to glide over the pavement and float across the divides that separated the buildings. Still, it wasn't enough to catch the bald-headed man, and moments later, his teacher disappeared from view.

Almost an hour later, he found Takash sitting comfortably on a ledge overlooking the city. Takash didn't say anything but nodded as Rohan trundled into view. It was a further fifteen minutes before the others started to trickle in, their grey shirts stained with sweat and dust. Rohan sat patiently on the ledge waiting for the stragglers. It was a brief moment of freedom, away from the regiment and structure of his daily life. He didn't sit down too long. He'd long since learnt that sitting around too much left him with stiff muscles, and as exhausted as he was, the day was not yet done. The afternoon was a tightly packed combination of workshops and physical training sessions.

The workshops focused on understanding the history of Central and building an understanding of militia tactics used before the fall. When Rohan started in these classes, it was tedious. He'd been forced to start with the alphabet, basic grammar, and mathematics. Things that were never taught at Shackle St. It came as quite a surprise to find that these lessons came easily to him.

The physical training sessions were more mundane. It was a mixture of strength training, hand-to-hand combat, and weapon handling. After a while it became mechanical, a regular series of moves, twists, and turns. Rohan genuinely believed that if he tried, he could complete the entire routine in his sleep. However, every now and then, Takash would pit the recruits against one another. These bouts were vicious, with the fight not ending until someone lost consciousness. At first Rohan didn't understand the need for these contests. They seemed brutal and unnecessary. However, as he witnessed more fights, he grudgingly recognised their usefulness. They made you innovate and respond to the unexpected. All those hours of repetitive training were important but couldn't replicate the feeling of actually hitting a person. You needed to have an opponent that could adapt, challenge you, and force you to out of your comfort zone.

The contests could be divided into two groups. Either they lasted for hours, each recruit clawing and kicking until one collapsed in exhaustion, or they lasted about twelve seconds. Usually when this happened, it was a case of poor strategy. Often a lighter fighter attempted to get inside the guard of a larger stronger opponent and failed dismally.

Rohan made this mistake the first time he fought one of the recruits affectionately known as "Oak". Oak was the only one of the recruits who could match Takash for pure physical strength. He stooped as he walked through most doorways, and his neck resembled corded ropes. Rohan knew that physically he was no match for his opponent and that speed would be his only advantage.

Rohan started the fight by trying to sound out his opponent. He pranced around, circling his prey like a hummingbird circles a flower. Occasionally, he would dart in, trying to ascertain how much reach Oak had over him. On one such occasion, he flicked the hair off Oak's brow and threw a whizzing fist past his ear. Finally, he decided he'd figure out exactly how to get inside the giants reach and do some damage. The last thing Rohan remembered was the whites of Oak's knuckles closing in on his face.

After training and classes, the day still wasn't over. At night, they were required to scrub floors, cut vegetables, and wash laundry. Rohan didn't mind so much, although he joined in the general whinging. For him it was a time to unwind and relax. Besides, he'd been required to do the same thing back at Shackle St. and they didn't feed him.

Whilst Rohan had fallen into the comfortable routine of the Grey there were still a number of things that confused him.

The most prevalent of these queries were simple. "Why were they here?" and "what are we training for?"

As far as he could tell, they had no enemies, they weren't trying to take anything, nor did the Grey seem to have any particular belief system they were trying to impart. As much as Rohan tried, he couldn't seem to find any pattern or method to the madness.

Rohan had tried speaking with the other recruits, but the competitive environment was not one that bred trust. Most recruits were focused on winning, and they had no room for enlightened discussion.

The only recruit that Rohan had been able to make any headway with was Oak. Since his training ground stomping, Rohan had begun to take notice of Oak, not just as a presence, but as a person.

Oak was in himself a contradiction. Whilst physically he was an imposing figure, his demeanour was one of gentleness. Rohan watched as he held back during combat training, so much so that he allowed others to hurt him. Rather than stamping his authority during training and showcasing his pure physical strengths, he was like a sponge absorbing the aggression of others.

Rohan once watched a new recruit, a girl named Mara, thrash Oak with a wooden staff. Unusually, the rain had been pouring all day and the Grey was at its miserable best. There were streams of water overflowing from the rusted-out guttering, pouring through the cracked balconies, and churning up the grime that covered the pen. Mara had barely been there for a week, but already the strain had tipped her over the edge. Her clothes were torn, her hair was a wild mess, and her skin was marked with a thousand miniscule cuts. She'd tried to fight Oak, hoping that he would put an end to her suffering.

She launched her attack when his back was turned, slamming a wooden staff across his broad shoulders. Water shattered like glass exploding off the giant. Oak had turned in an instant, his eyes blazing with a cool fury, the years of training and preparation coming to the fore. His huge fist swung in a horizontal arc with the speed of an unleashed spring.

Mara stood eyes closed, awaiting the contact, seeking some sort of joyous release.

Unfortunately for Mara, Oak's skills were so well tuned that he stopped his swing mere millimetres from her battered face. Even mid battle Oak recognised that this attack was not a grab for power, but a cry for help.

Mara trembled in the rain, the droplets coursing over her goosebumped skin. She slowly opened her eyes, confused as to why the pain was still pounding through her mind. When she realised that Oak was standing motionless in front of her, she stopped. He'd denied her a moment of peace, and in her madness she snapped. Her feelings of hopelessness were instantly replaced by a fury, reminiscent of heated metal hitting water. It was unpredictable, it was untamed, and it was explosive.

She took the stick in her hands and began to beat it upon the body of Oak, hammering his knotted flesh. She struck upon him time after time, trying to elicit emotion from the man before her. She struck his legs, back and chest repeatedly, her own hands leaking blood as the force of her strikes reverberated through the weapon.

Oak stood resolute. The rain continued to pour, washing over Oak's bleeding form, cooling the welts that had risen across his body.

Finally, Mara collapsed, knees scraping the coarse concrete of the Grey, head bowed in defeat. Her splintered and bleeding hands turned the water rushing around her body a diluted crimson. Tears no longer flowed, and all the fire that had been erupting from her left only an empty shell behind.

Oak leaned down and in a cool, practised move, picked Mara up, legs resting beneath his huge forearms as she curled her body towards his chest. He turned and carried her back to the sleeping quarters, never once uttering a sound.

Mara wasn't in her cot the next morning.

It was then that Rohan realised that he needed to get to know Oak better. Although they had shared the occasional conversation, they were barely acquaintances. That needed to change. If he were to learn anything more about the Grey, Oak would be a good starting point.

Surprisingly, it wasn't easy to speak with Oak. He was constantly training, forcing his hulking frame through sequence after sequence, far beyond the capabilities of any normal person. Rohan could only marvel at his inner drive, recognising that his skills weren't a product of natural ability, but were the result of thousands of hours of commitment. This only reinforced his suspicion that the giant knew more than everybody else.

"Hey Oak," Rohan started as he approached the giant after training. They'd just finished weapons practice and Oak was putting away the sandbags they used in place of people.

"Hey Rohan," Oak replied in a friendly but suspicious tone. Nobody at the Grey intentionally sought someone out unless they wanted something. "What can I do for you?"

"Actually… nothing," Rohan replied.

Oak looked at him curiously and kept stacking the sandbags.

"I just thought it might be worthwhile if we got to know each other. We've been here longer than any of the other Pups, and I don't know anything about you."

"What's to know?" responded Oak. "You're here this week, maybe next week you'll be gone. Why should I waste my time?"

Rohan blinked in surprise. It was not the answer he'd expected. It was true, they were the longest serving recruits in the Pup group. Everybody that had been a part had either been promoted to another group, another work program, or had cracked like Mara. They were the only ones that had lasted.

"Don't you wonder why that is?" Rohan asked. "Why are we the only ones that haven't moved on? What's wrong with us?"

Oak shrugged, hefting the last of the bags onto the stack.

"Don't you want to know?" Rohan asked again.

Oak didn't even turn around.

"Really, you're not even going to answer me?"

Rohan stood looking at the giant's back frustrated, not even expecting a response.

"Really?"

Rohan's patience was wearing thin. He would have been fine with Oak telling him to go away, but he couldn't stand being ignored.

"Have it your way," he said angrily, and rather than walking away, he launched himself onto the giant's back, wrapping his arms around his neck.

Oak spun quickly, leaving Rohan holding on tightly as the rest of his body went flying.

"What are you doing! Get off me!"

"Answer me!" yelled Rohan, still spinning.

"No."

"Yes."

"No."

Rohan was preparing to yell again when Oak suddenly stopped. For a fleeting moment Rohan thought Oak had given up. That notion disappeared when Oak reached up and instead of trying to dislodge Rohan's arms from his neck, he clamped down.

Rohan realised what was about to happen too late.

Oak launched himself into the air, diving backwards so that they stretched horizontally across the ground. Rohan's whole body tensed in expectation as they inevitably fell back towards the earth. Though it wasn't far to fall, the sheer mass of Oak's body crushed Rohan like a soda can. Every bit of air was driven from his lungs and his head exploded into a kaleidoscope of stars.

Comparatively, Oak rolled off Rohan's limp body completely unharmed. Without bothering to look at his victim, he brushed the dust off his trousers and started to walk away. He'd barely made it three steps when he heard a faint voice call out.

"Let that be a lesson to you, you ruddy Northerner."

He turned back to see Rohan raising his middle finger at him.

"Yeah, that'll teach you," Rohan wheezed as he slowly propped himself up.

Oak looked at Rohan, unable to comprehend what kind of idiot would taunt the person that had literally just crushed him. It was completely absurd. Seconds later, Rohan saw the edges of Oak's mouth start to curl upwards. That smile grew and grew until he was bellowing with laughter.

He laughed so hard that snot began to run down his nose and into his beard.

Rohan couldn't help but join in. It was infectious, and soon his entire body was racked in convulsions.

It took a full ten minutes for them to compose themselves.

Eventually Oak, still smiling broadly, offered Rohan a hand up, lifting him to his feet with ease. Rohan's entire body hurt, both from the beating he'd received and the laughter.

"You want to talk?" Oak asked, unable to wipe the grin from his face.

"Not if this is what it costs," quipped Rohan.

Oak roared with laughter once again.

It wasn't a friendship, but it was a start.

Over the following weeks, Rohan did his best to build upon the inroads he had made with Oak.

It wasn't easy. Life at the Grey wasn't designed to encourage friendship.

To start with, Rohan began to observe Oak more closely. As he watched, he began to understand the man more. Rohan corrected himself. Although Oak was the size of a truck, he was only a couple of years older than himself. His sheer size created an illusion that he was older than he really was. Still, those years made a difference. Whilst Rohan was still growing into himself, Oak had surpassed that stage. He was more confident in who he was than Rohan could ever have been. It seemed like he had made conscious choices in determining what kind of person he had become. Rohan hadn't even known that was an option.

This confidence wasn't lost on others either.

Once, whilst lining up for supper, Rohan noticed Oak frowning. He followed Oak's gaze and saw that one of the brasher recruits had pushed into the queue, forcing the others back. Rather than allowing this to happen, Oak stepped out of line and placed a single hand upon the recruit's shoulder. The man turned sharply, expecting an argument, but stopped when he realised who'd approached him. Instead, he hung his head and shuffled towards the back of the line.

Oak hadn't said a word.

Somehow Oak had built himself a reputation that encompassed both fear and simple reason. Without saying a word, he admonished the recruit in a way that was silent but meaningful. It was like being told off by a child. You couldn't help but feel ashamed of your actions.

Now this wasn't to say that Oak was perfect by any means; he had more than a few imperfections, none more evident than his lack of interest in the workshops.

For one to whom lessons came easily, Rohan was disturbed by the attitude Oak took to class. In lessons relating to strategy and history, Oak became sullen and moody, often complaining about the time spent in the stuffy rooms. At first, Rohan thought this was purely a response to the room and a desire to be outside, however, he soon realised that it was more than that. Oak had no desire to try or to learn.

When Rohan asked him about it, he shrugged.

"Rohan, I am a soldier. I am being trained as a soldier. I can kick, fight, and punch better than almost anybody," he paused, his eyes resting momentarily on Takash. "I am not here to make big plans or to make the clever decisions. I don't know why we are here, but I know that when the times comes, I am supposed to be at the front."

Rohan wanted to argue but found he couldn't. Oak was a combat machine. He was the perfect combination of brute force and technique. And he was right. Oak was being shaped into a soldier, whether he liked it or not. This revelation was disconcerting. He didn't like the idea of being forced onto a path without knowing where it led. Not only that, they were being forced along with a giant electric prod.

The other element of the Grey that Oak struggled with was the runs. After watching him for a few weeks, Rohan realised that Oak had been built for power, not endurance. He was a man mountain, made of bulging muscles, and as a result of the training, running, and diet, he was in peak physical shape. The problem was that moving such a large mass required an enormous amount of energy. It worked great in short sharp explosions of power, but the long gruelling runs Takash forced on them were a personal hell.

As the runs began to lengthen, Rohan noticed that while everybody else was able to push themselves further, Oak was left running laps of the compound late into the evening. Night after night, he would trudge around the crumbling walls, his feet scraping the concrete as they barely pried themselves from the cracked surface. His posture sagged in these moments, revealing a determined, yet sullen youth. In contrast, Rohan found himself running less. The long runs enabled him to stretch his legs further and use his slight frame to catapult himself across buildings and divides with almost as much ease as Takash. He was still a long way behind but no longer losing ground.

Rather than copying his fellow recruits and adopting the dog-eat-dog mantra of the Grey, Rohan took the opportunity to cement his friendship with Oak and maybe get a little back on Takash as well.

One night, whilst running laps, he sidled up to Oak.

"How's it going?" Rohan asked, trying to sound jovial. He stepped in close, his stride matching the giant's as he glided easily along the well-worn perimeter of the Grey.

Oak grunted.

"C'mon," grinned Rohan, "it's not that bad, it's only another forty laps."

Oak mumbled something rather uncomplimentary, Rohan wasn't quite sure what he said but he definitely heard the words "Northerner", "blasted", and "Takash".

"Ahhh, you'll survive," laughed Rohan. "Besides, you get me for company."

He looked around the compound. A few recruits were finishing up their runs, and there was one veteran stretching in the courtyard, but other than that, the yard seemed deserted.

He turned back towards Oak, still striding easily. "You must love running. You seem to be at it every night."

Oak's face darkened, his eyes piercing Rohan with a black stare.

Rohan laughed as his eyes twinkled in the moonlight.

Oak grunted again, clearly not enjoying Rohan's humour.

"I've been thinking about the runs," continued Rohan, "and it occurs to me that they are… counterproductive. Those of us that are good runners, run less, while others…" Rohan eyed Oak sceptically, "well, they run laps."

Rohan waited, trying to come up with the right words to convince Oak to accept the idea that had been bouncing around in his head.

"You see, it occurred to me that we don't actually need to follow Takash."

Oak looked at Rohan as though he had lost his mind. He may have even told Rohan that, but he was using all the air in his lungs to haul himself around the Grey.

"What I mean is that all we get judged on is how quickly we find Takash. He always hides somewhere near the Grey and waits for us to arrive. What if, rather than chasing him all over the city, I just signal you when I find him? You can jog over from the Grey and rather than being exhausted from running everywhere, you'll just be, well… there?"

Oak continued to jog. Rohan expected this from his friend. Oak was by nature honest. The proposal Rohan had presented him with, while not inherently dishonest, was clearly against the spirit of the exercise. He watched as Oak mulled the idea over, dissecting it, and rebuilding it over and over again in an effort to find some flaw or reason not to accept it.

After what seemed an eternity, he finally stopped, his feet coming to rest on the stairs that lead to the Clinic, a closed off section of the Grey.

Rohan waited expectantly, searching for an answer in the lines of Oak's face.

Instead, he barely had time to register what happened next. Oak grabbed him in a hug that felt like the warm embrace of a log cabin. It was composed entirely of love, gratitude, and hard muscle. As Rohan felt his spine begin to warp, he grinned.

The following week, Rohan and Oak enacted their plan. They had spent the last few days discussing their options, and how they could prevent detection. Unfortunately, that also meant that they didn't get a lot of sleep, and Rohan was now mid nap during the morning meditation.

Takash's jarring bark snapped him out of his stupor.

"On my count. 3... 2... 1."

Takash was never one to prolong the inevitable and immediately sprung from the compound. Rohan followed quickly, winking at Oak as he turned towards the exit.

The biggest challenge Rohan and Oak faced was finding a way to alert Oak to the location of Takash's final stop. They discussed whistles, elaborate smoke signals, and call signs. Rohan was particularly keen on a crow's caw, but Oak quickly convinced him that it would be too obvious.

Instead, the solution presented itself as though it knew they were searching for it. During one of their late-night discussions, Oak was momentarily distracted by a solitary plastic bag passing slowly through the compound. It tumbled with the grace of an acrobat, rising, and falling with the breeze. It barely made a sound on its journey, caring only about filling it lungs to propel itself onto its next destination. In a moment of inspiration, Oak raced outside and captured the bag in one enormous claw.

As he returned, Rohan looked at him quizzically. Ignoring Rohan's puzzled face, Oak proceeded to unwind some twine from a nearby garden fence. He attached the twine to the handles of the bag, tying them together into a tight knot. Then without another word, he threw the bag into the air, holding tightly onto one end of the twine. The warm breeze that seemed to constantly dry out Central, picked up the bag in one swift motion, lifting it onto its arc. It began to climb, higher and higher, only failing to reach the heavens due to the thin twine that anchored it to the earth. Soon, the bag reached its limit, rustling gently as it glowed in the moonlight.

Oak grinned. The impromptu kite was the perfect solution. It was small and compact, making it easy for Rohan to carry. It was also innocuous and nothing that would draw the attention of Takash or the other recruits.

The plan was simple. Rohan would chase Takash until he was certain he had stopped. Then, before presenting himself, he would release the kite. After that it was up to Oak.

They had decided that it was important for Oak to at least pretend to run. As such, he would begin alongside the other recruits as they left the Grey. However, as soon as was reasonably possible, he would separate himself from the group and search for a clear vantage point. After this, it was simply a waiting game. He was to watch for the kite, and upon determining its location, retrieve it quickly and present himself to Takash. Both Rohan and Oak were immensely impressed with themselves for thinking up such a devilish plan.

The run went as predicted with Takash outpacing the recruits with arrogant ease. Rohan still marvelled at his ability to lose the recruits so quickly. One moment, he was running into a dark alley, the next, he was escaping out the back door of a neighbouring building.

Rohan easily outpaced the next best recruit, ensuring he gave himself plenty of time to set the signal for Oak. The run was standard as far as Rohan was concerned. Takash led them through the rabbit warren of buildings that surrounded the Grey, but eventually looped back to the far side of the Grey, near where the Clinic stood. Rohan finally spotted him seated upon an old waterpipe that lined the rooftop of an old apartment complex. Rohan quickly released the kite, allowing Oak a direct line of sight to Takash's resting spot. He then sprinted the final few hundred yards to his destination.

As Rohan waited for Oak to arrive, his mind was filled with a number of possible scenarios. What if they were caught? What did that mean? Would they get a telling off, or would they get kicked out of the Grey?

Rohan hadn't considered these possibilities before, and the thought made him sweat more than usual. In fact, before Oak arrived, he had managed to grow the stain on his shirt, creating a dark patch that ran from his chin to the waistband of his trousers.

However, his fears were unfounded as Oak stumbled in last, only marginally quicker than usual, and panting with the gasps of a man searching for his last breath. He winked at Rohan as he lowered his head between his legs and pretended to recover.

Takash grunted.

Chapter 6

In an effort to repay Rohan for his generosity, Oak took a more active role in his combat training. Whilst Rohan was certainly not a novice, his attacks lacked power and his defence was about as effective as swatting the wind with a pair of chopsticks.

Oak took this as a personal challenge and began instructing Rohan on the best way to utilise his speed. Rohan had a natural evasiveness, born from many years of dodging shopkeepers and merchants, but once contact was made, he folded like a pack of cards. Rohan always assumed that it was his lack of strength that held him back.

In order to disabuse him of this notion, Oak arranged a challenge between Rohan and a slight girl named Daiyu. Daiyu was a recent recruit to the Grey but had been fighting most of her life. She stood out from the other kids from her region due to a streak of silver that ran through her pure black hair. While this made no difference to Daiyu, it made her a target of the other children, and she was often attacked for being different.

Rohan looked at Daiyu with pity. He was Grey trained and was physically superior, both in strength and reach. It should be a short fight.

Daiyu had other plans. As soon as Oak lowered his hand to signal the start of the fight, she was on him. Even Rohan's natural evasiveness was no match for the speed and ferocity with which she attacked. In moments she was inside his defences, clawing at his eyes with her sharp nails. She instantly drew blood, her tiny fists slashing Rohan just above the eyebrow. Then, as Rohan blinked the claret from his eye, he felt a sharp pain in his stomach. Daiyu had turned sharply and rammed her pointed elbow into his gut. Rohan doubled up with pain.

He closed his eyes and fell to the ground as Oak signalled the end of the fight. He looked up to see Daiyu crouched over him, her breathing still even and controlled. With a look of disgust, she stood, kicking the dust on the ground next to Rohan.

"Well, that was effective," laughed Oak as Daiyu stalked away. He leaned down and helped his friend to his feet. "Do you see now that size and strength have nothing to do with it?" asked Oak.

"It's alright for you to say," snapped Rohan. "If she attacked you, you would just swat her away."

Instead of getting annoyed, Oak just smiled. "Yes, probably, but at least now you can't use your spindly arms as an excuse."

Once Rohan started listening to Oak, he quickly learnt that speed was just as damaging as size. Being able to shift your weight into an attack provided velocity. It was like a bullet coming out of a gun. Sure, a cannon might blast a hole through your torso, but a single bullet in the right spot was equally as effective. Rohan started to learn where the weak points in the body were and where he needed to strike an opponent to immobilise them. Fighting became less about the brutality and more about the game. How could he outsmart his opponents? How could he find ways to win? Even this was a release for Rohan. Most of the other recruits thought of the combat sessions as a physical test. For Rohan it became a mental challenge. He needed to understand how he could defeat his opponent.

Rohan also discovered that Oak's technique was a lot more nuanced than he'd given him credit for. He always assumed that Oak had physically overpowered his foes, but by training with him, he now recognised that Oak rarely utilised the full extent of his strength. Instead, he guided his opponent's aggression into positions that would allow him to defeat them quickly, efficiently, and with devastating ease.

It was during one of these sessions that Rohan once again asked Oak the questions that disturbed him most.

"Oak?" started Rohan, his arms swinging over the ducking head of his more talented friend.

"Yes, Rohan," he responded exasperatedly, clearly annoyed and amused by Rohan's lack of focus during the exercise.

"What do you think we're training for?" Rohan ducked.

Oak didn't respond but waited expectantly as he flicked the sweat off Rohan's brow with a professionally controlled feint.

"I mean, we're practicing every day, but what is it for? When is it our turn?" rasped Rohan, his voice straining from the mock fight.

"To leave or to fight?" Oak asked this time, kicking Rohan gently in the chest, pushing him away.

"I don't know. To do something."

"Let me ask you a question then. Why don't they come back?"

Rohan had never thought about that before. He'd always assumed that whoever left the Grey was going somewhere better, wherever that might be.

A depressing silence settled over them as they stood apart, catching their breath.

"I don't know," said Rohan finally, shaking his head. "But I don't want the answer to be a surprise."

Following their conversation, Rohan started looking closer at the goings on of the Grey. He started taking notice of the little things he had let pass before. He started taking notice when recruits stopped turning up to morning runs, he started taking notice when Takash barked orders, and he started taking notice when things weren't right.

He noticed Oak doing the same.

This went on for months, and although he found more questions, the answers remained as elusive as ever.

Late one evening, following another day of ritual and structure, Rohan and Oak were left to clean up the compound after training.

"Well, I've got nothing," said Rohan, breaking the silence that washed over the Grey. His voice echoed slightly on the concrete walls that surrounded them, seeming to mumble their agreement. He looked at Oak, awaiting a reply, but was greeted with silence as Oak continued to sweep the compound, not even bothering to look up.

"I mean, it's been months and I have all the same questions as before," continued Rohan. "I feel like we've been swimming upstream. Lots of paddling, but we're not really going anywhere. I keep waiting for this startling revelation, for everything to make sense. Maybe we were wrong thinking there was anything more to the Grey. Maybe we're here to be tortured and that's it."

"Maybe..." grumbled Oak as he looked up from his broom. "Maybe it's all some trick, and we're the joke." He lowered his head and went back to sweeping the compound.

They worked in silence for the next hour, sweeping from one end of the compound to the other. Rohan had swept the same square of concrete three times by the time he spoke next.

"I think we've been looking at this wrong," Rohan mused out loud.

"How's that?"

"Well, we've been looking for things out of the ordinary right?"

"Yeah."

"Well, maybe that's our problem. We've been looking for strange things, in a strange place."

"Um, yeah."

"So how the hell are we supposed to see it? It's like trying to find a grain of sand in a handful of dust. Maybe we need to think of everything as messed up," exclaimed Rohan. "There must be a reason we are doing everything. It's too well organised for this all to be a 'just because we want to' kind of thing."

Oak considered this for a moment before nodding his head in agreement.

"Well, we can't figure out what's going on because we don't really know what we're looking for. But obviously somebody knows. I'll bet that Edith lady knows and Takash definitely knows. What we need to do is draw the answers out of them."

"Oh, and you think that if we ask politely they'll let us in on the secret?" Oak asked sarcastically.

"No, but maybe we can get to a point where they can't keep us out of the secret any longer."

"You've lost me."

"If we start pushing the boundaries of training, to a point where they can't push us any further, they'll have to do something. If we can beat them at their own game, they'll have to either promote us, or send us home." He looked at Oak seriously, "that means we don't hold back."

Oak looked unhappy. "But I don't want to hurt anybody."

"You could have fooled me," Rohan joked tapping his nose as a reminder of their last fight.

"True, but that's only because you were being… well, being a Northerner."

"Wow… a Northerner. Wow, that hurts, almost as much as your fist," laughed Rohan again.

Oak threw his broom at his friend.

"Ok, ok," laughed Rohan, "moving forward, we need to up our game. You fight, stomp, kill. Me, run, skip, jump."

Oak looked at Rohan sceptically but remained silent.

Pushing the limit was hard. Rohan always thought he worked hard, trained hard, and fought hard. He was wrong. He realised now that he had been coasting. He'd never truly pushed himself to the limits of his abilities. Every time he had been out for a run, trained in combat, or even taken part in the pre-morning meditation, he'd done it half-assed. He'd relied on his speed and natural talent to get him through, but it wasn't enough.

Even though Rohan knew there was a bigger picture in mind, he was enjoying the challenge of pushing himself. There was something freeing and rewarding about crawling into bed at night, exhausted. Even the other recruits started to notice the change in Rohan. In the past, he had always been middle of the road in combat training and average in the fights. Sure, he was fast, but he was dumb. He always went into everything headfirst at a million miles per hour. That was the reason he lost to Oak in their fight, the reason he could never catch Takash, and maybe the reason he was still at the Grey.

Now that Rohan was focused, he was a different beast. He started using his speed to decimate the other recruits. During combat training, he became a weapon. Sure, he wasn't as strong as Oak or as skilful as Takash, but with Oak's extra training and a renewed dedication, nobody could touch him. Rohan moved with the grace of a bird coming into land. He flew into the contest, moving left, moving right, back-peddling, and attacking with ferocious speed. His fists moved like pistons on a rotor, pumping in and out with brutal efficiency. It was devastatingly effective, and the other recruits started to avoid him, hoping they wouldn't be pitted against him.

Oak took brutality to another level. He not only defeated his opponents, he embarrassed them. Previously, Oak had always disarmed his opponents with cold efficiency, minimising any damage to himself or his challenger. Now he was hurting them. He was taunting his opponents, goading them into overcommitting on a strike or stretching too far on a jab. As they reached forward, Oak would step into their swing, leaving them face to face with their nightmare. He would follow up by ramming his knee into his opponent's leg, then as they fell to the ground in agony, he would pummel them with a giant fist to the face.

Very few were lucky enough to pass out after this initial spar. Most recruits sought to attack again, attempting to salvage a scrap of pride. They tried everything, from throwing sand into his eyes, grabbing weapons from the racks, and even charging him directly. Oak seemed to take this as an affront to his talents. As they edged closer, Oak would once again taunt his victims, jabbing at them with a flurry of strikes, tapping them across the nose, chin, and forehead before driving his fist deep into their stomach. He did this to showcase that there was nothing they could do to stop him and that he was in complete control. Opponent after opponent felt the wrath of Oak's violence. He wreaked havoc amongst the recruits and Rohan could have sworn that half of them were in the infirmary as a direct result of Oak's focused attacks.

As devastating as this was for the recruit's general population, it was worse for Oak. He hated what he'd become. He was not the character he was portraying, rather he felt like the villain in his own story. After one particularly devastating bout, Rohan found Oak sobbing uncontrollably in one of the disused storage rooms. He was broken.

"It's not right," sobbed Oak between gasps of air, "I can't do it anymore. Did you see me today? I was a monster. I nearly killed that kid. That's right, he was a kid. He's only been at the Grey for six months and I nearly killed him."

Seeing his friend being torn apart almost killed Rohan. He knew what they were doing was tough, he knew it. Oak was the best person he knew, and he felt like he was forcing him to mutate into some form of monster. It was wrong, and Rohan's heart cracked like clay baking in the sun.

He sat on the bench beside Oak and rested his hand on the hulking shoulders of his friend. "I'm sorry. I don't know... I... I just don't know any other way."

They sat together for a little while, neither of them speaking, but neither of them moving away.

"I... I... just can't," stammered Oak, finally breaking the silence.

"I know."

Oak looked at Rohan surprised.

"I can see it, you're not who you're pretending to be. Hell, you're not even who people think you are. But that doesn't matter, it's not about who others think you are, it's about who you think you are. What we're doing sucks for you right now, but if you can pretend a little longer, you might never have to pretend again."

Silence.

"Well, that was surprisingly poignant," mumbled Oak. His eyes red from the despair that threated to overcome him.

He looked at Rohan, "only a little longer?"

"I hope so," nodded Rohan, forcing himself to smile unconvincingly.

Chapter 7

Rohan prepared himself for his meeting with Edith. Each year he was paraded in front of the old lady where she would click her tongue and say, "potential, but it has to be earnt." It was the same every time.

Rohan couldn't quite figure Edith out. She was clearly the leader of whatever this was, but he had never seen her talking with anyone outside her rooms. She didn't eat with them or train with them, but she was revered as this all-knowing figure. As he thought about it, he realised that he'd never even had a proper conversation with her. This year he intended to change that.

Rohan and Oak had been discussing their options, and simply asking Edith seemed like too good an opportunity to pass up. Rohan had been preparing his questions for weeks. While he hoped to be clear and concise, he was fairly sure he'd just start screaming "what is going on?!!"

The day arrived and Takash sent Galvor to collect Rohan. Rohan had always liked Galvor. For one of the leaders, he seemed a bit more down to earth.

"How's it going Rohan?" asked Galvor with a casual nonchalance. "I notice that you're still letting Takash give you the run around."

"Yeah, well, I'm getting closer."

"Ha, close means nothing. It just means you're the first loser."

Rohan started to wonder why he liked Galvor.

They headed across the compound towards Edith's residence, passing the other recruits in the midst of combat training. Rohan took a moment to marvel at the recruits moving in perfect sync. It really was an art form. Step in, step out, slide left, shuffle, shuffle, shuffle, withdraw. It was rhythmic, graceful, and deadly.

The sound that rose from the compound was no less harmonic. It was a mixture of feet sliding across the rough concrete, weapons banging against one another and recruits panting from exertion.

Suddenly a scream rang out. Whilst this was not unusual, this was not a scream of pain, rather it was a scream of anguish, and it was a voice Rohan recognised.

It was Oak.

Rohan didn't know what had happened, but he started running towards the piercing scream.

"Oy, where do you think you're going?" shouted Galvor as Rohan pushed past him. "Edith's waiting."

Rohan didn't bother to respond. All he cared about was making sure that Oak was ok. He knew his friend had been struggling. Struggling to keep up the charade and struggling to keep it together.

Rohan charged across the pen, pushing past the other recruits who had come to a standstill.

Oak was standing still, eyes glazed in a near comatose state, hovering over the quivering body of a new recruit.

Rohan grabbed at Oak trying to pull him away from the situation. But Oak remained motionless, feet planted to the ground like the tree he was named for. He continued to stare into empty space, his face showing no emotion. Indeed, it was as though he had been turned to stone. The recruit at Oak's feet had curled his head into his knees, trying to appear as small as possible. His head was bowed, eyes scrunched, and hands over ears as though trying to keep the world out.

"What in blazes is going on here," huffed Galvor as he finally caught up. He glanced at Oak and immediately started barking commands.

"You," he yelled at a red-haired recruit standing nearby, "get Takash."

The recruit stood motionless, still stunned by the scene before him.

"Move," barked Galvor, spurring the recruit into action.

Rohan had never seen Galvor take charge like this before. Usually, he was the light-hearted guard, more interested in chatting than giving orders.

"You," he demanded, pointing at another recruit watching nearby, "what happened?"

The object of Galvor's point was a recruit, barely a week at the Grey. His face was as pale as a full moon on a clear night.

"He... h... he just snapped," blurted out the recruit. "For some reason, Sticks thought he could challenge Oak. We tried to convince him not to, but he was just being a cocky Northerner. He kept saying that we were all scared maggots and that given a chance, he would show Oak who's boss." He paused and looked at the cowering figure nearby.

"It wasn't Oak's fault, sir." He continued, "Oak was over there throwing rocks by himself." He pointed to a large pile of boulders used for training.

"Sticks challenged him. Oak tried to wave him away, but Sticks wouldn't let him. I think Oak's dismissal hurt Sticks' pride a bit. So rather than taking the hint, he waited until Oak lifted one of those rocks above his head and then hit him with one of those steel bars," the recruit continued pointing at the weapons rack.

"What!!!!" Rohan roared, "That filthy Northerner!!"

"Yeah, it was pretty dirty," agreed the recruit quickly, "but don't you worry about getting Sticks back, I think Oak's already done more than that."

A small crowd had gathered to hear the recruits' report, with even the more experienced recruits shuffling forward, straining to hear.

"Oak didn't even flinch. He just threw down the rock, turned, grabbed Sticks by the throat and slammed him into the ground. I don't think he even had time to react. I thought that was it, like, he'd sent a pretty clear message."

"C'mon boy, get to the point," snapped Galvor.

"Well, that's when he snapped. Oak picked Sticks up again and lifted him above his head. It was wild, like a beast brandishing a trophy. We could all see what was coming next, he was going to slam him across his knee. Sticks was barely conscious at this point... it was horrifying. As he was about to drop him, you could see Oak just... I don't know, it was kind of, like, the world became clear, as though he finally realised what he was doing. That's when he screamed and just let Sticks fall to the ground, like a sack of potatoes."

During this whole time, Oak hadn't moved, hadn't blinked, hadn't reacted. Rohan had to look closely to see if he was even still breathing.

"Alright," started Galvor, "you two, pick up Sticks here and get him to the infirmary." Two of the onlookers hurried over to the still quivering body of Sticks.

"Now, let's look after the big guy," he said, turning to Rohan. Oak seemed to wake from his stupor.

"No, no... no. Don't come near me," cried Oak in an almost panicked voice.

"It's alright," Rohan said softly. "It's over, it's all over now."

"I can't do it anymore, I can't," Oak responded still in a panicked, almost frantic tone. "I don't want to be a part of this, of any of this. I want to go home; I just want people to leave me alone."

"It's ok, we're done, no more," Rohan tried again in his most reassuring voice.

"No, leave me alone," snapped Oak, pushing Rohan's outstretched hand away. "You're the worst, you're the one that made me this way, you're the one that caused this, this... mess," cried Oak as he gestured to the now silent compound.

"I was just trying to find answers, same as you," hissed Rohan, hopeful that Galvor hadn't heard. He stepped closer to Oak, dropping his voice as he leaned in.

"This was never going to be easy. It was always going to push us to the end. They've made life hard. They work us from dawn to dusk and then expect us to say thank you. I know it's hard, I know you don't want to do this, I don't either. I also know that you can't give up like this. I need you to be strong, so that I can be. I need you to be ok," Rohan's voice cracked as the words spilled from his lips.

Oak looked at him, his body and soul collapsing in front of Rohan's eyes. "I'm sorry," he whispered, his words barely escaping.

"Ok, that's enough," barked Galvor, "get him back to the barracks, I'll send Takash over as soon as he gets here." Galvor stepped towards Oak to help him on his way.

"Leave me alone."

Galvor, somewhat taken aback, paused before placing his arm around Oak to direct him towards the barracks.

"Leave me alone," repeated Oak as he shrugged Galvor's arm away.

"Come on now, go to the barracks," said Galvor just a little more forcefully as he pushed Oak away from the training compound.

Oak planted his foot hard, smacking the concrete as his shoe hit the ground. "I said, leave me alone!"

"Alright, I'm done. Take him to the barracks now," Galvor motioned to a group of recruits standing nearby.

The recruits edged towards Oak, obviously aware of the short work he'd made of Sticks.

"Leave me alone," Oak warned ominously, his previous whispers replaced with a flat emotionless tone.

The recruits shuffled into position surrounding Oak, gently grasping his tense arms, two on each side of his body. Their fingers slowly clamped upon him, pressing deeply into his flesh, physically demanding his obedience.

Galvor stared at Oak, his eyes hard and focused, "alright now. Go."

Oak screamed, struggling against his captors, "LEAVE ME ALONE!!"

Oak flung his arms skyward, freeing himself from the clutches of those around him. His face betraying an anguish that he could no longer contain. It was as though he had been holding himself together like a tightly knit sweater. Normally, it was coarsely woven, with small breathable spaces allowing his pain to seep out in small controllable measures. This latest episode was like a nail catching upon the sleeve, pulling, and tearing, causing the whole thing to unravel. The other recruits jumped on Oak, forcing him to the ground. Oak raged against them, his body convulsing as though possessed.

"LEAVE HIM ALONE YOU NORTHENERS," screamed Rohan, leaping to the defence of his friend. "GET AWAY," he cried as he kicked one of the recruits in the stomach.

Rohan's blood boiled. In the instant his friend was dragged to the ground, he saw red.

A strong hand grabbed him and hurled him away from the fight. "Stay out of this boy."

Rohan looked to find Galvor holding him, keeping him away from the fight. He didn't know why he was being held back, but he knew he had to get back to Oak. He raged against the strong grip on his collar. He forced himself forward, urging himself towards the contest, straining against the strength of Galvor. His shirt ripped as the fabric stretched beyond its breaking point. His face was contorted with effort, his eyes red, and face flushed. When Galvor refused to surrender his grasp, Rohan turned on him. He spun quickly, coming face to face with his human prison. He could feel Galvor's breath upon his face. It was warm and scented by the gruel the recruits ate every morning. His eyes were hard. The laughter that Rohan had always associated with Galvor was gone. In its place was a seriousness that was reflected in his steely gaze. But there was something else behind it, almost a sense of expectation. But Rohan had no time to concentrate on that. He tried to wrench himself from Galvor's grip, hurling his body from left to right, but all to no avail.

Galvor grasped Rohan close, holding him tightly whilst Oak continued to battle in the background.

Oak was no longer on the ground at this point. He had pulled himself up, pushing the other recruits away with a show of pure force. With an almost arrogant ease, he forced his attackers back, intimidating them with his very presence. Galvor urged them on once again, demanding they bring Oak back to the barracks. More recruits had joined in, this time, crowding the now shaking Oak. They surrounded him like wolves, each hungry to exact payback for the ruthless beatings Oak had been dishing out.

Rohan watched on helplessly, knowing in his heart that Oak couldn't defeat that many opponents. Tears rolled down his cheeks in despair, the salty droplets evaporating as they hit the concrete.

Oak was still trembling, shaking almost violently as he tried to retake control of the situation. His muscles were tense, like the cords of a rope twisting around each other, tighter and tighter until they reached breaking point. His neck bulged and his eyes darted from side to side, desperately seeking escape.

Suddenly he stopped. He stood completely still, his eyes went blank as though all the emotion had been sucked out of him.

Rohan could barely hear what Oak said next.

"Enough," Oak whispered as though his words had the power to stop the world.

Then he slammed his fist into the concrete.

The result was incredible.

The cement sprung from the ground like a rose opening for the first time. It leapt and fell in a microsecond throwing everything and everyone away from the core. Fragments of concrete flooded the air showering the recruits in grey dust. The larger chunks of stone and steel transformed into projectiles slashing at sinew and flesh, tearing at clothing, and detonating as they collided with the walls of the Grey.

In that instant, the world was transformed. Everything Rohan knew to be true was gone. It was as though somebody had shaken Rohan like one of those old touristy snow globes. All the pieces of his life were displaced, floating around, waiting to settle on something true. Rohan watched the wanton destruction with a sense of awe and fear. He had known Oak for a long time and thought him to be a gentle giant, but this was different. This was primitive and brutal. More than that, it was a contradiction of everything Rohan thought he knew.

For one thing, the world does not explode without reason. Rohan had heard of powders that exploded when thrown in fire, but not when some crazy guy smashes his hand into the ground. Things like this didn't happen. Immediately, he thought of the Movers that appeared in the markets but dismissed the idea at once. He had only ever seen them move tiny rocks and sticks, nothing like this.

The recruits that had been surrounding Oak were now scattered across the courtyard like autumn leaves in a busy street. They were crumpled, beaten, and bent out of shape. They gingerly picked themselves up from the ground, stretching their limbs to regain movement, and check for broken bones. Their clothes were torn to shreds, ribboned where the concrete had flown past them. Their skin was red raw with scrapes and bruises and their hair was full of dull, grey dust. It scattered onto their shoulders and tumbled to the ground as they moved.

Oak stood resolute. Whilst those around him were scattered, Oak was a pillar of strength. He had absorbed the buffering like a giant tree in a storm. But where the tree would bend and sway,

Oak never wavered. The man that had once been Oak had been replaced by a mountain. He began walking towards the entrance of the Grey, striding purposefully towards the exit. Those that had experienced his force of power shied away from him, scrambling through the rubble, tripping in the rush to escape his presence.

Oak was almost out the front gate when Takash finally arrived. He strolled into the compound with an air of casual nonchalance and absentmindedly kicked some of the rubble from the footpath. He was dressed like he always was, simple, practical, and well maintained.

As Oak strolled past Takash, he turned ever so slightly and glared at his mentor, almost accusing him of turning him into this monster. Takash didn't even flinch, in fact, he didn't react at all. It was as if this kind of thing happened all the time. He didn't even seem surprised at the total cataclysm that surrounded him. Then as Oak strode past him, Takash swung a huge fist into the side of his head. As though in slow motion, Oak collapsed, his giant frame crumpling like a piece of paper. As he fell, his head slammed into the ground with a resounding crack that echoed across the compound. The sweat that had formed upon his brow sprayed the concrete, turning it a deep grey.

Rohan gasped, the colour draining from his face. Takash had killed him. He expected to see blood to start pouring from his head, seeping into the stone, forever crimson on grey.

Takash, nonplussed by the entire saga, leaned down and in a remarkable show of strength heaved Oak over his shoulder. Oak's body was still limp, like a soggy noodle hanging over the edge of a pan. Without even bothering to look back at the stunned onlookers, Takash strode purposefully away.

Rohan didn't know if he'd ever see Oak again.

Chapter 8

The next few months were a blur.

Following Oak's explosion, tensions ran high at the Grey. Nobody knew what had happened and for the first few days after the incident, it was all anybody wanted to talk about. How did he do it? What in blazes happened? And more commonly, where was he now? Conspiracy theories ran wild. They started simple and somewhat conventional and grew into wacky and disturbing. Rohan heard from one recruit that Takash had taken Oak to the top of the very tallest building and unceremoniously dumped him into the rubble below. As much as Rohan hated the idea, it was entirely plausible.

The next theory that Rohan heard was more obscure. All the recruits had seen the ease in which Takash controlled the situation. It was a stunning display of superiority. Maybe it was jealousy, maybe it was stupidity, but the theory was dark. It was whispered in the dark corridors of the Grey that Takash took his strength from the banished recruits. The method of theft was hotly debated with suggestions of cannibalism and soul stealing leading the way.

Dark, obscure, and certainly weird, Rohan didn't believe any of it. But where there is no truth, rumours will emerge. The stories raged about the Grey with none of the recruits immune to gossip.

Rohan tried to ignore the talk, tried to keep the image of Oak in his mind pure. Only he knew why Oak had been pushing himself harder and further than before. Only he knew why Oak had transformed from gentle giant into ruthless monster. Most recruits considered this hardened approach as the precursor to his brain snap, and in a way, they were right. If it hadn't been for Rohan pushing Oak to become something alien to him, he would never have exploded.

Rohan thought about this every day. In fact, there wasn't a moment that Rohan didn't think about it. It was as though he was walking around in a haze of smoke. It was always there hovering around him, clouding anything else that may be going on. The stench of the smoke clogged his nostrils with an overwhelming feeling of guilt and sorrow. Every night, Rohan lay in his bunk replaying the scene with Oak over and over again. He turned it over in his mind so many times, he could replay everything in reverse, sideways, and crossways. But no matter how many times he recreated the scene, he couldn't figure out what happened. There was no earthly way to explain it.

Rohan sunk deeper and deeper into despair. Even the challenge of chasing Takash through the streets couldn't rouse a smile. But no matter how much he wanted to, Rohan wasn't allowed to close the door and block out the world.

"Run, you useless little prick," screamed Takash at the barely aware Rohan. Rohan blinked slowly, vaguely aware that someone was speaking to him. He snapped back to reality when he felt a ham sized fist smash into the side of his face, knocking him to the ground.

"I SAID RUN," screamed Takash, almost foaming at the mouth in a fit of rage.

Rohan felt the red rush to his cheek as he snapped back to reality. He forced himself to stand and started jogging. Every step was like wading through tree sap. It stuck to his arms, legs, and body, pulling him down, trying to smother him in depression. Everything seemed less without Oak. The sky seemed greyer, and the buildings that used to hold fascination transformed into meaningless hulking structures.

The other recruits ran past him, screaming at him, but all Rohan could hear was nothingness.

Thump.

Rohan crashed to the ground. One moment he had been jogging the street, the next, Takash had rammed into him, shoulder first. It was like being hit by a bulldozer, only this bulldozer hit harder. Rohan's skin scraped along the rough concrete, tearing shreds of flesh from his shoulder and legs. He didn't even feel it.

"Get up, you useless waste of skin," sneered Takash, his face contorted into a sickening expression of disgust. His muscles were tensing and pulsating like a bag filled with snakes. "You are nothing," Takash continued, "less than nothing. Even your buddy Oak tried to fight before I got rid of him."

This happened every day, Takash taunting Rohan as he struggled with simply being. Maybe this was his plan, to taunt Rohan back to life, or maybe he was just a psychotic Northerner, whatever it was, it was starting to get through to Rohan.

With each run, Rohan could feel the ember glowing. He could feel the heat rising, slowly eating away the depression that had consumed him.

Finally, he'd had enough.

Takash's taunts caught fire, and in the blink of an eye, Rohan transformed from an empty shell into a hurricane.

The clouds that had filled Rohan's mind disappeared as they were pierced by white-hot anger. And as he lay bleeding on the ground, a guttural cry escaped his lips.

Rohan sprung from the ground intent on catching his tormentor. No obstacle was too much, no divide too wide, and no distance was too far.

In Rohan's mind, there was no doubt as to the outcome. He would catch Takash and he would destroy him. It didn't matter that Takash had defeated Oak with ease, or that Takash had years of combat experience. All Rohan knew was that if he found an opportunity, he would kill him.

It was as though Takash had been expecting it and without warning he began to run, exploding away from Rohan.

Seconds later, Rohan found himself sprinting after the bald man. The years of training had prepared him for this moment, and as Takash moved through the city, Rohan followed close behind.

He watched as Takash leapt across buildings, dived through open windows and exploded through buildings, literally knocking down walls as Rohan trailed him. Grey powder sprayed into the air behind him, clouding the path.

Rohan followed like a dog tracking a rabbit, never letting go of the scent. He trailed closely as Takash headed deeper and deeper into the city around them, his bulky frame expertly navigating the streets in front.

Rohan drew closer, lengthening his stride in an effort to catch the heavier man. The ground beneath him seemed to pulse with every step, driving him towards his prey. Rohan pushed harder, desperate to make contact, forcing his body beyond its limits. Then as he lunged forward, fist raised to strike, the impossible happened. Takash disappeared.

One moment he was there, the next he was gone.

Rohan stopped, whirling around the empty alleyway, scanning for any movement. He knew his fellow recruits has been left behind. It would be hours before they caught up.

Then he heard it, a soft, low whistle coming from the building to his right. Rohan looked quickly for an entryway, but all he could see was solid brick.

The whistle came again, this time followed by a soft cackle. Takash was still taunting him.

Rohan spun wildly, searching for his tormentor, his eyes glowing red as the fury seeped out.

Takash whistled again, and as Rohan turned, he saw him slide back into the alley, appearing from nowhere.

Takash hadn't stepped through an entryway or jumped out of a window, instead he'd emerged from the solid brick that separated the alley from the buildings that stood next door.

Takash walked towards Rohan, filling the space with his presence until he was mere feet from his pursuer, "see, even when you think you're close, you're still a step behind."

He pushed Rohan to the ground with the ease of a father disciplining his child.

"You are useless, a giant waste of time and resource," he started.

"We keep giving you chances. Push harder, train more, be nice. None of that works, you are a failure. The only value you ever brought was entertainment. But you never saw that, did you? You never saw your fellow recruits laughing as you befriended the oaf. You never heard them laugh at your inability to progress. For Northerner's sake, you've been here over two years and you are still a recruit. You are a disappointment. In fact, the only bigger disappointment was how quickly your stupid friend fell when I hit him."

Rohan didn't even hear him. His mind, now focused, was busy purging itself of all the fatigue and self-loathing he'd been drowning in. Things that had been blurry were now clear, and instead of feeling worn out he felt renewed.

Takash continued to berate him, towering over Rohan like a willow tree over a river. Rohan stood slowly, his muscles tightening like a spring winding down, tensing, waiting to explode. He didn't back away from Takash, instead he pushed forward, closing the space between him and his tormentor. Rohan could feel Takash's hot breath on his face. It washed over him like fog on a still morning, hovering in the silence. Takash's face was contorted, highlighting the lines of experience carved into his skin. Each wrinkle a story of the man before him.

"Never…" Rohan started to speak but was abruptly cut off as Takash's huge fist connected with his face. His nose broke instantly.

Rohan's vision blurred as he fell. It was either a concussion or blood, but his brain was too addled to know which one.

"Come on you little Northerner, you waste of food," taunted Takash, circling his prey like a vulture surveying its next meal. "You wanted to fight me… You wanted to take a swing ever since that lumbering friend of yours went down. I see it every time you look at me."

Rohan's head still swam as he staggered to his feet. "Come on!!" screamed Takash, smashing his fist into Rohan's head once more. Rohan went down again. Part of him wanted to curl into a ball, bury his head into his chest, and wait for the pain to end. For months that pain had burned inside his chest, like a small ember in a dead forest. It burned brightly, always there, always dangerous, always waiting to explode and turn the forest into an atomic fireball. This beating from Takash was nothing compared to his anguish. Maybe if he just closed his eyes…

"What? That's it?" Rohan faintly heard Takash exclaim. He closed his eyes again.

"No, no, that's not it," Rohan's mind screamed at him, "get up, get up, GET UP!!"

Rohan's body finally got the message, and his legs began to move, forcing him upwards. He was still a little dizzy and finding firm ground was like standing on a plate full of jelly.

"No," mumbled Rohan, standing with as much force as he could muster.

Takash moved towards him again, fist closed, preparing to pummel him again.

"No," said Rohan, this time firmly and without doubt. The world stopped.

The building around them started to tremble. The small pieces of rubble that topped every surface slipped from their resting places. The doorways began to warp as the locks strained against the frames and the few remaining windows shattered as the casings twisted. Dust and grey rock exploded as the steel beneath fought for freedom. Even the grates that rusted in the disused footpaths bent, warped, and shattered their foundations in an effort to escape.

The jagged metal flew towards Rohan like buck shot out of a shotgun. It was violent and terrifying.

Rohan himself seemed to transform in the blink of an eye. Gone was the depressed youth, barely clinging to sanity, and in its place, there stood a man, hardened by life, hardened by experience, hardened by the steel in his gaze.

The steel that had torn itself out of the walls now hovered around Rohan, turning slowly as the dust slipped off its rough edges.

Takash stood facing Rohan, feet firmly planted as the world shook around him. Even amongst all the chaos he remained unmoved.

"What about now?" screamed Rohan, eyes transforming from a blazing red to a steely grey, "is this what you wanted?"

As Rohan began to move towards Takash, the entire steel stratosphere he had created moved with him. The steel groaned as the shape transformed in motion, each piece warping as it moved. It was like watching a thousand thorns move in a symphony, each delicate piece travelling in perfect cohesion.

Rohan's muscles were tensed to the point of breaking, his veins pulsating, bursting from his skin like an underground current desperately seeking the surface.

Takash stepped closer into the dome of jagged steel.

"Rest now," he whispered in a voice as gentle as a spring breeze.

"Let it go. Rest now."

The steel dome crashed in upon Takash, cocooning him in a prison of serrated death. The scrapping steel grew silent as the tendrils of metal threatened to pierce the flesh of the bald-headed man.

"NO!" Rohan shrieked as though in agony. "You took him, destroyed him, you made him a monster."

The steel crept closer to Takash's skin.

"Look what you've done."

Rohan raised his arm, swinging it towards the ground in a slashing motion. As though a part of him, a shaft of steel crashed into the pavement spraying rock and dust into the air. As Rohan withdrew his arm, the steel stayed embedded in the ground.

"Rest now," Takash repeated, no less gently than the first time.

Rohan's sparkling grey eyes blinked, the dome beginning to lower.

"You…" that was as much as Rohan could choke out, his eyes starting to mist as the pain of his torment began to creep back into his soul.

"You killed him. You took Oak and erased him," Rohan managed to whisper, his voice hoarse with emotion.

The dome lowered further, scraping the pavement as it wavered.

"Rest," Takash repeated, this time closing his eyes as he did so, almost in a gesture of shared sorrow.

Rohan's body collapsed, and as he did, so the steel dome crumbled, dissolving into individual pieces once more. It was reflective of Rohan himself. What had appeared only moments before to be strong and ferocious, now lay broken and bent on the cold unfeeling surface of an unused street.

Chapter 9

Rohan woke to a beam of pure sunlight pounding into his eyes like a thousand needles.

He groaned and rolled away, trying to avoid the light.

His whole body ached. He felt as though giants had used him for a plaything and stretched out his body, tearing his arms and legs apart like an old-fashioned play toy.

Even his eyelids hurt. Was that even possible? Do eyelids have muscles? He supposed they must in order to hurt like this. He was somewhat surprised to feel the pain. He'd assumed that he'd died. Nobody could go through what he did and live. Come to think of it, nobody who lived could have gone through what he did. Was he already dead before that? Maybe he'd been dead a long time already, but just didn't know it.

He groaned again, too much thinking hurt and he was in enough pain already.

The next few days were a mixture of physical pain and excruciating boredom. The only respite was the daily delivery of food and water. Strangely, this provided comfort. It meant he wasn't dead, and somebody cared enough to feed him. It became blindingly obvious that he was there to recover. His body felt like a spring slowly beginning to unwind, creaking with every fractional release. Even his mind needed unwinding. Forcing his brain to run at such an elevated state had left him mentally fatigued. What had happened felt like stuffing an entire sweater into a sock. It didn't fit and ended up spilling over the edge, neither in nor out. As much as Rohan didn't enjoy staring at the paint flaking on the wall, he could see the benefits.

After a few days, he felt stable enough to start asking questions. Apart from "where am I?" and "what am I doing here?", a few others had crossed his mind. The one at the forefront of everything was "what the hell happened?"

He remembered only a few things. Dust, flying concrete chunks, and rather weirdly, floating steel spikes. He must have bumped his head or something. That didn't make any sense. How could... no, nothing made sense.

As he looked around his room, he was struck by a sense of irony. It seems as though he had been transferred back two and a half years. In fact, that sense of irony was further enhanced when Takash pushed open the door and strode into the room. Beside him stood Galvor, grinning like a child let out of school early.

It seemed as though Takash was about to speak when Galvor announced, "it's about bloody time."

Rohan shook his head in disbelief. What was going on?

"We've been waiting for you to come around forever," cried Galvor dramatically, gesturing at Takash. "I don't think the big fella could go on another run. I mean, look at him, he ain't build for running."

Takash grunted but remained stationary.

Rohan's face must have betrayed his utter bewilderment as Galvor grinned at him like a lunatic.

"Oh, come on man, lighten up. It's a good thing."

Rohan was still confused as Galvor pretended to dance a jig. Takash, however, remained still.

"What is going on?" asked Rohan, surprised that the anger he'd felt towards Takash had dissipated.

Takash looked at Galvor and sighed in resignation, then turned to Rohan, his face as stony as ever, "come on, I'll explain as we go."

Rohan stood gingerly, his muscles still sore and stiff.

"But I…"

The smile disappeared from Takash's face, "now."

He grabbed Galvor by the scruff of his collar and pushed him out the door, gesturing for Rohan to follow.

"Alright, let's fill in some of the gaps," started Takash as he led them down a long narrow hallway.

The hallway was painted a light, sterile green, the kind of colour that screamed of practicality. Even the flickering lights that decorated the ceiling were the purchase of an efficient, yet unimaginative architect. Every door along the hallway was perfectly spaced and trimmed in shiny steel casings. They were dented and marked, but smooth from the wearing of time.

Takash himself seemed to mirror the environment in which they found themselves. Clad in a tightly fitted shirt and well-constructed black trousers, he exuded the air of simplicity. Nothing was more than it needed to be, nor was it anything less.

"So," started Takash, "this is the Clinic." He waived his hand expansively.

Rohan looked around in astonishment. Sure, he had looked at the Clinic from inside the Grey before, but it was always just a disused area, a sectioned off part of the compound that held no relevance to him. He groaned, if only he and Oak had thought to explore the Clinic, perhaps Oak would still be there.

Takash was still speaking, "the Clinic is technically part of the Grey, in fact, we share the same walls, but what we do here is vastly different. Most recruits spend a year in the Grey before being transferred."

Takash turned back to look at Rohan, "it took you two and a half."

Rohan was reeling. He always suspected that there was something more to the Grey, but whatever this was, it seemed like it was more than he ever imagined.

"The Grey," Takash continued, "is designed to be a breaking ground. For most of the recruits this means breaking them physically and emotionally so that we can then mould them into something that suits our purposes. In exceptional cases, like yourself," he eyed Rohan slyly, "it's designed to test your Conviction. Not always an easy task."

Conviction? What was he talking about?

Takash continued, "that's why we persisted with you longer than the other recruits. You may have noticed that you were there for an extended time. The other recruits move onto being general soldiers, guards, or if they are completely useless in a fight, administrators. You'd be surprised how valuable a good administrator is. Anyway, breaking recruits is fairly standard. Usually, a lack of sleep and an angry sergeant does the trick. But for recruits with Conviction, it can take a little more. We needed to get you to a point where you felt you has no options left. You needed to rely completely on your Conviction, whether you even realised you had it or not."

"What do you mean by Conviction?" Rohan finally managed to splutter, the words sticking in his throat.

Takash grunted, "I thought you might want to know about that. I'm gonna give you a very quick overview of how it all works. Don't interrupt me if you want answers. Deal?"

Rohan bit his tongue, suppressing every fibre of his being, desperate to know more.

"Good. The recruits we find that we identify as potentially having Conviction tend to be the ones from less structured environments. Ones where nobody takes the time or cares to tell them the way of the world."

"The Unwanted," Rohan mumbled darkly.

Takash glanced at him but continued.

"This allows them abilities that most don't have. These abilities aren't something you can learn; they are based on Conviction. In basic terms, if you completely believe you can do something, you can. Whether that's moving rock, shifting water, or in your case, bending metal. But you must believe it completely and with 100% certainty. That's why we call it Conviction.

It's like, if I told you to walk through a wall, you would probably think that I was a madman. That's because you believe that walls are solid and that that is the natural order of things. But if you don't believe in that order and have developed a complete belief that it is possible, well…"

He lifted his hand and pushed it into the wall, passing between bricks until it disappeared to his elbow. He paused, shrugging slightly, "it's not an exact science. Each person we see brings a new perspective, hence a new ability."

Conviction, abilities, and he just put his hand through a wall!!!
What did it all mean? All he had done was… wait. He stopped.

Then it exploded out of Rohan before he could contain himself,
"WHAAAAAT!!! I have powers???" His words crashed out of
his mouth, spilling upon themselves like a waterfall shattering
onto the rocks below. His tongue barely able to convey thoughts
into a single cohesive sentence.

Galvor broke into peals of laughter, clearly amused by Rohan's
reaction. "This is why I came along Takash," he grinned, his
smile spreading across his face. "Also, I felt like I deserved it,"
he puffed out his chest a bit.

He turned to Rohan, "you see, I was the one that found you in
the market. I was there when you moved for the first time."

Rohan looked at him disbelievingly.

"What? How?" he managed to stutter as Galvor continued to
smile.

"Well, finding those with Conviction isn't easy ya' see,"
explained Galvor. "Most people don't have the stuff, or at least
don't think they do." He stopped to ponder his own words for a
moment, as though coming to some sort of realisation.

"So, we go out into the community to find the right type of
people. We dress up like beggars and thieves and perform minor
tricks to capture the imagination of those around us."

"What, like the Movers in the market?" asked Rohan.

Galvor laughed, "yeah, exactly like the Movers."

Rohan looked at him in disbelief. The Movers in the markets had
been around as long as he could remember. They were always
lying exhausted in the streets, their abilities greatly exceeded by
their limitations.

"You see," he continued, "they aren't really beggars. They're
spies, they're like us," he waved his hand gesturing around him,
"they're a part of the Clinic."

Rohan's mind was reeling. This changed everything. If the Movers at the market weren't broken…

"Does that mean I'm not broken?" he asked meekly.

Galvor burst into peals of laughter that echoed down the hallway.

"No, boy, you're not," answered Takash seriously as Galvor struggled to compose himself.

Although Rohan didn't entirely enjoy being the source of amusement for Galvor, he couldn't find the space in his brain to be annoyed. His mind was reeling. Sure, as a kid he thought he might have powers, but that's the stuff of fairy tales. It's not actually real.

That thought stopped him short.

He had just witnessed Takash put his arm through a wall. Takash was the most practical person he'd ever met. He was hard, blunt, and never used two words when one would do. Not the kind of man that believes in fanciful tales or silly tricks. In fact, it was who the man was, rather than his demonstration that convinced him that this might all be real.

With this jumble of emotion and possible brain explosion, Rohan didn't even notice that they'd come to the end of a corridor and were making their way down what seemed to be an endless staircase.

Takash hadn't spoken again, allowing Rohan to lose himself in his thoughts.

It all seemed too outlandish to be true. Of course he remembered that day in the market. He'd almost been killed by the Sun Bringers.

He could still picture the flash of the blade as it came towards him. He could still hear the ringing of the steel as it crashed into the stalls. It was like a bell in his head that wouldn't let him forget. He'd tried to convince himself that it was all in his imagination, and that the Sun Bringer had missed him, but as he rubbed his chest, he couldn't deny it anymore.

Takash led the way through a pair of large glass doors and into the sunlight. Having been cooped up for days, it felt good to step into the fresh air once more. As his eyes slowly adjusted to the light, he turned to see the building they had come from. In giant white lettering across the front of the building was the word "Hospital".

Takash paused briefly as Rohan took in his new surrounds.

"You think this is a surprise? What if I told you that this is the home of the Faithful?"

Chapter 10

Rohan slumped down in his new bunk. The room in which he found himself was bland as oatmeal. It could be summarised as blankets and paint. There was literally nothing special, different, or interesting about the place. The only light in the room filtered in through a small open window casting a single beam of light onto the hard-wood floor. You could actually see the dust flickering through the light as it made its way to the ground.

Takash had tried his best to educate Rohan on what the "Clinic" was, but there was so much going on, it was hard to take anything in. It was like drilling a small hole in a rock, and then trying to punch your fist through it.

In the whirlwind of emotions and new information, Rohan had somewhat pieced everything together.

The first revelation was the indisputable fact the Faithful existed and that he, one of the Unwanted from Shackle St. was going to be one of them. As shocking as it was, it was also an enormous relief. Ever since that night in the market, there had been a voice in his head telling him that he was different.

Takash had also assured him that the rumours about the Faithful were not all true, although Galvor's constant winking left Rohan a little uncertain.

Takash explained that the Faithful were not an order of bogeymen that stole children, nor were they the guardian angels of the downtrodden and misfortunate, although this was closer to the truth. The Faithful were the invisible arm of Central. They were the ones that stood up to the other regions and prevented Central from being a shopping cart. They did this in the shadows, hiding from the general public as well as the other regions. They hid because they knew how vulnerable they were. The North had too many spies and controlled too many of the gangs for the Faithful to be able to operate openly. If they had, they would have been crushed like a bug under the heel of the North.

He described the early years of Central, before the Faithful existed. Apparently, it was harder then. The other regions took what they wanted from Central, not limiting their greed to the occasional raid. They would empty gardens, crops, and living quarters of anything of value, from food to cooking pots. It was a time of fear, with no solution or defence.

In one of these communities there lived a girl called Edith. She watched as the North entered her village and stripped it bare. She had watched as the people around her died, and Central let it happen.

Somehow she survived. She didn't let the North or the gangs trample her. Instead, she took their cruelty and used it to strengthen herself. She refused to back down and stood tall when others wilted around her. Eventually she realised that she couldn't do it herself, she needed an army to break the shackles.

As she attempted to recruit soldiers, the people of Central shunned her. Her voice was too loud and her anger too real. They were scared of the attention she gathered and scared of the ramification of the North. Edith took it in her stride, refusing to cower to anyone that dismissed her ideas.

Rejected and frustrated by the downtrodden attitudes of her neighbours, Edith was forced to the fringes of the city. It was here that she stumbled upon another discard. This person, nameless and lost to history proved to be the catalyst for Edith's next move.

This outcast was a Mover.

They showed her abilities and insights beyond anything she had ever imagined. They showed her the truth of moving, rather than the distorted version accepted by society. In turn, she stopped seeing Movers as broken and helpless, and started seeing them as soldiers. These people were the answer she'd been searching for. They were a unique and powerful force, waiting to be galvanised into something greater. She saw in them an opportunity, not only to save themselves, but also the people of Central.

That was the beginning of the Faithful.

Over the following years, she collected Movers from across Central, visiting the small villages and outposts that surrounded the city. She searched amongst the poor and discarded, looking for those with Conviction, promising them a home and a purpose. Although not much, it was more than they ever had before. She didn't promise an easy life or one of comfort, but that wasn't what they were looking for. They were looking for acceptance, and in Edith they found it.

As time passed, the Faithful grew stronger. They found a place to call home and invested in learning and teaching. They studied the old books on war and strategy, learning from the past to understand how they could impact their present.

Edith knew then, even at their best, they weren't in a position to challenge the other regions. She also knew that the people of Central weren't ready to come together to build an army. Instead, she transformed the Movers into a guerrilla force, striking quickly and ruthlessly.

These attacks were like nothing anybody had ever seen.

They were brutal in execution and explosive in their impact. Movers of all types would descend on outposts or farms, destroying entire buildings in a matter of seconds. Then, as the dust settled, they would disappear, leaving only the memory of their presence behind. It was likely that these skirmishes were the source of their reputation as bogeymen.

At first, the other regions were confused by these attacks. They seemingly came from nowhere with no rational explanation as to why. However, over time, a pattern emerged. Every time they dipped a hand into Central to replenish their stocks, they were met with swift retaliation. Quickly, the cost of stealing from Central became unsustainable. This realisation had a profound impact on the regions. The Southern and Eastern regions withdrew, preferring to focus on their own people. The North didn't have that option. They needed Central to provide workers for their mines. They had grown too comfortable, and their own people wouldn't venture down into the earth. So they fought back, unleashing devastating attacks on Central, demanding more, and attempting to break the spirit of the region for once and for all. This included tearing Rohan's parents and neighbours from their homes.

This was the reality they now lived in. The North was still as demanding as ever, and as much as the Faithful fought them, it was like pounding a hammer on a cliff wall.

Rohan could only marvel at the woman he'd dismissed as a doddering old fool.

If it hadn't been for Edith, they would all be working in the mines.

She had saved the entire region by refusing to bow her head. He grimaced slightly when he thought about his previous meetings with her. He hadn't been rude, but nor did he show her the respect she deserved.

With the Grey established, Edith no longer had the capacity to scour the region for Movers. Instead, they sent out spies like Galvor to live amongst the fringes and seek out those with Conviction. It was pure fluke that Galvor had actually witnessed Rohan's abilities in the market that day.

Rohan thought about his own arrival at the Grey. Though not planned, or expected, he'd never been angry at being taken. He imagined that in a society where people had a future, family, or friends, they'd be upset, but for those with Conviction, there was nothing to be left behind. Being taken to the Grey was like a holiday. A chance to lead a life, that, while not normal, was theirs to lead.

However, it didn't always go as planned.

The Grey was designed to break recruits. Takash described it like plunging steel into a barrel of water. Blacksmiths and metalworkers did this to forge the metal and make it stronger. But if there were flaws or cracks in the metal, it could explode, leaving nothing behind but a molten mess. The same could be said for the recruits.

All in all, it was a horrifying example of the risks the Grey was willing to take.

Rohan discovered that the reason he'd spent so long at the Grey was due to his ability to compartmentalise. Most of the other recruits found the Grey oppressive because they never had a mental escape. They woke in the morning, and it was the Grey, they brushed their teeth, and it was the Grey, even when they lay down to sleep at night, they dreamed about the Grey.

Rohan hadn't been burdened by the oppressive nature of the Grey. He'd relished the challenges that had frustrated the others. This included chasing Takash, solving problems in the classroom, and even sweeping the compound. This had given him a purpose and a sense of belonging, whilst the other recruits felt theirs was being taken from them.

Even the early morning naps helped to blunt the harsh reality of daily life. Whilst everybody else was focusing on the torment of the day, Rohan was relaxing and taking the time for himself, something nobody could take from him. As a result, the abuse that broke other recruits washed over him like a wave on a sandy beach.

This made Rohan wonder about Oak. At first glance it seemed that though he had been dealt the ultimate hand. He was physically astonishing. A giant that could anticipate every move, every decision, every scenario before it happened.

But the more Rohan thought about it, the more he saw that this wasn't true. Oak wasn't gifted in the classroom, and the runs should have broken him. In fact, it seemed as though every torment offered by the Grey was designed to break him personally. Then it struck Rohan. Maybe that was why Oak had survived so long. He didn't approach anything as an individual.

Rather than being concerned for himself, he'd always focused on others. Even offering to train Rohan in combat was a selfless act, something no other recruit would have thought of doing. Maybe it was that aspect of his personality that allowed him to last so long.

Just thinking about Oak churned up Rohan's insides. He thought back to the tears streaming down his friend's face after each fight, each drop another dagger. It was agonising and Rohan couldn't help but feel responsible for every punch and kick that Oak inflicted. He felt responsible for Oak.

Rohan shook his head, trying to shake the clouds that threatened to engulf him. He was at the Clinic now, and he needed to focus on what he was doing.

The Clinic was different to the Grey.

Where the Grey was designed to break, the Clinic was designed to mould and create. It was designed to transform Movers into the Faithful.

Chapter 11

Rohan was forced into recovery for his first week in the Clinic. Apparently, students in the past had not responded well to their first breaking. They had responded in… unusual ways.

Sometimes when a recruit broke, their mind would follow. This left them unable to grasp their new reality and scared to re-enter the world. Others lost all inhibition and would run screaming from the Clinic, naked as the day they were born. Of the two, the first was the preferred outcome. Those that lost inhibition often retained their Conviction. Without encumbrance they became a danger to both themselves and the rest of the Movers. It was after a horrible accident that the Faithful implemented this enforced stay for new recruits.

Whilst Rohan was frustrated at being locked up, he was excited about what the next stage might bring. He was going to be one of the Faithful. There was still a long way to go, but somewhere deep in his heart, he knew.

As mysterious as Rohan had imagined the Faithful to be, Takash's explanation left him knowing one thing for certain, they were people. They were sons and daughters, mother and fathers, brothers and sisters. They got dirty, tired, and grumpy, just the same as everybody else. Hell, they even went to the bathroom.

After a week of inactivity, Rohan was at his wits end. Rather than relaxing and enjoying his respite he stayed on edge, desperate for whatever came next. His nerves were strung tighter than the purse strings of a Central merchant. His eyes were dry from the constant watching and his beard, or the few wisps that counted, stood at attention.

Rohan could barely contain his excitement as Takash entered the room. He had packed away his bunk hours ago and refolded his blanket a hundred times trying to fill the time. As he glanced down at his bunk, he felt a minor irritation that even after all those attempts at perfection, one edge of the blanket was still crooked.

"Alright then," yawned Takash, the words struggling to escape as his jaw expanded. "Time to go."

Rohan wasn't sure if he was doing it deliberately, or whether he was genuinely tired. He couldn't understand how anyone could act so nonchalantly on what promised to be the most exciting day of his life. No. The most exciting day of his life was when he yanked those steel girders from the ground. But this was a close second.

Takash meandered out of the room, signalling for Rohan to follow.

"All rested?" asked Takash whilst raising an eyebrow.

"So rested," exclaimed Rohan, "I was going crazy sitting there, waiting for… well just waiting."

"I know how you feel. I remember the first time I came to the Clinic. All I wanted to do was knock down the walls and start. Little did I know…" Takash's words trailed off, giving Rohan the impression that the Clinic was not quite going to be everything that he expected it to be.

So far, Rohan had only seen the recovery rooms of the Clinic, rooms that he hoped to never see again. But as he followed Takash, he began to see something more. The Clinic was indeed an old multi-levelled hospital. Unusually, it still maintained a neat outward appearance. Most of the walls were still standing, the corridors were clear, and there was almost no rubble. Even more remarkable was that half of the windows were still intact. For all intents and purposes, it was still a well-maintained building.

The building itself was composed almost entirely of cement sheeting and concrete. For seven storeys, all that could be seen was an architect's dream dying. In fact, it looked as though the building had been designed by a blind accountant. Everything about the building was square. From the windows down to the concrete paved footpaths that separated the buildings. The drainpipes were boxed, the vents formed a perfect grid, and the roof was as flat as a church choir. It was an entirely functional building. The only thing unusual about the whole structure were the walls that ran around the outside of the compound. Rohan didn't know if they were there from the beginning or had been added later. Perhaps that was why the Clinic had stood the test of time. It was so unappealing that even the scavengers were disinterested in what lay inside.

As Rohan followed Takash into the mess hall of the Clinic, he quickly realised that this mind-numbingly dull façade was a misrepresentation of what lay hidden inside.

Takash absentmindedly referred to this section of the Clinic as the mess but said most of the residents called it the "Cutting Room".

It was immediately obvious why. The entire wing that Takash loosely referred to as a mess had been stripped completely bare. Not just paintings removed and shelves taken down, but completely transformed. Gone were all the internal structures, walls, carpeting, and ceilings. Gone were the cubicles, beds, curtains, and hallways. In its place was a huge hall, something like a dilapidated recreation centre. The only difference was the height of the ceilings. As the floors that normally separated the different levels of the Clinic had been taken apart, there was now a cavernous space that stretched almost fifty feet above them. Across this vast openness ran hundreds of wires, cables, and pulleys. They criss-crossed the hall in all directions, like the web of an erratic spider. Each wire was bolted to the wall with industrial metal fasteners and tightened to varying levels of tension. Some were taut and hummed with each echo that carried its way to the ceiling, whilst others hung limply, as loose as an untied shoelace. On the farthest wall stood a small platform, the size of a garden bench. It was made from a collection of old air-conditioning units that had been pounded together and encased in a thousand feet of rusted wire. The bolts holding it to the wall were an inch thick and glinted as the light caught their jagged edges.

Hanging off the wires that criss-crossed the room were ribbons of a thousand colours. Each ribbon contained a small set of initials inked into the fabric. LZ, VM, SB, CV, TM. Rohan had no idea what they represented, but it made for a startling display. Some of the ribbons had clearly been there for years and had faded into a dull version of itself. Others remained vibrant, fresh, and had clearly been added recently.

The walls of the room had been painted white, a mild, but nonetheless welcome change from the pale green prevalent throughout the rest of the Clinic. Combined with the ribbons, it looked as though somebody had lost an argument with a barbed-wire fence. Yet, there was somehow something welcoming about it.

Below the web, the room housed what could only be described as a typical mess hall. It was lined with benches and tables made from thick planks of light-coloured wood. These were stained, scratched, and dented with the history of a thousand meals. Currently, these were about half full of every type of person imaginable. This part didn't come as a surprise to Rohan. Having lived at the Grey for so long, diversity was a way of life. However, he noticed that many of the older citizens wore darker shades of red, clearly distinguishing them from the younger crowd.

Just as he was about to ask Takash about the significance of this change, he heard a cheer go up from the crowd.

In the far end of the room, a recruit climbed up the wall towards the platform. It was a woman, dressed in fitted red leathers. The leathers appeared to be a quilt of mismatched garments, expertly stitched to provide full coverage. It gave her the appearance of a mercenary, eminently practical and hard as steel. With one hand she grasped a rail that had been attached to the wall above the platform. Her knuckles white and arm tense as she leaned out over the cavernous space beneath.

She wasn't somebody Rohan recognised, but the look of determination and excitement on her face was something familiar. Her stance gave the strong impression of a bird taking its first flight. A little unsteady, but fiercely confident and fearless.

She leapt into the air, hurling herself into the space above them.

Rohan gasped involuntarily, his sharp intake of breath causing Takash to turn.

Immediately the unsure bird was replaced with a snarling jaguar, expertly stalking its prey. She leapt with confidence, almost casually landing on a crossing wire about six feet away. Rohan felt a moment of relief, realising that it was a training drill of sorts, not a jump of desperation.

She didn't stop there. With the dexterity of a cat, she used the wire as a launching pad and catapulted herself higher, latching onto the wire above with the grace of a gymnast. The wires hummed as the vibrations of her movement reverberated across the Cutting Room.

Rohan watched in awe. This was not as simple as leaping from one wire to the next. No, this… phenom, for lack of a better word, utilised every bend, stretch, and flex of the wires to maximum efficiency. The tight wires she used to launch herself forward, whilst the slack lines were used for traversing difficult sections and descending from the heights of the upper wires.

Her feet scraped along the lines causing a soft rasping sound to echo through the room and every catch of the wire was met with the silent cheers of those watching below. Not a soul in the room dared make a sound for fear of upsetting the concentration of the woman soaring above.

Rohan watched astounded as this woman launched from wire to wire, gracefully twisting and changing direction as necessary. At one stage it appeared that she had traversed too low, only for her to launch herself into the upper echelons once more by landing on a particularly taut line.

As she progressed, Rohan could see the effort starting to take its toll. Her jumps were no longer as explosive and her movements no longer as swift.

Suddenly, mid-flight, her entire body lurched backwards.

Rohan started to run towards her, hoping he might be able to catch her as she fell. He had barely taken a step when the iron-like arm of Takash blocked his path.

In that fleeting second, Rohan knew that he was too late. There was no chance of him covering the distance in time.

He watched as the woman fell, her limbs flailing, too exhausted and too out of control to stop. His heart sunk, his eyes not willing to believe what he was seeing.

Then, as suddenly as she fell, she stopped.

Chapter 12

The woman hung from a long, black rope clipped to the belt around her waist.

In all the excitement Rohan had failed to notice the safety rope that trailed behind as she leapt from wire to wire.

The crowd, stunned out of its silence, began to cheer. Rohan heard a voice scream out above the others, "well done Jules! That's the furthest yet!!"

Hanging limply, the woman waved glumly back at the crowd, clearly embarrassed, but pragmatic about her failure.

Rohan's heart started to slow, the blood came rushing back through his body and he unclenched the fist that he hadn't realised was curled.

A ladder was rushed towards the hanging Jules, and as she was unclipped, she smiled and drew a long ribbon from her pocket. With a wave to the crowd, she tied a green, slightly tattered ribbon with a JR scrawled on the end to the wire where she fell. Then she scaled down the ladder and walked over to the crowd, receiving one final cheer before they settled back into their meal.

"What was that?" exclaimed Rohan as he trailed behind the now moving Takash.

"Hmmm, oh. That's the rookie challenge. Every year, all the rookies try and cross the Cutting Room without falling. They use the ribbons to mark how far they made it."

Rohan looked back up at the ceiling, noticing for the first time that the number of ribbons almost disappeared the closer it got to the far wall. In fact, the only ribbon at the other end was a single faded strip that must have been black at one stage, but had faded to a dark grey.

"Where's your ribbon then?" asked Rohan.

Takash stopped, looking up as though seeing the ribbons for the first time.

"There," he said, pointing to a purple strip about two thirds of the way across the room.

"And who's the black one at the end? It looks like the only one there."

Takash drew a deep breath, his eyes closing momentarily, his jaw clenching so minutely it was barely noticeable.

"Why did she fall?" he finally asked.

"Huh? What? What about the black…"

"Why did she fall?" Takash repeated, interrupting Rohan before he could finish his sentence.

"I dunno, maybe she lost her grip?" answered Rohan, "she was looking pretty tired towards the end."

"Try again."

"Ummm, she didn't make the jump?" Rohan guessed tentatively.

Takash sighed and pointed at the ceiling.

Rohan looked up, unsure what he was looking at.

"You see that black rope?"

"Yeah, the safety one?"

"Well, it's not just for safety," Takash explained. "She didn't fall because she was tired, or because she missed the wire. She fell because she ran out of rope."

Rohan looked back at the ceiling, the answer finally dawning on him. He had been so focused on the movement across the Cutting Room, he forgot about the rope. It was easy to see where the rookie had moved. She had moved up and down the wires like a zig zag, using up the length of the rope before she was even a third of the way across. As she leapt for the next wire, the rope pulled her back, no longer able to support her erratic journey.

"The challenge," Takash continued, "is not just about physical strength and stamina. You have to think your way through the wires. It's more of a puzzle than an obstacle course."

He continued walking, leaving Rohan contemplating just how quickly he could run the course.

"Alright, next is the training ground," announced Takash as they overlooked the sunken space in the centre of the Clinic. "As you can see, it's a little different from the Grey."

It certainly was. Where the Grey had been an open courtyard, the Clinic was a series of high walls designed to break the open space into a hundred mini spaces. Each space was composed of two walls, one long and one short, with large corridors separating each cell. At the end of each cell lay a variety of objects and targets. From bricks and rocks through to old metal pans and plastic tubs.

As Rohan looked closely, he could see that the space had once been a parking lot. He could still see the faint, white parking lines that criss-crossed the blackened tar floor.

The walls in the training ground were built from double brick cement blocks. They were thick, they were sturdy, and they were intimidating. It was as though each space was a cell. In fact, that was an excellent description thought Rohan. Each of these spaces was a cell, designed to keep anything that happened inside.

Suddenly the design of the space made sense to Rohan. They weren't dealing with ordinary folk at the Clinic. No, they were dealing with people with powers. After what Rohan had seen from people with powers, keeping them apart seemed like a good idea. Although missing in a few places, the top of the walls was like every other surface in the city, covered in a dull greenery composed of onions, cabbages, and beans.

"Come on," growled Takash for a second time. "Enough dawdling. We've gotta introduce you to your team."

Rohan was so engrossed in the scene below him, he almost didn't hear Takash.

"Hmm, team? What team?" Rohan mumbled, barely able to take his eyes off the cells.

Slowly Takash's words sunk in. "Wait, I get a team?" Rohan blinked.

"Everybody gets a team," explained Takash. "When you're one of the Faithful, you work as a unit. In order to be successful, you need to be able to trust your team. The way we build that trust is to eat together, train together, fight together, and live together. They will become your family."

"A family," Rohan scoffed. After what had happened to Oak, family was the last thing he needed. Family wasn't something that existed for people like him. Even at the Grey, other than Oak, there was nobody he could call a friend. Rather you looked out for number one. It's about survival, and you can't survive if you are always carrying others. No, family was for those that hadn't had to fight for survival.

Takash stopped mid stride. He turned to Rohan, who immediately saw that he had made a mistake. Takash's steely grey eyes flashed with anger and his fists clenched in restraint. Rohan could see the veins in his arms pulsing as he fought for control.

After a moment of silence, Takash breathed deeply and started to speak in a tone that demanded respect.

"Now you listen boy. This might be the only family you ever have." He clenched his fists tighter, "these people are the only ones standing between you and a knife in the back. If you can trust them, they'll save you a million times over, if you can't, you might find yourself pushing up daisies."

Rohan had never seen Takash like this.

"We clear?"

Rohan nodded automatically.

Takash turned and stalked down the hallway. Rohan stood motionless, trapped by the enormity of Takash's warning. It clearly meant something to the bald-headed man, and it wasn't just his words. As he turned, Rohan could have sworn that he had seen Takash's eyes glistening in pain. Something had happened to him. Rohan shook his head, collecting himself, and jogged after Takash.

Eventually Takash stopped, coming to a halt in front of an innocuous green door. Room 1103.

"I meant what I said," said Takash in a low tone, his voice having lost none of its seriousness.

He nodded at Rohan and pushed the door open.

Rohan squinted as the light streamed through the open doorway, pouring in from the window at the far end of the room. Like every other room in the Clinic, it was dull and sterile green. In his brief glimpse through the doorframe, he could vaguely make out several bunks lining the walls. They, like the walls, were dull. The mattresses were thin and covered in a single forest-green blanket pulled tight in the corners. Even the pillowcase was sterile green. Seated on these bunks were three figures, chins lifted in expectation.

Then, with almost inhuman speed, one of the figures charged Rohan, thundering into him like a bulldozer on a pendulum. In the brief glimpse of his assailant, Rohan knew this was no mere rookie. No, this was a gargantuan, a man carved out of stone. He could feel the whiskers of the man slice his face as he collided with him. He could even smell his breath, a mixture of gruel and mint.

The man grabbed Rohan with the ferocity of a child clinging onto their mother on the first day of school. It was pure emotion, and for the second time in minutes, the air was forced from Rohan's lungs. Then, rather than being thrown back against the wall, he felt two colossal arms drawing him into an embrace that at the very least would be described as robust.

Rohan's arms flailed unsure how to respond to the vigorous welcome.

"Rohan," he heard the gargantuan heave.

Wait. He knew that voice.

"Oak!!!"

Suddenly the onslaught made sense. Oak was here. Oak, the only person in the world that had any reason to attack Rohan.

Rohan's stomach dropped.

But Oak didn't let go. He didn't pick Rohan up and threw him over a ledge, nor did he squeeze him into a tiny ball and cast him aside. No, rather, he took hold of Rohan and hugged him tightly.

Rohan leant into the hug for just one moment, revelling in the only friendship he'd ever known. Then he remembered.

"Oak, Oak… I'm so sorry." The last part caught in Rohan's throat. He never thought he would have the chance to apologise, to tell him how much he regretted pushing him to breaking point. He thought he had destroyed his only friend.

He shoved Oak away, stepping back and wiping the dust from his eyes.

"Oak, I never meant…"

Oak pulled him in again and exclaimed, "man it's good to see you. I've been waiting ages for you to get here."

Finally stepping away from Rohan, Oak was beaming, his smile as wide as his chest.

"After I lost my mind and woke up here, I finally realised that this had been the plan all along. Sure, you and I didn't know that, but now we're here it makes so much sense. Thank you. Without you, I would still be at the Grey letting little girls beat me up."

A harmonious laugh came from one of the figures in the room.

"Let me beat you up? I think not, I took care of you fair and square."

A small girl, no, a young woman, Rohan corrected himself, walked forward.

"Rohan, you remember Mara?" asked Oak, his face reddening slightly as she stepped forward.

"Yeahhhh," Rohan replied hesitantly.

"Oh, you might remember me as the crazy girl that beat this big lug's ass down," laughed Mara as she slapped Oak on the back with all the grace of an elephant on roller skates.

Something about the woman was incredibly familiar, yet also frightening at the same time.

"Wait, you're not crazy Mara that tried to fight Oak in her first week?" asked Rohan, the answer finally dawning on him.

"Well, I prefer to be called amazing, genius, beautiful Mara, but I guess that is a fair summation of the last time anybody saw me at the Grey," she grinned, her smile reaching from ear to ear.

"Mara's come a long way since then," chimed in Oak, "she even hits a little harder now."

She certainly had. Rohan could barely remember Mara, but what he did remember was limited to the beating she gave Oak. In that moment, she was like a thunderstorm, wild and raging but almost indescribable. She was a mess of emotion, fury, and from what Rohan could remember of her fight against Oak, hair.

Standing in front of him now was a confident woman. She wore the same kind of leathers as the woman who attempted the Cutting Room earlier that day. Unlike most other recruits she wore her hair long, styled into a no-nonsense braid that stretched down onto her shoulders. Though it was mostly hidden when the light flashed across her face, Rohan could see flashes of purple intertwined with the braid. A subtle rebellion against the formality of the Clinic. Her eyes were violet like her hair and seemed to exude a sense of empathy that Rohan hadn't ever seen in a person before. In normal circumstances, she would be regarded as petite, but the life of a recruit had removed that word from her description. Instead, she was slim and muscular.

Rohan was stunned.

"Well, it seems you know two of the members of your team," interrupted Takash as Rohan continued to gape at the pair in front of him.

"Now let me introduce you to somebody you won't know. Meet Odger."

From the large shadow behind Oak, a short weaselly man appeared. He was much older than even Takash and immediately the silent warning bell in Rohan's mind began to sound.

"Welcome," crooned Odger, his voice oily like slick on a wet road. He stretched out a limp wrist, proffering a clammy hand.

Rohan shook it, releasing it almost before they clasped.

"Odger here," Takash started, "will be one of your teachers. Due to your more unique skill set, we are not blessed with… options. Odger here is one of the most skilled Steelers we have, even if he is here against his wishes."

Odger almost spat at Takash as Rohan made sense of this statement. It seems like the Clinic wasn't an amazing adventure for everyone.

"You see, Odger is not what you would call an upstanding citizen. For most of you, the Grey is where we break you to unleash your abilities. Odger was a little different. When we found him in the back streets of the city, he was using his abilities to sneak in and out of people's houses, taking whatever he wanted. He's a slimy little leech that compliments you with one hand and steals from you with the other."

Odger smiled, his yellow teeth flashing.

"Ah, but I am a changed man now. No longer I steal, but I am all about the Faithful," he smiled contemptuously.

"Yeah, that or the wooden rattle attached to your ankle that prevents you from going too far."

Rohan looked down to see a thick wooden band hugging Odger's foot. It was a strange band made from a single piece of wood. From a distance it looked ordinary, but even from where Rohan was standing he could hear something moving inside, like sand crashing over a waterfall. It sung like a whisper with every movement, not jarring, but clearly audible. Looking closely, Rohan could see that Odger had made several attempts to "liberate" the ring from his foot. It was criss-crossed with nicks and scratches, but nothing had managed to gouge into the grain. In fact, a good polish and the ring would have looked perfect once more.

"Well, yes, that has placed a slight hindrance on certain activities," smirked Odger. He spoke with a slight accent, indeterminate of origin but halting in pronunciation.

"You see, Odger is one of the rare few that has known about his abilities since childhood. Unlike you that exploded like a storm, Odger's skills are a more refined. He can't move massive volumes, but he has the rare ability to be able to manipulate steel like a blacksmith. Actually, he's better than a blacksmith, more like an artist. That's how he was able to steal from his neighbours for so many years."

"I wouldn't call it stealing," proffered Odger. "I prefer to call it assisted transitioning. And if I make a little profit on the side, all the better." He was almost rubbing his hands together in self-satisfaction.

Takash grunted, clearly unimpressed with Odger's explanation.

"And here comes the last member of your team." He motioned towards the slender, yet powerfully built woman who had appeared in the corridor behind them. As she made her way down the corridor towards them, Rohan felt the air in his lungs turn to cement. It was hard to breathe and the very prospect of sharing the same air as this woman intimidated him.

"Rohan, meet Amadyne." Takash motioned him forward.

"Ah, hi. I'm Rohan," he stuck his hand out.

"Yes, I know," Amadyne responded crisply without taking Rohan's hand. Rohan waited for her to say more, but as the silence grew he feared his new team mate already disliked him.

Takash coughed. "Amadyne here is one of the few dual ability fighters we have. She is both a Shard Shifter and a Water Torrent.

Rohan's face must have betrayed his confusion.

"It means she can move both glass and water," whispered Mara.

Rohan was surprised. He never knew that a person could have more than one ability. Actually, before he joined the Faithful he didn't know that even one ability was possible."

"How?" he blurted out, unable to contain himself. He regretted it the moment the word left his lips.

Amadyne turned to face Rohan, her impatience clearly visible. "I believe I can. Don't you get it? It's not a trick. Your ability is directly correlated with your Conviction. If you truly believe something, you can do it. Like Oak here," she gestured to the giant. "He can smash through rock and stone like a wrecking ball because he believes he can. But ask him to propel a single pebble and he's useless." She gave Oak a withering look, clearly emphasising her disappointment.

"On the other hand, I believe I can move glass." She reached into the small pouch at her waist and removed a solid glass marble. Then with a nonchalant flick, she threw the marble into the air.

Rohan watched incredulously as with the swift movement of her hands, she pushed the marble down the corridor, suspending it in mid-air.

Rohan had never seen anything like it before. He had seen Oak explode, and Takash provide a small demonstration, but he had never seen anybody showcase such control.

With a whipping motion Amadyne pulled the marble back towards them. It shot through the air like a bullet, stopping inches from Rohan's forehead.

Amadyne plucked it neatly from the air and tucked it back into her pouch. Rohan stood silent, his heart racing as he tried to comprehend both the extraordinary control and the danger she placed him in merely to prove a point.

She turned back to Takash once more, standing in a soldier pose.

"Permission to return to the training compound?"

Takash waved dismissively as Amadyne took her leave and walked briskly away from the group.

Oak and Mara stood to the side, grinning as Rohan stood shocked.

"Alright Odger, let's give these guys a chance to catch up." With that Oak and Takash followed Amadyne down the long corridor.

Rohan was still in a state of shock. This was not what he expected when Takash said he would have a team. From this initial joy of finding out that Oak was here and alive to the strange meeting of Amadyne. The Clinic was going to be weird.

Before Rohan could contemplate much more, Oak slapped him on the back, almost causing Rohan's eyes to pop from their sockets.

"She's something else, isn't she!" laughed Oak, the grin on his face growing wider as he enjoyed his friend's discomfort.

Mara gave Oak a sharp elbow to the ribs, making him laugh even more.

She sighed as she turned towards Rohan.

"Amadyne is… intense. She likes everything to be done in a certain way, and that way must be perfect. Being dumped with this big lug," she gestured to Oak, "and me was not in her plan. I kind of get it. We're both still rookies and really raw. She's a professional. Did you see the control she had over that marble? I could never hope to do that. We've only been part of her team for a few weeks, but it's pretty clear that we aren't living up to expectations."

Oak had stopped laughing now and was nodding along with Mara.

"Once we learned that we were getting somebody else, I think she was hopeful that it was going to be someone like Takash or Galvor, but to get another rookie, she's probably just a bit, um… disappointed."

"I guess that makes sense," Rohan said thoughtfully. "If I was an elite fighter or whatever, I'd be annoyed at being saddled with the new kids."

Oak scowled at this, but Mara nodded in agreement.

"But why Takash or Galvor? I know Takash is a beast, but I didn't know Galvor was anything special."

Oak laughed again, "ha, you thought Takash was special? You don't know the half of it, Takash is a freak. He can literally walk through walls."

Rohan almost laughed at the idea, but quickly caught himself as he remembered Takash's earlier demonstration.

"Yeah, he is a bit like me in that he can move rock, but his skill is more refined. Where I can smash like nobody's business, he can move it around his body. That's how he knocked me out at the Grey. He covered his fist in stone. Even in the runs, he used it. We never noticed because we were too far behind. He used to step through the brick walls and into buildings to lose us. That's how he was able to stay in front so easily."

Rohan shook his head in amazement. He was learning so much.

"What about Galvor then?"

"I can answer that one. He's a Bio-Mover like me." Mara smiled, clearly proud of her connection to Galvor.

"What? What is a Bio-Mover?" asked Rohan.

Mara smiled again, "a Bio-Mover is somebody who can move a living or previously living thing. Like plants or trees. Like all the other abilities, it can be different for everybody. It depends on what you believe. In theory, you can move anything as long as you have Conviction. Let me show you."

A few moments later, Mara had led them outside the main area and to a disused alley behind the Clinic. Here lay scraps of construction material that no longer offered value. There were scraps of tin, cracked and broken boards, and a few chunks of concrete.

Mara gestured and a piece of timber flew into her hand.

"So, I'm not very strong…"

Oak started to protest, but Mara waived him away.

"I'm not very strong, but I can move things made from wood in ways that most can't. See, watch."

Mara took the piece of timber and began to run her hands along its edges. Like the time Galvor had fixed the bowl in the market, he watched as the grains began to transform. At first, she took the piece, and pulling at both ends stretched it into a slender strip of timber about four feet long. Then, like rolling out dough in a bakery, she shaped it, removing the square edges with each motion.

In seconds she was done. Instead of a jagged piece of timber, she now held a smooth staff.

"See!"

She passed the staff to Rohan who held it as though it was made of glass. He marvelled at the workmanship and the ease at which Mara had transformed it. It was as smooth as the worn railings on a popular playground.

Mara was clearly satisfied with Rohan's reaction. "Bio-Movers aren't that well thought of at the Clinic. We're seen as a bit useless. Not much help in a fight you see, but we can do things that others can't. I think because we work with something real, something alive, we can move our materials in ways than most Steelers or Earthworkers can't."

Rohan continued to stare at the staff, comprehension dawning upon him.

"Wait, what you broke at the Grey. Didn't you hit Oak with a staff? Did you…" Rohan waved his hands about trying to find the words. "Did you do something to the staff to make it stronger?"

Mara looked sheepish.

Oak answered for her, "yes, and it hurt." He reached down and took Mara's hand, "but we've come a long way from there."

Rohan looked at them both. Oaks eyes had softened as he held the diminutive Mara in his giant paw. Alternatively, Mara looked up at Oak, the hint of a smile resting easily on her face. It was the face of contentment, of safety.

It finally dawned on Rohan. Oak and Mara weren't just teammates, they were together.

It wasn't overly surprising, surmised Rohan. In the Grey, there are very few partners to choose from. Sure, there are plenty of people, but someone who is willing to spend time with you by choice was a rare thing. People were typically too selfish and too ambitious for relationships to last long at the Grey. He hoped that wasn't the case between his new teammates, as it could very easily tear the team apart. But as he looked at them, he felt assured that it was more than just a strategic alliance.

He coughed, breaking the silence that had settled over the group and tried to change the subject.

"So, how many types of Movers are there?"

"Well," started Oak, "there are Earthworkers like me. We can move rock and stone and things like that. I think that anybody who does anything from the ground gets placed in my group. You could be able to throw mud and you would be an Earthworker."

"Then," interrupted Mara, "there are Bio-Movers like me, Steelers like you, Water Torrents, Shard Shifters, and Weather Wardens."

"Weather Wardens?"

"Yeah," continued Mara, "they are a bit of an anomaly. They don't do much except direct the weather. They can't control it or anything, but it's kind of like they have their own invisible raincoat. They are a bit weird because they have the ability to control lots of different elements but not with any great power. I think their greatest power is keeping dry in a storm."

"Wow," thought Rohan. It was overwhelming. For one of the Unwanted to suddenly be part of the Faithful, it was a big step. How would he, a discard from Shackle St. be able to compare with the likes of these heroes?

Rohan noticed Oak nudging Mara insistently. She flashed a look of warning at him, her eyes ablaze with fury.

"What?" Rohan asked cautiously.

"Nothing," snapped Mara irritably.

Oak nudged her again, but Mara, revealing a stubborn side, crossed her arms resolutely and remained silent.

Oak sighed.

"There are others as well. Mara doesn't want me to tell you yet cos it might freak you out, but there are other abilities." Oak paused, searching for the right wording.

"We know that there are those who use their abilities for their own advantage, and a lot of the time, I don't blame them."

Mara glared at Oak. He shrugged and continued.

"Take Odger, for example. Takash is hard on him because he used his powers to steal. But if you were desperate, wouldn't you do the same? If you had a power that gave you the ability to eat, sleep, and survive, wouldn't you use it?"

Rohan nodded in agreement. In Central, you had to take advantage of your opportunities.

"Well, there are those who used their abilities to do things like Odger. Then there are those with abilities that are a little… darker."

Mara elbowed Oak insistently now, but he ignored her.

"There are rumours about people who can move living things. Kind of like a Bio-Mover, except instead of moving plants and trees they move… well… people." He stopped, allowing Rohan to grasp the full implications of this.

"The reason Mara is so prickly about this," he continued, avoiding Mara's gaze, "is that they are a cousin to the Bio-Movers. In fact, most people believe they started as Bio-Movers and then graduated to become "Controllers". That's what we call them anyway. They can move a person the same as how you and I move metal or rock. We've never seen it," he gestured at Mara and himself, "but apparently they can fling people against rock or into the air easily."

Rohan shuddered. The thought of being controlled against his will was unfathomable and terrifying. No wonder Mara didn't want anybody talking about these people. They were terrifying, and from what he could understand, completely opposite to what the Clinic represented.

Oak lowered his voice further.

"Did you see the Cutting Room on your way in?"

Rohan nodded.

"Well, the story goes that the only person to ever reach the other side was a Controller. That's why nobody talks about the ribbon that's hanging at the other end of the course."

Rohan remembered seeing a black faded ribbon on the far side of all the wires. No wonder Takash had changed the topic so quickly. Rohan guessed that he didn't want to tarnish Rohan's first impression of the Clinic.

Rohan, Mara, and Oak continued to chat about the world that had been opened to them. They discussed their abilities, their goals, and how they saw themselves protecting Central in the future. Rohan could see that both Oak and Mara were convinced that they were on the right side. They spoke passionately about how they were going to use their power and openly guessed at when they would be sent on their first mission. Rohan on the other hand still needed to be convinced. It wasn't that he didn't trust Takash and the rest of the Faithful, it's just that he didn't really know them. Everything that had happened at the Grey before had been a deception, why should he trust them now?

Chapter 13

The Clinic, as per the Grey, started the day with a morning meditation. This was a time when Rohan would re-centre himself and prepare for the day ahead, a far cry from when he used to nap.

Following his discussion with Oak and Mara, his mind was too busy to settle. There were so many new questions. During his time at the Grey, the most pressing question was "why are we here?" Now it had been replaced with "how do I?", "what am I?", and "when will I?" None of these questions was answered easily and it made Rohan fidgety.

He noticed a number of the other members of the Faithful giving him dirty looks as he shifted his feet, wrung his hands, and hummed to himself during the morning meditation. He knew he was disturbing the silence, yet he couldn't help himself.

His nerves were partially freed when they moved from meditation to movement. Unlike the Grey, where they were forced into a breakneck run, the Movers transitioned into a series of stretches designed to limber up the body and focus the mind.

They shifted from back and shoulder stretches into lower body and core exercises. Though Rohan was unfamiliar with the order of the stretches, his body moved with the grace of a cat stretching in the early morning sun. His long limbs extending themselves in smooth deliberate motions. These simple stretches gave Rohan a sense of security and helped to settle his mind. He was still the man who had survived Shackle St. If he could survive that, he could handle anything the Clinic would throw at him.

Rohan's first lesson with Odger was to be held immediately after breakfast. Oak and Mara had warned him not to expect too much from his first lesson, but he couldn't help but be excited. As soon as his plate was clean, he leapt to his feet and raced towards the training area, worming his way between the cells until he found what he was looking for. Each of the cells had been assigned a number. These were a simple way of allocating training space for the Faithful. On the shorter concrete wall of each L-shaped cell was painted, in slapped on whitewash, an identifying number. Rohan's cell for the day was number 38.

Awaiting him were Odger and Takash. He wasn't sure why Takash was there. Rohan looked at him surprised, he'd thought it would just be Odger.

Rohan took a moment to look closely at Odger who sat hunched over on a small wooden stool. He was unnaturally dirty, as though he had been living in a dank alley for months. Even his fingernails were coated with dirt and grime. He was also sweating. While Central is hot, it was still early in the morning, and the slight sheen that covered the man's skin was repugnant. He wore a yellow robe that covered him from shoulders to shoes and brushed the ground with each step. The bottom of the robe was frayed and filthy, no longer yellow but a wet looking black. The sum of these parts gave Rohan the impression of a sick animal. He was skinny and his teeth were sharp and discoloured. He certainly wasn't like the Faithful from the stories.

He watched as Takash nudged Odger, alerting him to Rohan's presence. Odger scowled but reluctantly stood in response.

"Ah, you came," smiled Odger, the disappointment written upon his face. His voice was oily like the slippery scum on the bottom of a drainpipe.

Takash glared at Odger, annoyance flashing across his brow.

"Welcome to your first day of training," Takash started. "Odger here will be teaching you." He emphasised the word "will" causing Odger to slink back slightly, his eyes flashing with hatred.

"If you have any issues, let me know. I'm keen to learn more about Odger's… methods." He shoved Odger forward, causing the little man to trip on his robe.

"I am so pleased to be helping you start your journey as one of the Faithful," Odger rasped, his voice dripping with venom.

Takash glanced at the little man, sighed, and then made his way from the cell.

"Apparently I am going to be your teacher," started Odger, "although it is unlikely you have the skills or talent to be of any use." Odger eyed Rohan ruefully.

"What can you do?"

Rohan was taken aback. He hadn't expected such a blunt question.

"Um, I, um, I think I can move metal and steel."

"You think you can?"

"Yeah, well, I've only done it twice."

Odger spat on the ground in disgust.

Already Rohan was annoyed at the filthy little man. He'd been so excited for his first lesson, and now he was being treated like an inconvenience. He hadn't even started the lesson yet.

Letting his annoyance get the better of him, he snapped, "well, yeah, I've only done it twice, but it was a lot. What can you do?"

Odger glared at him and reached into his long robe withdrawing a small piece of wire.

Without speaking he held the thin piece of metal up to Rohan's eyes. It looked like nothing. It was a crooked piece of used copper wire, so small that it couldn't serve any practical purpose.

Odger began to rub his fingers over one end, causing the wire to spin quickly like an off-balance drill. It twisted and glinted in the soft morning light, whirling in a flash of colour. As Rohan watched closely, the wire began to transform, lifting and falling with minute precision. Odger continued to rub his fingers together, his eyes never leaving the spinning wire.

Rohan's eyes grew wider as the wire responded to his touch, each turn forming a new structure. Finally, Odger stopped, and in his fingers he held the perfect outline of a key.

Rohan was awestruck. This was more impressive than Amadyne's marble trick. This was an exquisite piece of mastery, almost an art form. It was like nothing he had ever seen before. Even though Mara had explained that each Mover's abilities were unique, he never imagined a person could be so in tune with their abilities. He thought of his own breaking and lack of control he'd had.

Odger flicked his wrist and in an instant the key turned back into that single piece of useless copper wire. He tucked it back into his robe and with a grim smile turned back to Rohan.

Rohan could only nod, words having escaped him.

Odger moved further into to the cell, gesturing for Rohan to follow.

"Do you see those objects?" he motioned to the back wall.

Rohan looked to where he was pointing. Leaning against the wall was a wide variety of steel objects. This included small items like spoons and cups through to some larger items like trash cans and street signs.

"I want you to call them."

Rohan looked at him, awaiting further instruction. Instead, Odger shuffled back towards his small stool, turning his back on Rohan.

Rohan paused. Calling an inanimate object seemed ridiculous. It was something that a crazy person on snuff did. He could see himself in that moment staring at the wall, looking like a lost child. He half expected Oak jump out and announce that this was all some sort of practical joke.

Odger glanced at him and nodded at the wall. It was clear that he expected Rohan to do something, only Rohan wasn't sure what he could do.

Hesitantly, he raised his hand as though he was reaching for a cup and mumbled the word "come." Out of the corner of his eye, he could see Odger listening as the word fell limply out of his mouth.

Nothing happened.

Odger sniggered, clearly amused by Rohan's ineptness.

Rohan looked at him ashamed. It wasn't his fault. He'd only ever moved something twice, and both times were by accident. How was he suddenly supposed to be good at this?

He lifted his hand again, and with more force this time he spoke the word "come."

Nothing happened.

Rohan stood with his arm still outstretched, his fears coming true. He felt like an idiot. Behind him, Odger was giggling now. In between chuckles, he looked at Rohan.

"Do it again."

Rohan took a deep breath and tried again, "come."

Still nothing happened.

Odger broke out into fits of laughter as Rohan started to turn red, both angry and embarrassed.

"Again," he laughed as Rohan's eyes hardened.

Rohan tried again and again for the remainder of the morning. With each failure, Odger smiled more, clapping his hands in delight.

"Enough!" shrieked Odger eventually, his eyes watering with tears of joy. "You are no Mover. You have no talent." He almost skipped as he said it. "Takash is going to be so mad. Ha!" He laughed uncontrollably and shuffled out of the cell, his robe swishing furiously as he walked.

Rohan watched him go, unable to utter a single response. Odger was right, he hadn't so much as tipped a thimble. He'd only had one reason to be at the Faithful, and he'd failed at the first hurdle. It might have been the quickest anybody had ever flunked out.

Rohan leaned back against the cell wall, letting himself slide to the floor. He didn't even know where to go next. Odger was supposed to give him some instruction but had long since left.

He considered going looking for Oak and Mara but didn't know where to start looking. They would be in their own training sessions or locked in a workshop.

Instead, he remained in the cell, allowing his thoughts to wash over him. He didn't know what the Faithful did with people that didn't become Movers. He remembered Takash mentioning administrators, but he probably wouldn't be any good at that either. He just hoped they'd let him say goodbye before they kicked him out. He thought of Oak and how disappointed his friend would be. They'd only just been reunited, and Oak was so excited that Rohan was with him at the Clinic.

He must have sat like that for an hour before Takash entered the cell.

"What's going on here? Where's Odger?" he looked down at Rohan confused. Rohan didn't even bother to look up.

"He left. Said there was no point."

"Did he now… shifty little blighter."

Rohan waited for Takash to leave but was surprised when he heard the sound of a large body sliding to the floor. He wanted to open his eyes but didn't dare break the silence he had created for himself.

He waited expectantly as Takash positioned himself beside him, but the silence remained. They stayed like that until the mess hall bell rang. It was a sign that lunch was ready and all the members of the Faithful would start making their way there.

Takash sighed again and finally spoke, "we can sit here all day if you like. It's not going to change anything. It's not easy you see.

Odger's always known how to use his abilities. The rest of us have to learn. Sometimes he doesn't understand that."

"He's a real Northerner," mumbled Rohan.

Takash laughed, "yes, sometimes. But he's also the best we've got."

Rohan grunted.

"I think it might be time for you to speak with Edith again. She helped me when I first arrived. Maybe she can help you."

"Not Edith," thought Rohan. As amazing as she was, all she ever did was make vague comments about his abilities. He wasn't quite sure what Takash thought she could do.

Rohan sighed, signalling his scepticism.

Seconds later he felt a rough hand grasp him by the collar and lifted him into the air. His eyes snapped open as Takash eased him back to his feet. Rohan looked at him shocked. Takash seemed no more bothered than if a fly had landed on his back.

"C'mon," Takash gave him the slightest push in the direction of the Grey. "It can't do any harm."

Rohan lowered his head and turned his feet in the right direction. There was no point arguing, and he didn't have the energy for it anyway. As they walked towards Edith's residence, he realised that she was one of the few members of the Faithful who saw the students grow from recruits into Movers. She really did get to see the whole picture. Hell, her room was placed between the two sections, providing her easy access to both sides. He assumed that was a deliberate decision, allowing her to scrutinise the new recruits, while still retaining in control of the Faithful.

When he had been at the Grey, he had seen her as a frail old lady, more of a figurehead that one with any actual power. Since learning how she had started the Faithful, Rohan had revised his first impression. She must have been incredibly tough to command a group of wild Movers and turn them into the army they now were. In fact, it was the single most impressive thing he had ever heard of, even more than the made-up stories of the Faithful. Going to see her felt embarrassing. She had overcome so much, and he couldn't even move a single pot. He wondered what Edith was going to do with him. She didn't seem like the type to berate him, although he wasn't quite sure. He would just have to wait to find out.

Soon enough, they arrived at her rooms. Takash knocked with military efficiency and pushed Rohan through the doorway.

As they entered, Rohan caught a familiar whiff of dust and moths. It was the same every time he visited, she even wore the same dress. Rohan guessed that she wore it to appear non-threatening and relax some of the more stressed recruits. It certainly worked, Rohan couldn't help but see her as a tiny old lady, one that didn't possess a threatening bone in her body.

Rohan watched as her dress hovered over the threadbare carpet once more. Takash stepped backwards, clearly deciding that whatever was said was between Edith and Rohan.

"What seems to be the problem dear?" she asked, her voice a gentle rasp that spoke of age and wisdom.

As agitated as Rohan was with his situation, he couldn't find it in himself to be rude to this lady. "I... I'm not a Mover," he stammered. "I tried to move the metal in the cell today and nothing happened. And it's not like I only tried once, I tried a lot but nothing happened. I don't belong here, I don't know how to do anything and I... I just..." the words gushed from his mouth until he could no longer breathe.

She smiled and walked towards a desk that was pushed against one of the room walls. "You know, you're not the first person to come in here with that problem."

Rohan waited expectantly, his head bowed. He never thought he was the only one to fail, maybe the quickest, but not the only one. He waited to hear what happened to the rejects, what was going to happen to him.

"No, certainly not the first," she repeated. "But you should know, just as the others found out, that at the Clinic, we never make mistakes." She looked around, as though looking for someone, "not when it comes to identifying talent."

Rohan raised his head confused.

"The problem," Edith continued, "is that students forget. They forget that they don't need to find their Conviction. That's what brought them here in the first place."

She seemed to look right through Rohan, as though seeing the students who'd passed through the room before him.

"Remember the first time you used your ability?" she asked.

Rohan remembered as though it was yesterday. He still thought it was a fluke, that knife should have claimed another victim that day.

"There is a strong chance that it was an accident," stated Edith in a matter-of-fact tone. "In fact, I can almost guarantee that it was. When we recruited you to the Grey, we needed to see if that accident was a one-time occurrence, or something that could be nurtured. So we took a risk. We took a risk that you could find your Conviction again."

Rohan nodded, unsure where she was going.

"At the Grey, we use a variety of techniques to ensure that our recruits have the best chance of finding their Conviction once more."

Rohan nodded. A lot of things that Takash and Galvor had told him were making sense now.

"So when you broke, it wasn't a surprise. It was a confirmation for us. You see, we don't promote anyone to the Clinic until they have proven their Conviction. Now you just need to recognise that in yourself. Besides," she added her eyes sparkling, "how many people do you know who can do what you did?"

Rohan smiled at this. He had made a mess the day he broke. Metal and steel had gone flying everywhere. It was carnage. No, that was certainly not a fluke. Through the chaos he'd been in control.

That simple realisation lifted the weight that had planted itself on Rohan's chest. He hadn't thought about it that way. He didn't need to prove himself at the Clinic. He'd already done that. If he hadn't, he wouldn't be there. He smiled for the first time that day.

"Now, it may help you to understand the nature of Conviction," started Edith. "At first, your belief is like a seed, one that is covered in a hard shell, designed to keep it safe. The first time you find and use it, that shell cracks. It gives you a glimpse into what lies inside, but not enough that you can reach in a take it. That crack continues to widen each time you find it, giving you more and more access to what lies inside. At the Grey, we take it further, we design your training to not only crack the shell, but to pull it wide open. We want you to be able to grasp your Conviction like a torch and show it to the world. We want you to display it with confidence. You're almost there now. The shell is open, and the seed is sitting there, asking to be used by you. You don't have to do anything other than accept it."

Rohan blinked. It couldn't be as easy as that, could it? He had been trying so hard to make something happen out of nothing that he forgot that his Conviction was his own. He had surely cracked the shell when he broke. Nothing like the mayhem he caused could be contained by a brittle shell. No, it was his and nobody else could take it.

Edith smiled as Rohan's face betrayed his awakening. "Yes, it really is that simple," she murmured as Rohan stood stunned by the revelation.

Edith started to wander around the room, moving without any specific purpose. Rohan looked at his hands, scarcely able to believe the power that lay in his fingertips.

He looked at Edith with a new-found respect, perhaps even awe. She had been able to remove all his fears and shame with only a few sentences. He'd barely said a word. Now he understood why everybody held this woman in such regard. She was an oracle, at least to him.

Takash crept up behind Rohan and leading him by the shoulder, slowly guided him out of the room once more.

As the sunlight beat down upon them, Rohan turned to Takash. He wanted to ask what to do next? Could he see Edith again tomorrow? Should he start practising right now? Instead, he stood, unable to muster the words.

With a knowing look Takash nodded at him, "training starts again in the morning. Make sure you're on time."

Rohan watched as Takash walked towards the Clinic. He took a deep breath and fell into line behind the bald-headed man.

Chapter 14

Odger placed the steel objects against the back wall of cell 38 once more. He moved slowly and with obvious reluctance. It was clear that Takash had forced him out of his cot, and he wasn't happy about it. With each step he scowled at Rohan, cursing him under his breath.

Odger trudged back towards Rohan and like the previous day, lowered himself onto the small wooden stool.

"Alright, let's waste some more of my time," said Odger as he waived dismissively at Rohan. Rohan tried not to hate him in that moment but found himself failing. Odger had no right to dismiss him. If Edith and Takash believed in him, then so should he. Rohan turned his eyes from his teacher before they could betray his inner thoughts.

As he looked at the steel objects, he knew they were his to command.

He raised his hand, just as he had the previous morning. "Come."

Nothing happened.

Not again, though Rohan. He lifted his hand, "come."

Nothing happened.

The panic started to rise in Rohan's chest. This is not how Edith said it would be. She said his Conviction was already there, and he just had to reach for it.

"Come."

Nothing.

"Come."

Nothing.

"Come, Come, Come!!!"

Rohan was screaming in frustration at this point. Why wasn't it working?

"COME!!" he bellowed again, but nothing happened, not even the slightest whisper of movement.

Rohan's face began to turn purple. They lied to him. They told him it would work. They told him he belonged.

Behind him, Odger started to laugh. It wasn't a pretty laugh, or one that brought a smile to the face of others. No, it was a derisive laugh, one that opens wounds with its high-pitched snort and wheezing exhale.

Rohan watched as he rocked to and fro, barely able to contain his glee at Rohan's failure.

He mimicked Rohan, lifting his hand and yelling "come", then burst into peals of laughter.

Rohan's anger grew from a simmering kettle into a raging volcano, his face contorting as Odger mocked him mercilessly. But unlike the day before, Rohan didn't lower his chin, he wouldn't let Odger defeat him again.

"No," cried Rohan.

He looked at the steel at the far end of the cell, and knew he wanted to hurt Odger with it.

"Come."

This time Rohan knew with a sense of certainty that it would work.

Even though he was expecting it, the result was more than Rohan could have imagined. Rather than just a single spoon or pot flying towards him, everything rushed directly towards his outstretched hand.

Both Rohan and Odger dived to the side, as the metal projectiles flew over their heads and smashed into the brick wall behind them. The metal menagerie clanged with an enormous boom, almost deafening Rohan and Odger as they hunkered down to avoid the spray. One solitary pot lid rolled away from them spinning on its edge. It travelled between two other cells, humming softly as it went. Now, out of sight, Rohan only knew it had stopped by the rotary ringing of its final clang.

Rohan rolled over, his knees and elbows bleeding where they had grazed the rough ground.

Odger's eyes flashed red, furious at Rohan. He picked up one of the metal tins that had collided with the wall and threw it at Rohan. It bounced of the bitumen near Rohan's head and rolled to the side.

Rohan looked at him darkly, his anger threatening to overcome him. But as he looked around, he recognised the damage he had caused. He had done this. He had called the steel and it had responded. It was his to control. He looked at Odger who was glaring at him angrily, but it didn't bother him. He had moved the steel. He was a Mover!

Odger sneered at Rohan.

"It seems that you have a least a little range, but no control."

Rohan didn't understand what he meant but smiled broadly, unwilling to let Odger take this moment from him.

Over the remainder of the morning, Rohan was able to eke out the smallest crumb of actual teaching from Odger. He grudgingly explained that range was the distance between the smallest object you could move and the largest.

While Rohan still harboured a small fear that his earlier explosion was some form of accident, these fears proved to be unfounded. Each time he called the steel and metal, he envisioned it doing the same thing it had that morning. It was so much easier to believe when you had recent experience. The steel flew towards him as though he had been doing it all his life. By the end of the lesson, moving steel and metal seemed like a natural extension of himself. It was as easy as catching a ball. Well, maybe not that easy. Although he had mastered calling the metal, stopping it from rushing towards him at a million miles an hour was proving more challenging.

Once Rohan felt more confident in his abilities, Odger announced that they needed to find the limits of Rohan's range. He explained that once they had a clear understanding of a Steeler's range, they could then work on controlling the elements within it.

Unfortunately, this turned out to be difficult. Following Rohan's initial explosion, Odger knew that Rohan's range extended from a spoon through to a trash can. At first, he asked Rohan to move some of the larger items, starting with a large cooking pot and working his way up. However, he soon gave that up as a bad idea. As Rohan started moving objects bigger than himself, it was no longer safe. This was evidenced by a flying refrigerator that nearly decapitated them both.

Odger quickly changed tactic and started working backwards, placing objects smaller that a spoon in front of Rohan. He started with a small tin soldier, an egg cup, and a thimble. As Rohan moved all these with ease, Odger looked at him curiously. Next, he placed a single coin at the far end of the cell. After Rohan called that, he tried a key, a metal ball bearing, and finally, a nail. When Rohan moved all these objects easily, Odger stopped looking at him with boredom and started looking at him with loathing.

"You know boy," Odger smirked as he looked at the cuts and scrapes that Rohan had received whilst avoiding projectiles, "I think this is a challenge I am going to enjoy. Tomorrow, we will do it again."

He shuffled away, his long yellow robe kicking up small stones and bits of dirt.

Rohan felt himself disliking Odger more and more. Every comment was one of derision and every activity felt like it was designed for Odger's personal amusement. He felt like a test subject, being poked and prodded without any care for the patient. Besides, he'd thought that once he could move things, it would be more fun. Being put through a series of tests wasn't exactly thrilling.

Though Odger had dismissed him early, this didn't bother Rohan at all. He was happy to be away from the slimy little man and couldn't wait to share his progress with Oak and Mara.

Rohan sat at one of the long pale wooden benches that lined the Cutting Room floor, staring up at the wires above him. He was the only one in the giant room, and it seemed to echo softly as it amplified the sounds of the Clinic. Rohan could hear the distant cracking of brick, the shattering of glass, and the distinct thud that came as gravity worked its magic. He had been hoping for an early lunch, but even the cooks hadn't made their way to the kitchens yet.

As Rohan stared at the wires, he wondered what drove the Faithful to attempt the challenge. It certainly wasn't a challenge of Conviction. It was more an obstacle course than anything else, but each of the Faithful seemed to hold the challenge in some reverence. Maybe it was a rite of passage, something that connected them all together. A common failure, Rohan mused.

Almost absentmindedly he began to plot his own course through the maze. He began analysing the distance between jumps and the force required to bridge the gaps. The more he looked at it, the more he respected the woman that he had seen attempting the challenge on his first day. Not only was it an incredibly difficult obstacle course, but you had to completely trust the rope that held you as well. One slip could mean a very nasty fall.

Rohan was so lost in thought that he didn't notice Galvor coming up behind him.

"She's an impressive sight ain't she?" Galvor noted staring at the web.

Rohan jumped in fright before nodding slowly.

"Yeah, I remember the first time I tried it. I think I made it about three feet before I wet the inside of my trouser leg. Don't like heights you see. No, I can think of much better things to do with my time than pounce from wire to wire like a frightened cat. Still, it is a challenge…" He let the sentence hang and resumed staring at the ceiling.

"What route you thinking about?"

Rohan snapped out of his stupor, "oh, what, um…. well, I hadn't really thought about it," lied Rohan.

"Don't lie," Galvor quipped. "We all think about it, it's just that most of us can't figure it out. But it's worth a shot. By the time you're done here, you'll have tried it at least a dozen times. If you can get past halfway, you've done better than most."

Rohan was about to explain to Galvor that it looked impossible, and he didn't know how anybody got past the first five metres, let alone past halfway, however at that moment he saw Amadyne enter the hall.

He waved, hoping to appear friendly. She was going to be his new teammate, so a little bit of effort wouldn't kill him.

Amadyne saw him waving and deliberately turned away, making her way to the far side of the room. The cooks were starting to arrive now, and a few others were filtering into the room also.

"Don't let it worry you lad," consoled Galvor, patting Rohan on the back. "I don't think she likes anybody. Don't know why, but it's been like that since she arrived." With that, he wandered away to chat with a few of the other Faithful.

Rohan watched as Amadyne settled down on a table as far away from him as possible.

Maybe she was like him? Maybe she was so used to being alone, that she didn't know how to get along with others. Heck, if it hadn't been for Oak, he wouldn't have made a single friend in the whole time he was at the Grey. Maybe she just needed somebody to give her the chance.

He shrugged to himself and returned his gaze to the wires above.

Chapter 15

The next day, Takash introduced the team to Za'Niyah, a veteran of the Faithful.

Za'Niyah was not what Rohan was expecting. He'd assumed that, like Takash, she would be a hardened warrior, barking gruff commands as she watched on in silence. Instead, she wore a long flowing dress, her hair was tied back with a single piece of string, and she smiled pleasantly as Takash completed his introduction. Rohan almost had to rub his eyes to comprehend the difference between the two. As he glanced at the others, he could tell they were thinking the same thing. Oak looked as confused as he was, Amadyne was scowling, while Mara was grinning like a merchant on market day. It appeared that she hadn't realised that there was an alternate to the sensible but stiff leathers.

"Good afternoon, everyone," Za'Niyah began, her voice deep and melodious. "I know that many of you were expecting another combat class, or at the very least some theory lessons..."

Oak groaned.

Za'Niyah smiled, "but our focus will be on building connections. These connections are what bring us together and allow us to grow as people and as a cell."

She motioned towards them, her palms opened outward.

"We are like the walls of a cell. On our own, we are easily knocked down, but when we work together, we can withstand anything. What this class will teach you is how to support your cell mates, to make each other stronger and forge connections that go beyond that of necessity. Once you understand these connections, and how powerful they can be, you will see your cell mates not only as friends and confidants, but as family."

Rohan couldn't help but roll his eyes. As much as he liked the idea of teamwork, the idea of "connections" and "confidants" was a little much. It appeared as though she hadn't lived in the real Central for a long time. The closest thing he'd had to a friend on the outside would have robbed him twice before he'd rolled out of bed. Perhaps the only person less excited about the classes was Amadyne, who was looking thunderous. It was clear that she expected to be the domineering force in their team, or cell as Za'Niyah referred to them. The idea of working together, rather than demanding obedience, was not a part of her plan.

"Wonderful," Za'Niyah announced, ignoring the expressions on the faces of the group. "Let's get started. This way," she strode between them, heading towards the nearest stairwell. Rohan gave Oak a wry smile before falling in behind.

As Rohan followed Za'Niyah, he realised that they were heading towards the old maternity ward. Where most of the Clinic was sterile and green in colour, the maternity ward had been painted a soft pink that somehow felt welcoming and warm. All the harshness of efficient design had been removed and replaced with thoughtful touches that subtly blended into furnishings. Elements of the Clinic, like the steel railings and door frames, still existed but the window coverings were brighter, and the lighting was somehow different. Perhaps it was the stark change that rankled Amadyne, and she sighed audibly as they entered the room.

Za'Niyah gave her a questioning look, raising an eyebrow slightly, but said nothing.

Inside they found half-a-dozen plush chairs set up in a circle. Za'Niyah took a seat in a high-backed grandfather chair and instructed them to sit. Oak and Mara took a seat in a sofa so soft that it sunk to the floor under Oak's weight. Mara giggled as she fell sideways into the giant. He grinned and attempted to prob himself up with the cushions that lay scattered around the room.

As they shifted uncomfortably in their new surroundings, Za'Niyah stared at them each in turn, as though assessing them through sight alone. This went on for what felt like an exorbitantly long time before Amadyne sighed again.

This time Za'Niyah turned to her, smoothly and silently, like a hunter setting a trap.

"Yes Amadyne?" her words though soft and pleasant, carried an edge none of them failed to recognise. "Is there something you wish to share with the group?"

Not expecting to share her thoughts, Amadyne froze.

"Uh, um, I…"

"Yes, dear?"

Amadyne looked positively terrified. She had no defence for her poor attitude and apologising was simply not in her nature.

Mara giggled.

A look of irritation flashed across Za'Niyah's face.

As though contemplating her next words, Za'Niyah sat back in her chair.

"These classes are not mandatory," she began, clasping her hands together, "and if you so choose, you may leave."

Rohan couldn't help glancing at the door.

"However, should you fail to meet my expectations, you will not progress to mission work. If you are unable to prove yourself capable of working as part of a team, we will not risk sending you out. Do I make myself clear?"

Rohan and the rest of his "cell mates" nodded.

Za'Niyah smiled, satisfied her point had been made.

"These rooms," she continued as though nothing had happened, "were designed to create a peaceful and harmonious environment. From the floor coverings to the lights, they were crafted to promote a sense of calm for women as they braved childbirth. The soft pinks represent a mother's warm embrace, the large windows, opportunity, and the large furniture, strength."

Though he knew he shouldn't, Rohan couldn't contain the smile that had spread to his lips. As he glanced at the others, it was clear he was not the only one. The concept behind the room was unlike anything they had experienced in Central.

Za'Niyah smiled, "I can see you all smirking, and I understand. These thoughts are so far removed from the lives we lead here in the Clinic that they are almost laughable." She paused, drawing them in.

"However, the lessons remain. As teams, or as a family, we need to find different ways to live together and to work together. It's not easy as we come from different places, and we are not raised to be understanding or forgiving. But in these rooms, we need to find harmony."

With that, she stood and began outlining the afternoon's activities. These ranged from staring into one another's eyes to sketching each other's faces.

Rohan could hear Amadyne's eyes rolling before they even started.

These sorts of activities didn't endear Za'Niyah to the group, and as much as he hated to agree with Amadyne, he suspected these classes were going to be a waste of time. After five minutes these suspicions were confirmed. Mara and Rohan broke into fits of giggles every time they looked at one another, while Oak was trying so hard to take it seriously that his face hurt. Amadyne, who didn't appear to have a sense of humour, remained stone-faced throughout.

This went on for weeks before anything that could be described as a breakthrough occurred. Before that, it was agony in the form of soft pillows and hugs.

The cell was divided into pairs and tasked with building a cardboard shelter. Revelling in some form of competition, Rohan found a willing partner in Mara. Utilising a previously unknown ability, she sketched out a plan involving a number of pillar-like boxes and flattened panels. Each piece would slot into one another, interlocking to provide strength and structure, like a giant puzzle coming together. It was elegant in its simplicity and Rohan marvelled at the speed at which she created the concept. Mara was certainly more than a Bio-Mover. She was incredibly intelligent and driven.

On the other hand, Oak and Amadyne's partnership seemed doomed from the beginning. As always, Amadyne took charge of the project. Her plan was to stack the boxes on top of one another and connect them with a series of cardboard spikes, like nailing plaster to a wall. However, the creation of each spike required a great deal of dexterity. Amadyne was able to make these with ease, but Oak's giant paws lacked the finesse to mould the spikes together. Though Amadyne remained positive on the surface, Rohan could see the rage growing behind her eyes. They persevered with their approach, miraculously managing to create something that resembled a small room. Although the ceiling sagged in places and the spikes were limited in their effectiveness, it was standing nonetheless. Unfortunately, that was when Oak noticed one of the spikes slipping from its hold. In an effort to save the structure, he entered the cardboard shell. As he did so, it became painfully clear that the doorway had not been designed for a person of his stature. The cardboard tore like tissue paper and he watched in horror as the entire structure fell to the floor around him.

Oak turned quickly to Amadyne, his face aghast. The room went quiet as they waited for Amadyne to explode. Rohan could see her face contorting as she struggled to suppress the rage building inside. Her face turned a strange red purple colour and her grey eyes bulged as the pressure built. Rohan turned to look at Oak and could see the remorse written across his face, evident to everybody in the room.

What Amadyne did next shocked him. Rather than berating her cell mate as they were expecting, a high-pitched squeal escaped from her lips. At first, Rohan thought it was the steam leaking from her ears, like a whistle announcing the end of shift. But then it broke into something more. She laughed. It was almost like an accident, as though it had escaped her lips before she had a chance to stop it. It started with a single bubble, and then grew into a hearty chortle and finally ballooned into an all-out laughing attack. It completely changed Amadyne. Gone was the frenzied perfectionist and in its place stood a person, a person who could be part of the cell, a person who could be more than a disgruntled teammate.

Then in an instant, it was gone. As though remembering who she was, her back straightened and her eyes snapped back to same steely gaze that had unnerved Rohan at their first meeting. When she had been laughing, they had warmed, becoming a light blue as though life had been poured into her soul and brightened her face. As she composed herself, Rohan saw this light flicker and disappear.

Whilst he and Mara won the competition, he felt as though they had all won. They'd seen that there was another Amadyne below the shell she'd created. Maybe Amadyne also learnt something. Maybe she started to understand her cellmates better. Rohan wasn't entirely sure, but he was relieved to find that there was more to Amadyne than what was on the surface.

Chapter 16

Rohan's lessons with Odger continued in much the same way as the first. Each morning, Takash ensured that the little man appeared in the cell and at least gave the pretence of teaching. This meant that Odger was forced into helping Rohan find his range. They tested objects of every shape, size, colour, and texture. From steel funnels through to corrugated iron sheets. It didn't seem to make any difference to Rohan. He believed that he could move any steel object because that's how he understood Conviction. It wasn't necessarily taxing work, but every time he called an object towards himself, he ended up sprawled on the black asphalt dodging missiles. The worst was the sheet of corrugated iron. It flew with such a ferocity that it became a giant blade that threated to take his head right off his shoulders. As a result of all this dodging and diving, his legs and arms resembled a tartan mat, a crosshatch of red and black. While Odger laughed sadistically every time Rohan fell, Oak and Mara looked at him with growing concern.

"Is he trying to kill you?" asked Oak one night as they made their way to the Cutting Room.

Rohan shrugged and kept walking.

"This didn't happen to me when I started my training," Oak continued, "I spent one day learning how to catch stones and rocks, then we moved onto punching and kicking." He held up his fist, swinging it through the air as though destroying some invisible opponent.

"Yeah, that's because you have the range of a toothpick," laughed Rohan as his giant friend started to shadowbox the air around them.

It was true. Oak had almost no range. He was for all purposes a wrecking ball. Ask him to do anything delicate or with finesse and you might as well ask pigs to fly. Rohan suspected that it was Oak's size that limited his range. In his day-to-day life, he didn't have the dexterity to manipulate small objects, so it made no sense that he'd be able to do this as an Earthworker. It was the perfect example of abilities being unique to each Mover.

"I didn't take that long either," Mara offered, her eyes cast endearingly over Oak. "It took me a couple of days, definitely longer than this oaf," she gestured towards Oak who was now practising his kicks. "Galvor basically had me move as many different types of plants and trees as I could. Once we figured out what was possible, we then tried the same types of materials with different sizes and weights. It really didn't take that long."

This didn't make Rohan feel any better. There seemed to be no end in sight to Odger's testing. He sighed, looking at the cold linoleum beneath their feet.

Mara looked pensive as she peered at Rohan.

"Is he using the same materials over and over again?" she asked, "or keeping the weights the same?"

Rohan shook his head, "no, it's always something different, it's only the results that are the same."

Mara stopped walking abruptly, even Oak who was apparently in his own world stopped kicking the air and looked at Rohan.

"Rohan, how many objects have you moved?"

Rohan shrugged, "I dunno, fifty, a hundred?"

"And is there anything you haven't been able to move?"

Rohan paused, suspecting that this was some form of trick question, "nothing yet, I guess."

Oak's jaw dropped. Even Mara seemed shocked.

"You mean that all these weeks and after all your complaining, you've been able to move everything that Odger has put in front of you?"

"Well, yeah," Rohan responded confused. "I mean, I haven't tried anything too big yet, just a couple of girders and beams but no cars or anything."

Mara and Oak continued to look at Rohan awestruck.

"That's normal, isn't it?" asked Rohan, now a little nervous.

A silence broke over the group as each cellmate comprehended the answer.

"No, no, it's not," Mara finally managed to say, her eyes still bulging slightly. "You are only supposed to be able to move a few things. If we were to break range down to a number figure, say, one to ten, most people can move things between three and five. If what you're saying is right, your range is like one to thirty-five."

"Oh," was the only word, or partial word Rohan could get out. That would explain why the testing was taking so long. Maybe he was some sort of freak. His stomach started to fill with butterflies, unsure how to take the news. He didn't want to be different to everybody else. Being part of the Faithful was enough.

Oak and Mara continued to glance at Rohan as they reached the Cutting Room. While they didn't say anything, Rohan could tell that something had changed, he was no longer just Rohan to them.

Chapter 17

As much as Rohan hated his lessons with Odger, he loathed the lessons in the maternity ward. He'd thought that after Amadyne's outburst that things would be better, but instead, they had gone markedly downhill.

While Oak, Mara, and he seemed to work well together, Amadyne now refused to partake in any of the exercises. When she was feeling particularly irritable, she would start muttering insults or bemoaning the general incompetence of all those involved. She was like a poison that infected all those around her.

This is how it usually started. An innocuous comment or mild insult burying itself into the group and feeding on their insecurities. This led to hurt feelings and members of the cell acting defensively in an effort of prove Amadyne wrong. The problem was that there was always a hint of truth in Amadyne's comments, and the words rubbed them raw.

After one particularly explosive lesson in which Oak had berated Rohan for not taking things seriously, Rohan felt the need to escape. He was tired. He was sick of the constant bickering, and he was sick of the Clinic.

He thought that once he knew what his purpose was that he'd be fulfilled. What he hadn't counted on was all the work required to get there. He was also struggling to come to the realisation that he wasn't alone anymore. It was a dramatic change for him. He couldn't do what he wanted anymore, he needed other people, and what was worse, they needed him.

He thought about Odger and Takash. Without them he might not ever be a proper member of the Faithful. Right now, he was a liability, a Mover without any control or skill. It was a scary prospect and without the right training, he could be a danger to those people around him. He thought about his breaking and shuddered at the memory. If it happened again, he could kill someone. He could kill Oak or Mara.

That thought filled him with dread. Oak and Mara were the best things about the Clinic. When they weren't bickering, their companionship was more than Rohan could have ever asked for. Oak was his best friend, somebody that Rohan knew he could depend upon, and Mara was the most generous person he'd ever met. That's not to say that she handed over her food or anything, but she was always there answering his questions with patience. She gave more of herself away than she kept to herself. Rohan could see why Oak loved her.

Watching their relationship was like watching a pair of birds fly together. They would dart in and out from one another, stealing moments when they could. Then they would dance, spiralling up and up until they finally came together in a lasting embrace.

Rohan felt lucky to be a part of it, even if he was the third wheel a lot of the time. It was something very normal in what was a very abnormal place.

With these thoughts flowing through his head, Rohan left to find the only retreat that was still entirely his own, running.

The pressure that had been weighing Rohan down began to release itself as soon as his feet started to move. It was as though he had been tied down by a thousand boulders and one by one, each was letting go. It felt like a tremendous relief after the intense training they had been going through these past weeks.

At first, Rohan thought the pressure came from Odger's lessons and his struggle to find his range. However, he soon realised that it was more than that. It was the experience of being thrust into a new environment, one with teammates and rules and responsibilities. Being one of the Faithful meant taking in a lot at once, and Rohan was finding it overwhelming. His mind felt like a balloon filling with water. At first, it had seemed ok, and he swelled slightly as the information and newness poured into him. However, as it continued, he found himself swelling more and more, straining at the sides. The pressure kept mounting, forcing him into a shape that wasn't his own. Even recognising his own weakness added to the pressure.

It was a lot, and Rohan knew that he wasn't the only person feeling the strain.

He watched as Oak and Mara became testier, bickering with one another to relieve their own tension. He watched as Amadyne physically tensed as she entered the classroom, steeling herself for another session. Even the instructors, Odger and Za'Niyah, seemed to be on edge, as though holding their breath in expectation.

It created an atmosphere alive with static, feeding upon the doubts and frustrations of the group.

Running was the only thing that provided momentary relief.

He rejoiced as he stretched out his long limbs, feet slapping the pavement like a chorus. It was rhythmic and relaxing. He felt the wind caress his face as his brow began to glisten with sweat. He floated across the uneven ground easily, barely touching the earth before he was carried forward with his next stride. Over walls and gates, he moved with a motion embedded in his being. Every movement had purpose and required no more, and no less energy to propel him onwards. Unlike his runs with Takash, Rohan had no destination in mind. He let his mind wander freely with his feet being led by whim and fancy. He ran down main roads, crossed buildings, and scrambled over walls. He felt no restraint, no shackles holding him back, and it felt wonderful. With sweat now dripping from his face, he slowed, determined to catch his breath. As good a runner as Rohan was, even he had his limits. He spotted a disused balcony on a low-rise building ahead and let himself be carried towards his resting stop.

The balcony was nothing special. It was everything it seemed, a dark grey projection on a concrete structure. Whilst to others this may have felt disappointing, to Rohan it was reassuring. Not only was it familiar, but it provided a sense of safety and strength. He grinned wryly at himself. Often on runs with Takash, he had led them across perilous structures, rusted with age and sagging on their last bolts. They would often creak or bend as you landed on them. It made Rohan nervous every time this happened. He glanced around at his surroundings, trying to find his bearings in the sea of grey. Finally, he spotted a building he recognised. It was a long way away. He'd travelled further than he thought. Inwardly he was a little annoyed at himself. He had wandered too far off the beaten track and wasn't sure how long it would take to get home. He resigned himself to a long run back.

As he waited for his breath to catch up, he found himself musing over the events of the past few weeks. The run had taken the edge off his anger, he was left with a simmering frustration, like a stone stuck in his shoe. He felt like he was being punished but couldn't understand why. It was as though Odger felt some personal animosity towards him. Oak had suggested that perhaps he was jealous. It was evident that Odger had a small range, limited perhaps to the size of the small wire in his hand. Rohan knew this because after every test Odger would physically maneuverer the next test object into place, rather than using his abilities. That was one of the strange things about the Faithful. Once they discovered they had abilities, they became incredibly lazy. No longer content to waste their energy on menial tasks, they would use their abilities in every situation. He was sure he had seen a Bio-Mover call a wooden bowl across one of the Cutting Room tables, rather than reaching for it himself.

Rohan was looking forward to being able to call objects with control. He still hadn't figured out how to stop himself from making objects fly at him like they'd been shot out of a cannon. Whenever he asked Odger about it, Odger would give him an oily smile and suggest that they focus on one thing at a time.

None of it really mattered. Rohan had to do whatever Odger wanted. If he didn't, he could hurt himself or someone else. No, for the time being he would keep doing whatever the Faithful asked.

He was about to run back to the Clinic again when he spotted movement below. It wasn't a lot, but there was a flicker of light and shadow that cast itself across the building for a split second. Rohan knew enough from his time at Shackle St. not to take any risks. He crouched behind the wall of his balcony, resting on the balls of his feet. He saw the shadow lengthening as something made its way into the alley below. He assumed it was a person but was unsure who it could be. The gangs of Central didn't go anywhere alone, nor were they stealthy in their approach. Normal citizens wouldn't wander down an alley alone and nobody from the Grey could have followed him. Of that he was certain.

He watched and waited.

After what seemed an eternity, a figure emerged. It was Amadyne.

Rohan was stunned. Of all people to find, she seemed the least likely. As he watched her, he felt uncomfortable. Seeing somebody outside the Grey or the Clinic was like seeing them naked. They hadn't had a chance to put on their shield or their mask. They were vulnerable.

It certainly seemed like this was the case for Amadyne. Gone were the confident strides and the rigid posture. Instead, she seemed almost nervous. He watched as she peered around each corner before proceeding, moving with purpose but also hesitation. Rohan followed her, moving across the roof tops. He bounded easily across the divides that separated the buildings, landing each time with the grace of a bird in flight. She glanced up a few times as though looking for a pursuer, but Rohan leaned into the corners of the building, hiding himself from her gaze.

Finally, she came to a small courtyard. It was surrounded by large, opulent buildings. Rohan assumed that fancy people had once lived there. He could tell because all the balconies were made from formed steel, bent into elegant shapes. The steel had once been painted white, but this was now peeling and cracked, leaving flashes of red and brown to melt down the sides. It gave the courtyard a sense of elegance and beauty, not normally revealed in Central.

Rohan watched as Amadyne began to stretch, her strong body moving into a series of familiar exercises. She moved with a confidence born of years of practice. Rohan could see that these simple movements brought her confidence and the nervousness that had been evident before was now replaced with a silent sense of self. Her gaze was steadfast and focused as she moved from motion to motion, her pace quickening as she worked further through the exercises. Rohan was transfixed. He had never looked at Amadyne like this before. There was something breathtaking about the way she moved. It was precise, powerful, and graceful. She moved with such ease that Rohan could only marvel at the control she had over her body. As she quickened, Rohan could see her breathing in and out in perfect unison with the series of jabs and kicks she was doing.

For the first time, Rohan noticed how beautiful she was. Perhaps it was the relief of being outside the Clinic that did it, but in this environment her face softened. Gone was the sneer that seemed to be a permanent fixture on her upper lip. Gone was the hardness and gone was the arrogance. All that was left was beautiful. It's not to say that she was perfect, her chin was perhaps a little too pointed and she was marked with cuts and bruises from combat, but these imperfections only seemed to add to her beauty. They complemented her confidence and attitude. Oddly, the thing that Rohan noticed most about her was the shape of her nose. It was small, slightly upturned, and as symmetrical as two sides of a mirror. It seemed to punctuate her face perfectly, as though sculpted by an artist. Rohan shook his head in wonder. Could this be the same person who yelled at him each day?

Maybe all they saw at the Clinic was a mask, maybe this was the real Amadyne, like the one that had laughed at Oak in Za'Niyah's class.

All too soon, she wound down her exercises, finishing with a simple stretch to ensure her muscles cooled appropriately.

Rohan didn't know whether to be disappointed or relieved. He had watched in near reverence as she worked but felt relieved that she hadn't noticed him. He imagined her anger if she had caught him. He could picture her face darkening as she shattered the glass around them, threatening his life with the razor-sharp shards. It felt all too real.

He waited on the balcony for a long while after she left, making sure that she was gone before he left his perch. His mind was now swirling with thoughts beyond those of Za'Niyah and Odger. His run, which has been so cathartic, was now the cause of his confusion. Was there more to Amadyne then he thought? Then again, all he had seen was her stretching. It wasn't like she had saved a drowning child or rescued a puppy. Maybe he just liked the way she looked.

His mind awash with thoughts of Amadyne, he began his journey back to the Clinic. He took a much safer route this time, sticking to the street-level roads that criss-crossed the city. As he grew closer to the compound, he once again found himself relaxing, so much so that he almost didn't see the lone figure hovering in the darkness.

"Agghhh!" he yelled, bludgeoned abruptly from his daydream. "What?!"

He ducked as he felt a fist swing over his head, grazing the very top of his scalp. He stepped to the side to see another fist coming directly at his face. He tilted his head, again just avoiding the strike.

He was stunned. Where had this person come from? And why were they attacking him? He glanced at them momentarily, but their face was obscured by a dark hood, the failing light unable to give him any insight. Before he could think to ask, they attacked again launching a series of punches, each designed to take his head off.

The training from Oak kicked in and soon Rohan wasn't just avoiding being kicked, he was fighting back. As his attacker struck, he found himself grasping their arm and wrenching it over his turned shoulder. Surprised, they flew involuntarily over Rohan's back, somehow landing on their feet on the other side.

Rohan blinked. It wasn't often somebody landed on their feet. This was one seriously talented fighter. But so was Rohan.

Rohan launched his own attack, moving swiftly to capitalise on his opponent's surprise. He stepped towards his smaller opponent and loosed a flurry of punches, each delivered with the speed of an adder striking. Not even Oak could dodge when Rohan put his mind to it. He finished with a kick to the chest of his opponent, slamming them into the brick wall of the alley.

"Oomph," he heard his attacker gasp as the air was driven from their lungs by the combined force of Rohan's kick and the wall behind.

Rohan hesitated, "Amadyne?"

The hood fell from her face as the faint light reflected her features.

She grunted and looked at him, her face a thunderstorm.

"Why were you following me?" she demanded, moving back into a fighting stance.

Rohan shifted uncomfortably. He hadn't been following her, and he was sure she hadn't seen him in the courtyard. Even then he'd left her plenty of time to get back to the Clinic so she wouldn't catch him.

"What?" he changed position, mirroring her stance. "I wasn't following you."

"Really," she snarled, "then why are you out here so late?"

"I was running," stammered Rohan, thrown by her aggressiveness. This was a stark contrast to the Amadyne he had seen only an hour or two before. "I run at night sometimes. It... it helps me clear my mind."

"Bullshit, you little Northerner."

"No, it's true. You can ask Oak or Mara," said Rohan as he lifted his hands in mock surrender.

Amadyne remained in a fighting stance, clearly considering whether this merited a sufficient response.

Finally, she relaxed. Straightening, she glared at Rohan.

"Fine. But if it happens again, you won't live to tell anyone about it."

Happens again? thought Rohan. It was a fluke the first time. What were the chances that he found her in the first place, let alone ran into her a second time? He was still thinking about her practice routine in the courtyard.

"What are you doing out here then?" asked Rohan, realising that he now had a convenient excuse to ask.

Amadyne snarled at him.

"Hey, you asked me... actually you attacked me and all I was doing was running," snapped Rohan, getting angry now. She wasn't special. He had as much right to know as she did.

"None of your damn business," rasped Amadyne, glaring at him.

"No... I mean, yes. Yes, it is," stammered Rohan. "I find you randomly out on the street and you physically attack me. I want an answer. You don't get to brush it off."

"I can do what I want. Nobody tells me what to do. Not Takash, not Za'Niyah, and certainly not you," spat Amadyne, her voice edged with venom.

"Yeah, that's right, isn't it?" sneered Rohan. "I forgot, you don't listen to anyone. You think you're too good for the Clinic, right?"

All the frustration that Rohan had been feeling towards Amadyne was coming to the fore and spilling out of his mouth before he could stop himself.

"You've been a stuck-up Northerner ever since I arrived. Always walking around like you own the place. For some reason, you seem to think that Mara, Oak, and I are beneath you. Well guess what? It's not us that's the problem, it's you. You make life difficult. Rather than being a leader and working with your cell mates, you take petty swipes at us and act superior. You're not a leader. You're a self-entitled waste of air that has a false impression of her own abilities. You're not even that good," lied Rohan. "I heard that you've been one of the Faithful for ages, but this is your first team. And why is that? Because nobody wants you. You're a pathetic Northerner that only thinks about themselves."

Rohan regretted the words as soon as they left his lips. He knew what he said was harsh and exaggerated. He had targeted all the hurt and pain he had been feeling directly at Amadyne.

Looking at Amadyne, he could see that his words had hurt more than any kick or punch could have.

She looked at him, her mouth agape in shock.

Rohan had the distinct impression that nobody had ever spoken to her like that before.

She stood still, her body shaking as she strained to control herself.

Rohan stood resolutely, looking directly into her eyes as though daring her to contradict him.

Finally, after what seemed like an eternity, she shifted her feet and lowered her head, not in defeat, but in resignation.

"You don't know anything," she whispered, her voice barely carrying the short distance to Rohan.

Rohan was taken aback. He had not expected her to back down. He had expected her to yell, to scream, to destroy him with a single slash of a glass shard, anything but what happened.

He watched as she turned on her heels and trudged back to the Clinic, the arrogant stride gone.

Rohan was now more confused than ever. He didn't know whether to be scared, angry, or depressed. Amadyne was a giant pain in the ass, but she deserved better than he had treated her.

He sighed and plodded slowly after Amadyne.

Chapter 18

Za'Niyah's classes gradually began to change from team bonding into team-sharing sessions. It was even less fun and a lot more talking. Rohan did not like the change.

Za'Niyah insisted that getting to know one another was a key element in building trust. She believed that there needed to be complete honesty between cellmates and that understanding one another's history was a part of building that trust.

Following Rohan and Amadyne's recent encounter, he couldn't envision a worse time. Amadyne had returned to her usual abrasive self, regularly correcting the others, and trying to take over group activities. The only difference was that she refused to make eye contact with Rohan. It was as though she feared looking at him would break the delicate walls that hid her emotions. Rohan doubted that was true. Before that night, he could have sworn that she had no emotions. Still, it was a nice change from the usual glares he received from her, even if he did feel a little guilty every time she looked away.

On the other hand, Oak and Mara seemed to relish the sessions with Za'Niyah. Rohan personally believed they used it as a couples' counselling session. It was filled with a lot of oohs and ahhs from Mara and some serious mooning from Oak. Rohan felt sick as he watched the two of them.

For Rohan, Za'Niyah's classes were a new experience. He had never really taken the time to get to know somebody before. What did he care about somebody's parents, home, or background? If it didn't affect him, it was irrelevant. Every time Za'Niyah asked him to talk about growing up in Shackle St., he would shrug, responding that there was very little to tell. Why did they all need to know about the constant fight for food, for space, for survival? It was Rohan's scar, and they didn't need to share it. Amadyne responded in a similar way, grunting in response to Za'Niyah's probing.

As the sessions continued, Rohan remained silent, but found himself being drawn into the stories of his cellmates. He had never realised how much there was to people, probably because he had never cared. He was especially ashamed that he didn't know anything about Oak. He didn't know that his only friend had once been held captive, forced to work in the underground subways that criss-crossed the city. He didn't know that he had a family, and that he hadn't seen them since escaping.

It explained so much about his friend. It gave Rohan insights into why Oak had such a protective nature and why the ability to move rock and stone made so much sense.

As he listened to Oak describe his path to the Clinic, he noticed the giant taking large pauses, clearly struggling to put into words the emotion he felt.

Oak started by describing the place where he was born. Even though Rohan was sure Oak's memory was clouded, he described it like a haven.

"It was beautiful in its ugliness," he started. "It was like finding a room that had been trashed by one of the gangs and painted with cuss words and dirty pictures. If you looked at each of the drawings or words separately, you would be disgusted," he grinned, "but if you take a step back and look at it as one big picture," he shrugged, "it's something more. It's beautiful. It's a clash of colours and lines that screams of pain and anger. In that way, it's not a jumble, it's a story. I think that's what my home was like."

He explained, that like all of Central, his home was hot, dry, and dusty, but unlike the urban jungle Rohan had experienced, his was desolate, a wilderness inhabited by only his community. He talked about the nights and how he would stare at the sky and watch the stars pass.

After one of Oak's pauses, in which he seemed to become lost, he continued, "I think that's what I miss about being there. It's not the food, or the sheds where we lived. It's the silence." He described how the silence in the city was different to the silence he experienced. He explained that his silence was not the silence of anticipation or of fear, but a silence that required no words, a silence that was his alone.

Oak paused again.

"You know what?" he asked the group rhetorically. "At the time, I hated it. I hated the emptiness and quiet. I used to think that we lived in the most boring place in the world. It's funny what you miss isn't it?"

He looked at the faces of each of his cellmates in turn. They smiled at him, nodding slowly, none truly comprehending the life into which he had been born.

Oak continued, gesturing as he spoke. "I was born on one of the old plantations outside the city, a long way from where they were now. In fact, growing up, I didn't know anything about the divisions of Central, North, South, and East. In fact, I didn't know much about anything except farming. We lived in a collection of abandoned warehouses and sheds. I think that they had once been used to store huge amounts of wheat and corn grain."

Rohan looked at him sceptically but didn't interrupt.

"My mother was sick. She had one of those coughs that gurgled with every vibration. It was her lungs. The dust where we lived caked her insides and it was slowly choking her. She found it particularly difficult at nights. I can still remember feeling completely helpless when her coughing shook the tin sheets that surrounded us. She always tried to hide it, smiling whenever anybody asked, but we all knew she was getting worse. My little brother and sister were like her. They caught every cough, cold, or fever that everybody else managed to avoid. It meant they spent a lot of their time indoors, shut away from the rest of the community."

He paused, composing himself.

"I don't really remember my dad. He was a myth, a person about whom everybody told stories, but nobody ever saw." Oak grinned. "Apparently, he was huge and as strong as an Ox. I think that's where I get it from. The men in the sheds told me a story about how he had carried three men back from a hunting party gone wrong. They had been out hunting wild dogs and were cornered by the pack. They managed to escape, but two of them were bleeding out and a third had a broken leg. With a man on each shoulder and the third dragging behind him on a makeshift stretcher, he brought them back to the sheds where they lived. It took him two days, but he bought them home."

Oak paused.

"I don't know what happened to him, nobody ever said, but I think that's why they always looked after my mother. The other kids didn't understand, and they picked on me and my brother and sister, calling us weak because we had to ask for help. I fought them for it, but it didn't do anything."

Rohan disagreed. He imagined that this was where Oak had first learnt to fight.

"We used to farm the fields that surrounded our home. It was really poor ground and getting anything to grow was difficult, but we got by. Because I was big for my age, I had to help with the farming and for as long as I can remember, I was carrying buckets or planting crops," he grinned, "I started to get pretty strong, and the men outside started calling me Oak. That's where my name came from. I can't even remember my real name anymore. I remember the first time my brother and sister were allowed to come and help in the fields," smiled Oak, his eyes glistening as he recalled the memory.

"They were so small and were more hindrance than help. They were constantly underfoot and ran around chasing the moths that fed on the turnips. I think they were relieved to be let outside. But at the end of the day, when we were exhausted and headed back to the sheds, they ran up to me, so excited."

Oak paused.

"They were so excited…" he wiped his eyes, the pools that had been forming, now slid down his cheeks. "They were just holding a few rocks and a small potato, but they were so proud. They were so proud that they had helped." He mashed his giant paw across his nose, smearing the tears and snot across his face.

Mara sat looking at Oak as though he were a hero. He could see that she longed to throw her hands around his neck, but her eagerness for the rest of the story held her back.

"Anyway," sniffed Oak, finding his voice again, "it was soon after this that the gangs began to arrive."

Rohan's head snapped up. He hadn't known that Oak had experienced the torment of the gangs.

"At first, we didn't really notice. It was just a few missing turnips or shovels, nothing too major. Stuff goes missing all the time. It wasn't a bit deal," he shook his head.

"I wish we realised at the time. We… well, we might have been able to do something."

Amadyne grunted, clearly bored with Oak's story.

Mara gave her the filthiest look Rohan had ever seen. If there was a way that Mara could have melted Amadyne with her eyes, this look was it.

Amadyne sank back into her chair sniffing but didn't contribute any further.

"They started to get more and more confident, until we couldn't ignore it further. Our crops were disappearing, our tools were gone and there were boot prints around the sheds each morning. Eventually, they must have decided that simply taking our food wasn't enough anymore. I remember, we were out in the field when we were approached by this gang leader." Oak's face darkened.

"He was wearing full black, and he carried a huge knife like a scythe in his hand. He was grinning like he was some sort of maniac and walking across the field like he owned the place. Worst of all, he wasn't alone. There was probably another five or ten of them behind him, all laughing and carrying on like a pack of dogs. I was too far away to hear what he said, but when he walked over, he spoke to Gar Teke, one of the oldest men there. Apparently, he was demanding that we give them our food. Not all of it, but enough that we wouldn't be able to survive. He threatened to kill us if we didn't."

Rohan was shocked, was that real, could that happen?

Oak continued, "at first, we didn't believe him. We didn't know who he was, or how he even found us. So we ignored him. The next day he turned up again, still with the stupid grin, but this time there was a truck full of gang members. There was probably thirty of them, all laughing and jeering at us. He strode up to Gar Teke again asking for the food. When Gar Teke told him there was none, he grinned more, like he was a madman or something. He waved at the truck, then turned and punched Gar Teke in the mouth, knocking him to the ground."

Mara gasped.

Oak eyed her sadly, "that's not the bad bit. When Gar Teke fell, the man laughed, and once again demanded that we give them the food. Right then, we probably would have, but it would have killed us. We couldn't survive on what they were willing to let us keep. So we ignored them. He didn't come again the next day, or the next. We thought he had given up. We were wrong. It was a few nights later..." He paused, steeling himself.

Even Amadyne was listening intently now, the tension as thick as tar.

"I don't know who smelled it first, but suddenly there was panic. There was light in the sheds, which never happened at night, and we could see smoke creeping up under the edges of the tin. Actually, they were glowing red, heated from the fires they had lit on the outside of the building. The smoke started to pour in as the tin warped and twisted. I remember everybody coughing and spluttering as the smoke threatened to smother us. They had locked the doors from the outside, and there were no windows to speak of. People were banging on the walls trying to escape. It sounded like corn popping in a pot, banging, and clattering on the steel. I... I was scared. All I could think was that the smoke was bad for mom and the twins. All I wanted to do was get them out of there. The walls were like fire now and too hot to touch. People's hands were blistering as they struck the tin, and they were falling like flies as the smoke engulfed them."

He stopped. "Actually, it was the first time I moved anything. I was so scared, so terrified of what was happening, that I started swinging at anything that moved. I couldn't see anything properly, and I didn't know if they were in the building or not. I was panicking and I'm not sure what happened next, but suddenly, there was hole in the ground between the floor and the wall. I didn't even realise that I had done it. All I knew was that suddenly there was a way out. People were scrambling for the hole, pushing past one another to get out. Eventually, we managed to crawl out, me and probably another twenty of us. I could see the twins crying as they were held by gang members, and there were a few people with cuts and bruises sitting on the ground... but that's all I remember."

A silence that was shared by the group followed.

"What happened next?" prompted Za'Niyah, her eyes tinged with anticipation and sadness.

"I'm not sure," replied Oak softly. "I passed out. It could have been the smoke, or maybe somebody hit me, I don't really know. What I do know is that the next time I woke up, I was attached to a giant steel chain in the bottom of a subway tunnel."

"What about your home, your family?" cried Mara, her voice cracking as she felt the pain of Oak's story.

Oak shook his head slowly. "I dunno. I haven't seen them again. I don't remember the journey to the city, where we stopped, or even where we slept. Maybe the saddest part is that I don't even know where to look. I don't know where home is."

With that, Mara transformed into a blubbering mess. She threw her arms around Oak and sobbed gently into his chest. Even Amadyne had fallen silent, shaken by the moments that transformed Oak's life.

Maybe Za'Niyah's strategy had some merit. Knowing just a little more about Oak had started to bring them together.

Chapter 19

"Enough!" cried Rohan, his patience with Odger coming to an end.

Though Mara and Oak had told him to wait, he found himself squaring up to Odger in the middle of his lesson. Rohan felt as though he hadn't done anything new since he had arrived at the Clinic. Every exercise Odger put him through was a repetition. He felt like he was on a constant loop. Train with Odger, complain to Oak and Mara, repeat.

Odger looked at Rohan lazily. Rohan had snapped before, actually, he had snapped a number of times. Rohan estimated that he argued with Odger at least once per week, but it always ended the same way, with Odger ignoring him and delivering more punishments.

"Can we please try something different?" pleaded Rohan as he lifted himself off the floor for the tenth time that morning.

"Different you say?" mused Odger, a hint of disappointment crossing his face. "Are you not enjoying the lesson dear boy?"

"No, I am bloody well not!" snapped Rohan, "and you know it you... you, sadist."

Odger chuckled, his laugh more disturbing than all the lessons combined.

"I suppose we could try something new. Is there anything you had in mind?"

"Could we try moving an object away from me, rather than at me for once?" Rohan asked Odger wearily, knowing what the answer would be.

When Odger shrugged indifferently, Rohan's heart leapt.

"Really?! We can try?" Rohan asked in disbelief.

Odger grunted and placed a small frying pan on a small wooden stand in the middle of the cell.

"Well, boy. It seems that finding your range has bored you, and I don't care for your complaining and whining. If you don't want to do it properly, what do I care?"

Rohan was too excited to be perturbed by Odger's indifference.

"But," continued Odger, "you should understand why we only pull objects right now, as opposed to pushing them."

Odger always referred to the pushing and pulling of objects, rather than simply moving them. He had once explained, in a rare moment of actual teaching, that any idiot could move an object, but only a true Mover had the ability to control their actions. Pushing and pulling required control, not just ability.

"When you pull an object towards you, the only person in danger is yourself. You can see the object coming and can take steps to avoid it," he gestured towards the cuts and scrapes that covered Rohan's arms and legs. "When you push an object, you put others in danger. They may be unprepared or unaware of the object that you have pushed towards them. Now you are responsible for not just yourself, but for everybody else… including me."

Rohan hadn't thought about it like that before. He had just thought about it as another skill that needed to be learnt. He had forgotten that the Clinic wasn't just there to teach him to use his abilities, it was there to turn him into a weapon.

"Additionally," continued Odger, "when you pull an object, the object is locked to you and will travel in a straight line. When you push an object, you have to give it its direction. Now, call the pan."

Rohan sighed internally, he had done this a thousand times before. He lifted his hand and commanded the pan to come towards him, "come."

As usual, the pan flew at him at a thousand miles per hour, but this time, something else happened. As Rohan dived out of the way, the pan seemed to follow him, changing its trajectory mid-flight. It smashed into his elbow shooting vibrations up his arm and into his shoulder.

"Owww!" yelled Rohan, more in frustration than pain. "How did that happen?"

Odger laughed gleefully, clapping his hands in delight. "Haha, a little push is all it takes."

"What?"

"That my dear boy was the power of control. All I did was give the pan a little push and it was able to change direction and follow you to the ground."

"You could have just told me," grumbled Rohan as he climbed to his feet.

"Yes, I could have," grinned Odger, his mouth twitching in sadistic delight. "You see, not many Movers could do such a thing," his chest puffing out at this statement. "Instead, they summon great amounts of pushing power and throw the object completely off course. It's like using a fan to move a feather, rather than a single puff of air."

Rohan considered this for a moment. He hadn't realised it before, but what Odger had just done was incredible, no wonder Takash said he was one of the best Steelers. He glanced at his teacher as Odger collected the frying pan and placed it back on the wooden stand. Odger was a lot more talented than he had realised, even if he was a Northerner.

"But you are a child. It is unlikely that you will ever be able to do such a thing. We need to start with something easy."

"That would be nice," grunted Rohan, dusting the gravel off his trousers.

"It's actually quite simple," began Odger, "each object responds to the strength of your command. The more forceful you are, the quicker it moves. Like the difference between Takash yelling and Takash asking. I know which one would make me move quicker."

Rohan looked at him. It couldn't be that simple, could it?

He moved into his stance preparing to call the frying pan once more, but before he could speak, Odger stopped him again.

"Also, you don't need to do all that," he waved at Rohan dismissively.

Rohan looked at his feet and hands confused. "All what?"

"All that moving and shouting. It gives me a headache."

Rohan was more confused than ever. He's seen Amadyne and some of the others do this when they moved things. In fact, every time he walked out of the training area, he saw different Movers shaping up.

He straightened, still confused. "What?"

Odger sighed, then turned to him with a fake smile.

"All that moving about and shouting. It's unnecessary."

"But everybody else…"

Odger raised his hand before Rohan could continue. "Everybody else is an idiot." He almost spat the words. "All that movement and loud talking is just for show-offs. If I did that every time I broke into a house, I would have been caught immediately."

Rohan was stunned. How could everybody else be wrong? He thought of Amadyne's elaborate stance the first time they met. She had moved her entire body, using her arms and legs to push and pull the small ball of glass. Even now Rohan marvelled at the control she possessed.

"Again," snapped Odger, interrupting Rohan's stream of thought.

Rohan started to move into his stance once more, before catching himself. What Odger said kind of made sense. It wasn't him lifting or moving anything. It's not like he physically did anything, it was all Conviction.

He straightened his back and moved back into a casual standing position.

Odger smiled.

"Come," he commanded, his hand stretching out involuntarily. Once again, the frying pan flew at him with the velocity of a bull being let out of its pen.

"Idiot boy!" screamed Odger, his rat nose practically steaming. "What did I just say?" he raised his hands to his head as though failing to comprehend Rohan's stupidity. "Let me say it again, but this time I'll dumb it down so that you can understand it. Big talk equals big move. Small talk equals small move." He used his hands to demonstrate the difference between big and small.

Rohan was quickly reminded why he didn't like Odger. He was a bloody Northerner. Now fuming, he stood again, picking up the frying pan as he climbed to his feet. He stalked to the podium, slamming it onto the wooden top and marched back to his starting point.

Odger glared at him.

Rohan glared back. He held out his hand and without saying a word whispered to the frying pan, "come."

The pan lifted itself off the podium and gently transported itself into Rohan's outstretched hand. He grabbed it with one swift motion, then threw it into the wall. Without uttering another word, he walked out of the cell and left the training compound.

The next day Odger seemed to have forgotten Rohan's tantrum. He treated Rohan with the same indifference as he always had, but for the first time he didn't start the lesson by setting steel objects against the wall. Intrigued, Rohan watched as he moved, slowly shuffling his way around the cell, his wooden bracelet ringing gently. Instead of setting up new projectiles, he packed them away. Rohan couldn't help but smile. It seemed like the days of testing his range had come to an end. He was faintly perturbed that they hadn't come to an answer but felt relieved to be moving onto something new. As the last items were packed away, Odger picked up what looked to be a bundle of twigs. As Odger undid the strings that bound it together, Rohan realised that it was in fact a straw mat about the size of a towel. It was covered in dust and mites and seemed to be on the verge of falling apart. Facing away from Rohan, Odger flicked it hard a number of times. A puff of dust escaped with each flick and Rohan heard a small array of stones and rocks scatter on the bitumen. Eventually, he seemed satisfied and spread the mat out in the middle of the cell. He turned to collect something from the back wall and quickly looked back to see the mat roll itself back up again. Muttering, he wandered to the wall and picked up a small case as well as a number of the heavier items he had just packed away. Rohan watched with amusement as his teacher spread the mat out again, spreading his body across the straw, placing the heavy steel objects in the corners to hold it down flat. Finally satisfied, he motioned to Rohan.

"Sit," he beckoned to the mat.

Rohan sat to one side, allowing Odger to sit cross-legged next to him. As Rohan shuffled slightly to the side, he caught a whiff of stale sweat and snuff. He blinked in surprise. The smell of sweat was not a surprise, but the presence of snuff caught him unaware. He had not expected anybody in the Clinic to be addicted to the tobacco mixture. He hoped that Odger was mixing his with basil or mint, not some of the chemicals that were common outside the walls of the Grey. Judging by Odger's acrid breath, he doubted it was mint.

Odger leant forward and unzipped the small case he'd collected earlier, his small hands struggling to grasp the edges. Whatever it was, it was heavy. Rohan leaned forward in expectation.

Inside the case, sitting in their own moulded pockets, sat three scratched and dented steel balls. They looked like giant ball-bearings that had been discarded after years of service. Whatever Rohan was expecting, this wasn't it. Odger pushed the case towards Rohan, and withdrew three similar, albeit much smaller, steel balls out of his ripped pocket.

"Yesterday, we spoke about control. Control is difficult to achieve. You will most likely not, but Takash demanded that I show you." He sighed again, apparently disappointed that his days of forcing Rohan to dive onto the floor were over.

Although Rohan had only seen Odger demonstrate his skill a few times, it had left a lasting impression. His control over his ability was undeniable. Rohan remembered when he had created the key out of the piece of wire he kept in his pocket. It was an incredible piece of artistry. That was the only way Rohan could describe it.

On the other hand, he had listened to Oak talk about his lessons. He spoke gloriously about using his giant fists to smash through brick walls and concrete foundations. He laughed when describing the falling debris and the ease with which he pulverised large structures. There was nothing subtle in that and it didn't seem to require a large amount of control. Even Mara only spoke about working hands-on with her bio-abilities. She revelled in contorting plant matter into new shapes and structures, but admitted that the plant often followed the path of least resistance, rather than the one she had designed. Apparently, this was one of the challenges of working with a living substance.

Rohan looked at the steel balls, wondering how they could assist him in controlling his powers.

He turned back to Odger who had separated one of the smaller steel balls out from the rest and was levitating it easily a few inches above his hand.

Rohan gasped involuntarily. He had seen a number of Movers shift objects, but not once had he seen them levitate an object as easily as Odger was now demonstrating.

Casually, Odger picked up a second ball and as though placing it upon a shelf positioned it a few inches to the left of the first. It remained perfectly motionless, held as though by an invisible string.

He repeated the process with the third ball, leaving Rohan wide-eyed as he levitated the three small objects above his hand with the air of somebody going for an afternoon stroll.

Rohan stared at Odger, his brain boggling in disbelief. How could this filthy rat of a man possess such control? As Rohan continued to stare, he noticed a small bead of sweat run down Odger's cheek. This was followed by another, then another until the rat-faced man was drenched, sweat dripping off the end of his hooked nose. It had happened so fast. One moment he was calm, cool, and collected, the next, he was a sweaty mess.

Without warning, Odger shook his head and the balls crashed to the ground, clattering loudly as they smacked onto the hard floor.

Rohan jumped. He had been so engrossed in Odger's demonstration that the sudden noise was a rude awakening. Odger smiled and slowly collected the steel bearings, depositing them into his pocket once more.

"The secret to control," he started, wiping his face with a tattered yellow sleeve, "is concentration. Holding one ball, easy, eh, even a child can do that. Holding a second ball. That requires skill. To do this, you need to find a way to split your mind and to concentrate equally on two separate objects." He glanced at Rohan slyly, "typically, women are better at this."

Rohan grinned despite himself. He was sure Mara would tell him the same thing.

Odger reached into his pocket once more, retrieving one of the small steel balls. He held it up as he had before and left it to levitate.

"You see, I can hold this ball here at the same time as having a conversation, probably because speaking with you is not challenging. Once I start adding in other elements, like more balls, it becomes more challenging, splitting your concentration like that is difficult."

He plucked the steel ball out of the air once more.

"The control of any ability is not dependent on a person's size, muscles, or intelligence, which is good news for you. It is limited by their ability to concentrate. That is why moving abilities still follow Newton's third law of gravity, although the others are up for debate."

"Who's Newton?" asked Rohan sheepishly. He thought he knew everybody at the Clinic by now, maybe not personally, but at least by sight.

Odger gave him a withering look. "Newton was a great scientist. He discovered gravity and made sure things didn't just float off into the great unknown." He waved his hand skyward.

"Newton's third law," Odger continued, "is easily summarised. What goes up, must come down. While we, as Movers, can delay this, inevitably it holds true. In order to keep something from falling, we must concentrate on it. As we all know, it is impossible to concentrate on a single thing for an extended period. Even if we could, a little thing called sleep would get in the way. So, for today's lesson," he reached for one of the larger balls in the case, "your job is to levitate this ball for as long as possible."

Rohan was intrigued. Levitating a ball was something new. It was something none of the other recruits were being forced to do, but for the first time, he could see the value in what he was doing. He guessed that Odger didn't have the range to lift these balls, which was why he demonstrated with the ones in his pocket. The size didn't make any difference to him; he'd figured that much out over the past few months.

He clasped the ball offered to him by Odger and held it at arm's length. He stared at it, trying to focus his full attention upon it. He thought about how to hold it there. The only command he had used so far was "come" and that didn't seem appropriate here. Maybe he would use "levitate", no, that sounded ridiculous, he wasn't a magician. "Stay," he thought. That sounded perfect, it was simple, relevant, and captured the essence of what he wanted the ball to do. He had realised early on that the actual words used are largely irrelevant. It was the strength of your belief that caused an object to adhere to your will. The stronger your Conviction, the more receptive it was to your commands. But this was something new, this wasn't just moving an object. This was control in its purest form.

He slowly removed his hand, leaving the ball floating in mid-air.

"Nobody likes you!" screamed Odger suddenly.

Rohan turned to him, and the steel ball immediately fell to the ground, clanging loudly, and rolling away.

Odger smiled with a look of smug satisfaction. "Not so easy, is it?"

Rohan sighed and clambered after the ball, returning to the mat to try again.

Chapter 20

The next few weeks had Rohan wishing for a return to Odger's old lessons. He thought that Odger had forgiven him for his outburst, but it turns out that changing to control exercises merely gave him another opportunity to torment Rohan.

As Rohan sat staring at the floating steel ball, Odger would pelt him with rocks, stones, coat hangers, or whatever else was within easy reach. At first, Rohan ignored him, allowing the stones to bounce off him as he gritted his teeth. However, after one particularly well-aimed coin hit him in the back of the head, Rohan turned on him angrily, ready to throw the steel ball directly at his rat face. Odger just grinned at him, pointing at the mat.

"Concentrate," he reminded Rohan. "If you can't overcome such a small distraction, how do you expect to add a second ball?"

Still fuming Rohan returned to the mat. He lifted the ball to eye level and watched as it fell from his hand and onto the ground.

Odger giggled, revelling in Rohan's failures.

Rohan gritted his teeth and clenched his fists to stop himself throttling the little man. He was so angry he couldn't focus on the task. This meant that every time he tried to hold the ball up, it would fall to the ground. This both frustrated Rohan and delighted Odger, who laughed louder with each attempt.

The lessons continued in much the same way, with Odger hurling projectiles while Rohan tried desperately to ignore him.

The only thing that kept him going was his determination to improve. He was quite proud when Odger reluctantly told him that he should add a second ball into his training. For Rohan, this was a validation of his hard work. He had successfully outlasted Odger and moved onto the next stage. For Odger however, it was a sign that he needed to double his efforts. As such, Rohan was pelted with many more annoying objects aimed at breaking his concentration.

On a brighter note, Za'Niyah's classes had come to an end. As much as Rohan had grown to understand their value, it was still a class he didn't enjoy. He longed for the study of history and strategy. He longed to feel as though he was learning something, as opposed to being taught how to feel. He couldn't deny that Za'Niyah's classes had made an impact on their cell. Once Oak had shared his story, it gave the rest of the team confidence to share more about themselves. Rohan spoke of his upbringing in a very matter-of-fact manner. He didn't try to create a story, although he knew he could have left the entire group crying. Instead, he listed his daily routine, giving Oak, Mara, and Amadyne an insight into his solitary upbringing. This time there were no sobs of tears, but silent nods of comprehension and understanding. Oak nodded especially hard when Rohan spoke about his fear of the gangs and the options left to the children from Shackle St. when they timed out.

Mara spoke about her upbringing, which was something none of them had experienced. Her family had owned one of the larger rooftops in the city and due to her mother's careful planning and skill, was able to grow large crops, more than enough for her small family. Her father was also clever and managed to trade their extra food for a multitude of luxuries, including blankets, mattresses, and even soap. In the minds of the rest of the cell, Mara had grown up in the lap of luxury. How she came to be part of the Faithful, they weren't quite sure. She tried to explain that just because she had food, safety, and shelter, it didn't mean she was looked after. Her father was barely home, preferring to spend time with the other merchants in the city, and her mother was searching for a life outside her family. She grew silent at this point, as they watched her with curiosity. She tried a number of times to continue and to explain but found herself unable to find the words. Eventually, she admitted that her mother would work hard during the day but disappear at night to take snuff and drink with "friends". With barely a mother or father present, Mara spent a lot of time with herself, playing with her dolls and reading. She shrugged at this, supposing that because she was alone so much, she didn't really have anybody to make boundaries for her. She did what she wanted, and as she grew older, that included roaming the city and making friends with gang members. Oak gasped, eyeing her with suspicion. Mara patted his arm and reassured him that she was brought to the Grey before she had the chance to join. He looked placated but shocked. She realised there was something different about her one day when she destroyed her family garden. She told them how angry she had been, how the rage that had been simmering inside her forced its way out. Her father and mother had both left for the day, her father for the market and her mother… just out somewhere. Mara had been left alone again, and the black cloud that normally sat silent but threateningly in her mind, transformed into a thunderstorm, raging inside her head. She needed to do something, to show them that she was angry, to show them that she needed more, more of anything. The only way she could think to do that was to destroy something they loved, and the thing they loved more than anything else was their stupid garden. Mara's fists were clenched at this point, her knuckles turning white as she suppressed her remembered rage.

She ripped out plants, vegetables, and fruit trees, turning the perfectly manicured garden into mulch. She pulled down the planter boxes and tore at the vines that covered the walls. She even destroyed the seedlings that her mother had been cultivating for the market. It was the vegetation equivalent of a massacre.

It was only then that Mara realised what she had done. She described standing over the scene, hair wild, dirt covering her hands, and clothes shredded from all the thorny bushes and panicking. She hadn't simply hurt her mother and father, she had sentenced them to years of suffering. By destroying their crops, she had sentenced them to starvation. They might have been able to survive for a while by eating some of the dried fruits or selling the mattresses, but eventually, they would run out.

Hopeful that her mother would be able to grow something before the food ran out, she scrambled around the garden, trying to repair the damage she had caused. She picked up the planter boxes, scooped the soil back into place and planted new stakes, but it was a disaster. It looked like a wrecking ball had collided with the garden, destroying everything in its path. She fell down, head in her hands, and started to cry. Through that haze of tears she took hold of a broken plank of wood and tried to force it back into place like a piece of a puzzle. It was no good. It was broken, short, and splintered upon one edge.

She looked at the broken plank in her hands as though failing to comprehend how it couldn't fit. She was about to throw it away when she felt it change. She felt the rough edges become smooth in her hand. She looked down and saw the wood straining and stretching like a rubber band. She watched it transform into the shape it once was, albeit a little thinner. She held it up to the box. It fit perfectly, just like she had imagined it would. Although surprised, she was also strangely reassured. Now that she had done it once, there was a confidence that she could do it again. Consequently, she wandered around the garden repairing the broken boxes and stakes. She placed broken ends together and watched them intertwine once more, clasping together as though shaking hands. Within an hour, she had restored the garden to a version of itself. It wasn't perfect but was at least a representation of what there had been. The plants were another issue. Although she tried to restore them using the same method, she found that they didn't respond in the same way. Mara smiled at this, exclaiming that she could have done a perfect job if only she knew what she knew now.

When her parents came home, they were curious about the change and the destruction of the plants but seemed reluctant to ask too many questions. Mara now realised that they were more than a little afraid of her. They could see the destruction, but also the lines of regrowth and what had been fixed. It wasn't natural and if there was anything that scared Mara's parents, it was something that wasn't natural. She guessed that her parents' mutterings and whispers to friends were what had led the Grey to her in the first place. Not that she minded. In fact, she rather liked being surrounded by people for a change. She grasped Oak's hand happily.

Even Amadyne took a turn, explaining in as few sentences as possible about having a difficult father and an absent mother. She explained that her father had been a believer in the Faithful for a long time, and that as a child, he had encouraged her to find her abilities. While technically possible, it meant telling her a lot of lies and keeping her in the dark about a lot of things.
Privately, Rohan thought that her father sounded like a crackpot. For Amadyne it meant that she found out about her abilities a lot earlier than most and had been crafting her skill since the age of eleven. That explained how she had so much control.

She didn't say a lot more and remained sullen for the remainder of the day.

Now that Za'Niyah's classes were done, Takash had taken over. Rohan couldn't have been happier. He had been longing for some kind of physical activity. Though he spent every day outside with Odger, that tended to be a purely mental exercise. He needed something to stretch his muscles.

Fortunately, Takash did have something in mind, even if it wasn't running. He explained that the reason they had been grouped together was that they all had complimentary abilities. In order to become an effective cell, they needed to understand how to work together. Step one, he clarified, was to work with Za'Niyah and to build a level of trust. Step two was to use those relationships and one another's abilities to achieve team success. He clearly emphasised the words "team success", looking pointedly at Amadyne as he did so.

The new sessions were a welcome relief for everybody. Rather than sitting in a stuffy room at the top of the stairs, they had the chance to show off their skills and find new ways to utilise them. Rohan was a little reluctant at first. He had only started to learn how to control his abilities, and still hadn't figured out his range. Compared to the others, he felt like a child.

But after the first few lessons, he realised that he wasn't the only one with doubts. Oak seemed embarrassed that his range wasn't overly large and would often try to remove himself from an exercise stating, "I think it'll be better if I sit this one out." Mara, on the other hand, had full confidence in her abilities, but recognising that others viewed Bio-Movers as useless, kept trying to insert her abilities where they weren't needed. The only one that seemed at all ready to get to work was Amadyne. She was, as always, the ultimate professional. She was cool, in command, and ruthlessly efficient.

Rohan was still unsure how to feel about Amadyne. Since he had spied on her during his run outside, he had felt that there was more to her. When he first met her, he had pencilled her in as a disgruntled Mover, one who had grown sceptical of the Faithful. She was like a manager that was constantly passed over for promotion: effective and capable, but bitter. He suspected that it had a lot to do with her father and having been a Mover for so long. To watch those less capable than her being sent on missions must have been a tough pill to swallow. So, rather than trying to grow alongside her cellmates, she hid behind a veil of sneering comments. To anybody else watching their cell, this façade hadn't changed. She was still the same Amadyne, but when Rohan watched her closely, he found hints of something more. These hints came in the form of a nod or smile, so subtle that nobody else would notice. So Rohan watched, waiting to see if he was right.

This afternoon, Takash brought them outside for their lesson.

"The task today is simple. I want you to move all the trash at the far end of the compound over to the dustbins." He motioned to the large metal containers behind him.

Rohan grinned and winked at Oak. Oak was so big, he could probably carry it all himself. They were going to finish in no time. Oak was also grinning wildly. Unfortunately, neither of them had predicted Takash's cunning.

"You can move the trash in any way you like, however, you are only allowed to make one trip each. Additionally, if you drop or spill anything, you fail the task. The punishment for failing is fifty laps of the Clinic."

Oak groaned audibly, causing Amadyne to roll her eyes.

Rohan's hope of completing the task quickly were dashed when they crossed the compound to get started. The pile of trash was taller than Oak and about three times as wide. Even if they had been able to make multiple trips, it would still have taken them all afternoon to move. Worse, it was made from every variety of junk that could be imagined. In Rohan's cursory glance he spotted plastic wrapping, garden weeds, concrete blocks, a steel girder, and an array of broken and disused furniture. Even with their abilities, there was no way they could carry everything in a single journey.

Rohan looked at Takash helplessly, but the bearded man ignored him and told the group to get to work. It was at this moment that Rohan suspected it was less of a lesson and more of a chore that needed to get done.

Amadyne and Mara immediately started picking through the pile working to identify exactly what needed to be moved. Both women started barking orders at Rohan and Oak, forcing them to move some of the larger objects out of the way. In order to keep the peace, they submitted to the requests and spent the next hour sifting through the large stack and sorting the rubble into piles. Once divided up, there were almost thirty distinct groups. These ranged from a bucket of tiles through to a stack of plastic chairs.

At first, Mara suggested that they create a platform of some type and load everything on top. She gestured at Rohan, suggesting that if the platform was made primarily from steel, that he may be able to shift it. They all knew about Rohan's challenge with finding his range and were keen to take advantage.

Unfortunately, Rohan pointed out that the only steel that was present in the entire pile was a single girder that was twisted and bent in a thousand directions, hardly the ideal base for any platform.

Amadyne looked at each pile separately, examining them in detail, looking for something they were missing. Meanwhile, Takash sat to the side, watching them in silence, his steely gaze thoughtful. When they finally broke and asked him for a hint or for some guidance, he waved them off, exclaiming his willingness to wait until the job was done, even if it took all night.

As the sun started to set and the light in the yard dimmed, the piles of trash remained unmoved. Eventually the dinner bell rang and they watched glumly as the other Faithful began to make their way to the Cutting Room. They'd been at it for hours and were no further along than they had been when they started. Their stomachs were grumbling, and their frustrations were starting to get the better of them. Eventually, Amadyne snapped and picking up one of the plastic chairs, she threw it against the wall. It bounced off easily and tumbled away, barely a scratch on it. One of the passing Movers looked at Amadyne in surprise before nonchalantly kicking the chair back in their direction. Rohan watched him go, wishing he could follow.

Suddenly he had an idea. Rushing over to the pile and picking up a bulging bag of weeds he ran to the edge of the training compound. The others watched him in confusion.

"Hey, hey, excuse me!" yelled Rohan at the nearest Mover.

The Mover, one Rohan didn't recognise, turned to face him.

"I'm sorry to bother you, but would you mind bringing this bag to the dustbin on the other end of the yard?"

"Um… why?"

"Well, you see Takash over there?"

"Yeah."

"Well, he bet that we couldn't move all this trash from this end to that end without making multiple trips."

The Mover looked at him blankly, "why would he do that?"

"Why would he do anything?" Rohan responded exasperatedly.

"Look, all you have to do is carry this bag from here to there," said Rohan pointing. "If everyone does it, we win, and more importantly," he said with a wink, "Takash loses."

Rohan could see the gears turning as the man's mind worked at snail pace. Finally, he smiled.

"I would like to see Takash lose..."

Rohan grinned and handed him the bag.

Word quickly spread that there was an opportunity to get one over Takash. It seems as though he had an annoying habit of winning and the rest of the Clinic were keen to get one back. For the next hour, Rohan organised willing volunteers into lines, carrying the trash from one end of the compound to the other. Even Galvor and Za'Niyah got involved, and laughing, carried two small plastic chairs across the floor.

Takash watched the whole thing in silence until the last piece of trash had been dumped into the bins. As it landed in the pile, a rousing reception erupted across the training ground. Rohan, grinning wildly, turned to Takash, and with an imaginary flick of his coat tails, bowed deeply.

The now rather large audience broke into cheers and laughter as the rest of Rohan's cell clapped along. It was in this moment that Rohan thought he saw the real Amadyne. Her face was radiant. She cheered and hollered as loudly as anybody, forgetting for that instant her cold demeanour. Rohan could see the colour in her cheeks rising as she smiled at Takash. This was the Amadyne Rohan had seen outside the Clinic. This was her, unencumbered by the image she had worked so hard to create. This was the real Amadyne, and it was something Rohan liked a lot more than he cared to admit.

After Rohan's stunning victory over Takash, the exercises became progressively more difficult. Takash developed a series of scenarios and tests to push them to their limits. Often this involved utilising one another's abilities to maximise their effectiveness. For example, Mara would often use her Bio-Mover abilities to weaken a structure. She did this by allowing some form of biomaterial, usually a plant or tree, to infiltrate the cracks and gaps in a wall. This would weaken it significantly, allowing Oak to smash it into a million pieces. On their own, they may have been able to accomplish the task, but together they were more efficient and more effective. Rohan and Amadyne also found a new way to utilise their abilities. Although Amadyne's water moving was seen as a less useful ability, it was incredibly effective when combined with electricity. As Rohan had the ability to move metal, this gave him easy access to the wiring that ran throughout the city. Suddenly they were a lethal combination. They discovered this accidently during one of the training sessions when Rohan was attempting to electrocute one of the dummies Takash had set up. As he attempted to manoeuvre the steel towards the fake guard, his concentration slipped. In the corner of his eye he had seen Amadyne sending a jet of water towards the eyes of the same dummy. At first, he was furious as taking out the guard had been his responsibility. However, his anger disappeared immediately as the dropped wire connected with the pool of water at the guard's feet. It sizzled and crackled like popcorn on a hotplate, and the guard shuddered violently as the electricity coursed through its body and transformed it into a blazing torch.

Rohan and Amadyne looked at each other in disbelief. Then Amadyne nodded, "I knew you'd be good for something."

It was probably the nicest thing she had ever said to him.

These tests went on for months, giving each member of the team a sense of purpose. Gone were any lingering doubts about whether they belonged or whether they could match it with the other members of the Faithful.

It was this, perhaps overconfidence, that led to each of them giving the Cutting Room run a go. Unsurprisingly, it was Amadyne who suggested it one day over lunch. They had been congratulating themselves on the previous day's training in which Oak had launched his cellmates onto a second story building using a large slab of concrete. It was an impressive feat, and one that could definitely be used in battle.

Amadyne, who usually remained silent during their meals, had been examining the wires that criss-crossed the hall. "Do you think you could try that then?" she asked, interrupting another one of Oak's retellings.

He looked at her, both stunned that she had spoken during mealtime and surprised at her question.

"What? Do that?" Oak puffed out his chest. "Of course, I could do that. Did you see me yesterday? I can do anything!" he lifted his arms to flex his muscles.

"Pfft," snorted Amadyne. "Sure, yesterday was impressive, but running the wires requires much more than physical strength."

Rohan looked at her surprised. For the past few weeks, Amadyne had seemed to be cooling down. She was less derisive and actually seemed to want to be part of the team. This comment seemed like a return to the old Amadyne, the one that they could only tolerate.

Mara, never one to take a backward step, stopped smiling and turned to Amadyne.

"And what exactly do you mean by that?"

Amadyne rolled her eyes as Mara's eyes flashed with warning. "Nothing. Just that running the wires isn't just about ability or strength," she eyed Oak, who had slowly lowered his arms, "it requires strategy and planning. I just don't think that Oak has the skills required to make it far."

"Oh, and you do?" snapped Mara, her face contorting into a vicious snarl.

"Well, yes," responded Amadyne matter of factly, as though surprised by the question.

Mara leaned in close, her voice a hoarse whisper, "hear this. Oak is worth ten of you. He is strong, he is kind, and he is loyal. Even more so, he cares about his friends. Hell, he even cares about you, although personally I can't see why. He mightn't be one to talk about how smart he is, he just shows it in everything he does. He doesn't need..." Mara emphasised the word, her eyes searing into Amadyne's, "to talk himself up like you seem to do. He is perfect the way he is."

Oak, looking rather embarrassed, tried to pull Mara back across the table, but she wouldn't be moved.

"You think you're so great. I bet we could all make it further than you." She spat in Amadyne's direction emphasising her disgust.

"Well then, let's find out," said Amadyne slyly, as though she had anticipated this response.

"Fine."

"Fine."

Rohan looked at the two women. What had just happened? He didn't say anything, although he agreed with Mara. Oak didn't have anything to prove.

"Tomorrow after dinner."

"I look forward to it."

Amadyne picked up her plate and left, leaving Rohan, Mara, and Oak sitting alone on the long wooden table.

Oak placed his hand over Mara's, holding her gently as she shook with anger.

"She just makes me so angry," said Mara finally. "She thinks she's so much better than us, and I'm sick of it."

She looked at Oak and Rohan, "I really do think that we could beat her."

Oak nodded supportively, but Rohan could see the doubt in his eyes. Amadyne was incredible. Her control over her abilities was far better than any of theirs, and she had spent more time at the Clinic than any of them. Rohan knew first-hand that she could hold her own in any fight and he didn't doubt her ability to think through a problem like the wires.

He sighed as Mara looked at him.

"I know, I'm an idiot. She will probably make us all look stupid and it's all because I couldn't control my temper."

Rohan shrugged as Mara lowered her eyes. They finished the meal in silence, each thinking about the following day.

Rohan looked up at Oak as he stood on the rusted air conditioners that composed the platform above the Cutting Room. Even now, forty feet above the watching crowd, he looked gigantic. Actually, he looked like a monster about to leap into the pit. His hair was its usual untidy mess, and he was covered in a fresh sheen of sweat. For those that didn't know him, he could be an unnerving sight.

Rohan saw something else. He saw his friend looking nervous. Although he had seen Oak run along ledges and leap across buildings, the Cutting Room was something else. There was nothing below you except the wires that threatened to trap you in their dangerous web. Rohan could see the apprehension on his face and could only feel anxious as Oak gripped the metal railing that prevented him from falling.

Mara stood beside him, her face stony as she struggled to contain her composure. Oak meant more to her than any person ever had before. Seeing him forced into this situation because of her temper was almost more than she could bear. She knew that breaking down in front of him would only distract him, so she buried her emotions and clipped the safety rope to Oak's belt, not daring to look into his eyes. She stepped back, giving him the space to jump.

Amadyne stood below, leaning against the wall of the Cutting Room. She smiled as she watched Oak edge closer to the end of the platform.

Rohan watched as the muscles in Oak's neck tightened as he shifted his feet preparing to jump. Earlier that day, they had discussed who should go first. Mara felt it was her responsibility as she had been the one to volunteer them. Oak had strongly disagreed. He pointed out that she was only defending him when he had failed to defend himself. He looked a little ashamed of that. He stated that since Amadyne had insulted him, that it was his decision, and that he should go first. As much as Mara tried to dissuade him, he would not be moved.

Oak leapt, catching the closest wire in his paw-like hands. As his full body weight transferred to his new perch, Rohan could hear the bolts straining with the tension. Oak hung like that for a moment and then started to rock his body, back and forth, back and forth, each time gaining more momentum. He swung again, this time landing on a slack line and sinking quickly as he took in the extra wire. He managed to keep his balance momentarily but started to panic as the wire moved beneath his feet, forcing him to jump again almost immediately. This time, he didn't have a plan, he leapt into the air, reaching for the wire that wasn't there. He fell quickly, bouncing off the wires below. Eventually he stopped, the rope tied to his belt catching him well before he reached the ground. As he hung in mid-air, spinning slowly, he flashed the crowd below a toothy grin and a big thumbs up. They erupted into applause, cheering loudly for the giant. Nobody expected him to make it far, but they were all encouraged by his attempt.

Mara was up next. She stood on the platform, hands on hips, determined to succeed. In contrast to Oak, she seemed tiny. As she stood on the platform, Rohan wondered whether she would even be able to reach the first wire. He need not have worried. With a running jump, she launched herself into the air. Unlike Oak, she moved with confidence, carefully planning her steps and leaping from wire to wire with purpose. Rohan and Oak watched from below as she moved lower and lower down the wires, trying to find the easiest way through. Even though she was moving well, Rohan could see that she wasn't going to make it as far as she'd hoped. With each leap, she utilised more of her rope and moving downwards had taken up a lot of the slack. Sure enough, only a few jumps later, she hit the end of the cord. It wrenched her back in mid-air, only a third of the way across the Cutting Room floor.

She screamed in frustration. It wasn't her lack of ability that had held her back, it was her path. Rohan could see that in order to get further, she would have to find a way of approaching the target more directly. As she was lowered to the floor, Rohan could see the anger in her eyes. He started to walk towards her, to congratulate her on her effort, but Oak held him back. Instead, Oak walked forward, and instead of consoling or congratulating her, he lifted her onto his shoulders. He did it with ease, leaving Mara surprised and gasping for air. Oak laughed and started to run around the room with Mara in tow. She held on for dear life as the crowd laughed and cheered them on. Mara's face transformed from one of shock and anger to one of jubilation. She threw her head back and laughed, using one hand to pretend to whip Oak.

In that single act, Oak had turned a disappointment into a celebration. He didn't want her to feel disappointed about achieving her best. He wanted her to celebrate her first attempt at running the wires.

In all the commotion that Oak caused, almost nobody noticed Amadyne climbing to the platform above them. The only person watching was Rohan. With nobody to connect her to the safety rope, he watched as she clipped herself in. She connected the rope expertly, with minimal fuss and only a slight adjustment to her belt. She stood on the edge, watching the people below cheering Oak on. He was slowing down now but still pretending to be a wild horse. Tears of laughter running down his and Mara's faces.

Amadyne looked out across the wires and unlike Oak and Mara, she stepped back, taking the time to plot her course. Rohan immediately saw the benefit of doing this. It gave her the chance to strategize and determine how to best approach the task in front of her. It made Rohan think. The best path across the wires was different for each of them. For Mara, she needed to find wires that were strung closer together. This would have allowed her to cross the distance without making hopeful leaps. Alternatively, Oak needed space, he needed clear air that would enable him to stretch his massive frame out and cover the distance that way.

Amadyne waited on the platform allowing the noise from below to die down. Eventually the crowd settled, and still panting, Oak and Mara made their way to the tables to join the other onlookers. Amadyne stepped up to the edge once more, but unlike the others, she didn't leap into the web in front of her; instead, she stepped off casually, as though hopping off the curb.

She fell like a rock. The watchers below gasped. They had never seen anybody do this before, not in all their time at the Clinic. They watched as she fell, almost to the bottom of the wires, and then throw out an arm, catching a wire in the crook of her arm, swinging wildly as she did so. Rohan watched her carefully. What was she thinking?

He watched as she found her balance, and started to climb the wires again, aiming diagonally upwards for the far wall. It was a risky move, and one that used up a lot of rope quickly. As Amadyne climbed, moving in slow deliberate steps, Rohan began to understand. She wasn't trying to get to the other end of the Cutting Room, she was only concerned with winning. He watched as she made her way through the wires, moving in a straight line towards her target. He was stunned by the simplicity of it. Amadyne had known that the rope wouldn't be long enough to carry her to the bottom of the wires, and then back to the top. It was likely the reason nobody had attempted it before. Instead, she was climbing with a singular purpose, to travel further than Mara. Looking closely Rohan could see that her path upwards was clear and direct and would easily eclipse Mara's mark. He wasn't the only one to recognise the strategy. He saw Mara groan and as she buried her head in her hands.

The other members of the Faithful watching were confused, until Oak clarified the situation. They watched in fascination, half applauding her craftiness and half expressing their disappointment. The purpose of the Cutting Room was not to defeat one another but to challenge yourself. They saw Amadyne's strategy as a stain on the exercise. Consequently, when she finally met her limit, the crowd responded with scattered applause and murmuring. There was none of the celebration that followed the attempts from Mara and Oak, and as Amadyne was lowered to the ground, the crowd remained silent. Amadyne didn't care. She looked at her cellmates with triumph plastered across her face. She had crossed just over halfway, and as she took her seat, the ribbon with her initials was tied to the wire where she finished.

Rohan didn't know whether to be impressed or annoyed. He was impressed with her thought process. She had entered the challenge with one goal, to defeat Mara. She had implemented her plan perfectly and left no one in doubt that she had won. On the other hand, Rohan shrugged, it didn't make her popular, not that it seemed to bother her. She was singularly focused on being the best, even if it meant ruffling a few feathers along the way. Rohan was lost in these thoughts when he felt a sharp elbow nudge him in the side.

"Your turn." It was Mara, looking hopeful.

"Huh," responded Rohan. He hadn't made the bet. Even though Mara had volunteered him, he didn't think he would have to run the wires as well.

"C'mon," pleaded Mara, "we can't let her win."

Rohan could see the rest of the crowd watching them. It seemed like a number of them agreed. They nodded silently, eavesdropping on their conversation.

Amadyne turned her head towards Rohan. Clearly she had not been expecting him to try either. She glared at him, as though challenging him to cross her.

Rohan shrugged. He'd been wanting to try it anyway. He put his hands up in mock surrender as Oak clapped him on the back and Amadyne turned away in disgust. He wasn't going to let her get away with her sneaky tactic. No, he was going to beat her doing it the right way.

Rohan climbed up to the platform, wiping his sweaty palms on his pants as he reached for the rungs. It was strange, there was a slight tightening in his chest and his breathing was coming a little faster. He was nervous, not about the height or the challenge, but about his own expectations. He had watched Mover after Mover try to cross the void, each falling without getting much further than halfway. As he watched them, he developed a strange belief that he could do better. Whether this was based on arrogance or confidence he didn't know, but it put a pressure on him that he couldn't shake.

Oak climbed behind him, shaking the ladder with every step. He had declared that it was his responsibility to ensure that Rohan's safety rope was properly tied. Rohan suspected that he was there to make sure he couldn't back out.

As they reached the platform, Oak gripped the railing, almost denting it with his grip.

"Do you think you can do it?" he asked Rohan in earnest.

"What?" asked Rohan confused, "run the wires?"

"Well, yeah," responded Oak. "It would mean a lot to Mara if you could beat Amadyne."

"Oak," said Rohan, inhaling deeply, "Amadyne has been at the Clinic a lot longer than any of us. She's probably run the wires before. Also, she is really good. I don't know if you've noticed in training, but she is better than most people. It's not an act. If I can get anywhere near her, I'll be surprised."

Oak looked at him in surprise.

"Rohan, I don't mean to sound mean, but are you an idiot?"

That was not the pep talk Rohan was expecting. "What?"

"I mean, did you get dropped on your head or something? In all the training sessions, it's you and Amadyne fighting it out. Mara and I talk about it all the time. It's not that we're jealous or anything, but it's pretty obvious that you and Amadyne are a level or two above us."

Rohan looked at Oak in stunned silence.

Oak shuffled his feet uncomfortably.

Rohan didn't know what to say. He'd never thought about it before. All he ever wanted to do was make his cell better. If that meant coming up with an idea or taking on a difficult role, then he was going to do it.

"Um..." he stammered, "I'm really sorry Oak. I never meant to make you feel like that."

"No, that's not what I mean," said Oak quickly. "Mara and I, we know who we are. I told you, I'm a soldier, and Mara, well, fighting isn't what she is passionate about. But you, you seem to thrive on it. You are always looking for an edge or a backup plan. The way you think is, well, it's beyond me. That's why I'm glad you're on my team."

Rohan looked at Oak, words escaping him.

"Now, if you could get out there and beat that Northerner," he nodded at Amadyne below, "that would be great." He clapped Rohan on the shoulder, finished tying the safety rope, and headed back down the ladder.

Rohan stood there, unable to think straight. What did they think of him? Was he really all that? He shook his head, this was not the time to be thinking of those things. He needed to concentrate on the job at hand.

As Rohan looked out across the wires, he realised that he had judged his fellow Movers harshly. It was a maze. There was no discernible path to the other side. Every way he looked was blocked with another web or a loose wire. How anybody had managed to make it to halfway was beyond him. It felt like an impossible task wrapped in a non-existent solution. He studied the wires closer, identifying the paths that Oak, Mara, and Amadyne had taken before him. It was easy to see where Amadyne had gone. He immediately dismissed the idea of following her, that wouldn't prove anything. He could see where Oak had leapt and laughed to himself. That was clearly not an option, he didn't particularly like the idea of falling like a stone.

Mara's route was the best of the lot. It was clear that she was trying to make it to the end but had been caught in the obstacles in the way. Every time she had tried to manoeuvre herself forward, she had been forced to move up and down, taking up the slack the rope offered. Rohan looked closely at her planned route. There was definitely something there, a path that opened up if he could just...

Taking off his shoes, he placed them neatly at the back of the platform and leaned against the handrail. He could feel his feet moulding to the rough metal surface, seeking out the ridges and notches that formed its structure.

As Oak stepped off the ladder and back onto the ground below, Rohan threw him a quick glance. While he had been waiting for Oak to complete his descent, he remembered the first time he had watched a Mover attempt to run the wires. She had been magnificent. She had propelled herself along the wires using the tension to rocket her upwards and forward. It had given her tremendous momentum and allowed her to cover the wide divides between the wires. While she hadn't been successful,

Rohan could see the value that this offered. It would allow him to make moves many of the other Faithful couldn't comprehend. The crowd below watched in expectation. They had heard rumours about Rohan's running ability and were curious to see if it would help him cross the Cutting Room. They didn't have to wait long. Rohan, like Amadyne, stepped off the edge of the platform, falling like a stone. Unlike Amadyne, Rohan had no intention of letting himself fall to the bottom. Instead, he landed on a taut wire that ran the length of the Cutting Room. It flexed as he landed, stretching as the weight pulled it downward. Then, like a rubber band, it reached its maximum tension and leapt back, firing Rohan like a bullet out of a gun. Suddenly Rohan was flying, moving with a speed unseen before in the Clinic. In contrast to the other Movers to attempt the strategy, Rohan didn't use the momentum to move towards the top of the wires, instead he used it to drive him forward, into the web that spread out before him.

Below, the crowd gasped. It was a risky strategy. The idea of hurling oneself into a maze of wires that could trip, cut, and strangle at a thousand miles per hour was madness.

To Rohan, it seemed as though the world slowed down. His mind was operating on super speed, and he was making decisions in the space between seconds. He knew what he wanted and how to achieve it. All his years of chasing Takash along the streets and roofs of the city were coming to the fore. He knew that taking the traditional path wouldn't lead him to success, he needed to try something new, something that nobody else would dream of doing. As such, he knew that swinging between wires wasn't the right answer. Instead, he needed to travel on them, running on a horizontal plane. As he launched forward, he searched for a place where the wires intersected, providing a clear landing pad for his foot. He found it, close to the central corridor of the maze. The slack that he used falling caught up to him now, looping slowly as he altered direction. Rather than taking the time to consolidate his position, he moved forward looking for his next landing, another crossed wire only a few feet in front of him. His goal wasn't to achieve the greatest distance with each stride; instead, it was to provide him with the clearest footing. It meant that he had to bound from side to side, moving like a small child running across a storm drain. As he moved, he ducked under wires that hung limply from above and skipped over those that threatened to trip him. To those watching below, it looked as though Rohan was sprinting across the maze of wires. They watched at the wires hummed upon release and sent reverberations back into the walls.

Rohan was growing confident. His strategy was working, he had already eclipsed Mara's mark and was fast approaching halfway. His feet hurt where the coarse wires gripped at his feet. He had taken off his shoes to allow his feet to mould to the wires better, but now it was tearing at his skin. He gritted his teeth and pushed on. He had to keep going. He ducked, barely avoiding decapitation from a razor-sharp wire that crossed in front of him. Next, he eclipsed Amadyne's mark. Relieved, Rohan allowed himself a smile. Had hadn't done it the easy way and now it was paying off. He zig-zagged across the wires, making decisions about his next landing place in a millionth of a second. His mind was racing as fast, if not faster than his feet. The number of fabric markers was growing thinner now. For the first half of the Cutting Room, they covered almost every wire, marking the failures and achievements of all the Movers before him. Now he was in rare company. He could see the far wall. It was no longer obscured by the thousands of wires that blocked his path, it was within reach.

He looked longingly at the faded black marker at the far end. If he could just…

Snap. Rohan's body was jerked back so fast his legs and shoulders didn't know what had happened. They were still moving forward as the belt around him tightened and heaved him towards the ground. Only his didn't fall far. As he hung spinning gently, he saw the rope that had been trailing behind him. It was completely taut. He had used up all his slack. He shook his head. He thought he had been so close, but as he spun back towards the wall, he could see that he still had a long way to go. He was, at best guess, only three quarters of the way across.

As he waited to be let down, he looked back at the rope to see where he had gone wrong. Though he had avoided the trap of moving up and down the wires, he had been too lateral in his path. He could see where the rope had become tangled in the loose and vertical wires. That was where his slack went. He cursed inwardly, wondering how he didn't realise as he was going. He looked down at the crowd below, wondering what was taking so long. Unlike Oak and Mara's attempt, this time there was no cheering. In fact, the room was so silent you could have heard a mouse sneeze.

He looked around. What was going on?

The crowd of Movers was staring at the ceiling, their eyes never leaving Rohan, even as he was finally lowered to the floor. He landed with a soft thud, his feet smacking onto the cold concrete.

Oak pushed past the gawking Movers and looked at Rohan in awe.

"Wow man. That was incredible."

"What's going on?" whispered Rohan as Oak continued to beam at him.

"You freaking smashed it is what happened," exclaimed Oak. "Nobody has made it that far in years, let alone on their first try."

Had he really done that well? As Rohan examined the faces of the people around him, he realised that what he had done must have been special. They were looking at him with a sense of reverence.

"All I did was run the wires," hissed Rohan, "heck, I didn't even make it the whole way."

"Nah, that doesn't matter. I told you, you are special. Now you've just proved it. Not just to me, not just to them, but maybe to you too. Now you can stop doubting yourself."

Rohan didn't know what to say. He was in as much shock as everybody else. He stood silently as the crowd slowly began to disperse. Some congratulated him on his run, but most seemed content to whisper amongst themselves.

Somehow Rohan had become more than a Mover to those in attendance. He was… well, Rohan wasn't quite sure what.

Chapter 21

Over the next few days Rohan was treated like a minor celebrity. Everywhere he went there was pointing and whispers. Members of the Faithful were as bad as a group of teenagers. They gossiped and made-up rumours about how Rohan had managed to get so far on his first attempt. Some were saying that he took off his shoes because he had glue on the bottom of his feet to help him stick better. That was ridiculous Rohan complained to Oak and Mara, it didn't even make sense. If he had done that, his feet would be stuck in his shoes, not to the wires.

Rohan had never been this popular, even Takash gave him a nod of approval when he saw that Rohan had beaten his mark. Still, Rohan didn't love his new-found popularity. He felt as though people were treating him differently. Amadyne certainly did. Ever since he ran the wires, she had treated him as though he had insulted her grandmother. During training sessions, she actively ignored him, going so far to talk over the top of his suggestions. Rohan was both frustrated and a little hurt by this. He thought he had been making headway with her and before the Cutting Room challenge she had definitely been sneering at him less. Oak and Mara noticed as well, giving Rohan a sideways look when it happened in an exercise briefing.

"Don't you get it?" asked Mara as they sat down at the long wooden table in the Cutting Room. "She's threatened."

"Ahhmm," agreed Oak though a mouthful of bread and gruel.

"Ever since we started at the Clinic, it's been pretty clear that Amadyne's the leader of our cell. She's the most experienced, the best Mover and probably the smartest."

Oak pretended to look hurt, then grinned and went back to stuffing his face.

"Anyway, the balance shifted a bit when you ran the wires. Now people are looking at us wondering who is in charge. Is it you, or is it still Amadyne? Worst of all, she can't run the wires again to show everybody that she's just as good as you."

"Why not?" asked Rohan confused.

Mara sighed, "Because, if she does it now, they'll just think that she's copied you. It would make it look like you are the leader."

Rohan hadn't really thought about being the leader of the cell before. He was happy being part of the team. It was strange that people were looking at him like that now, all he did was run across a few stupid wires. He sighed and turned back to his lunch.

Mara looked at him strangely, as though she knew something that he didn't. "Is there a reason you're concerned with what Amadyne thinks?"

Rohan looked at her with one eyebrow raised, "huh?"

"It just seems like you might care a little too much about poor wittle Amadyne's feelings," teased Mara, her voice impersonating that of a baby. She pouted dramatically and winked at Rohan.

Rohan looked at her in disbelief. Had she noticed something he hadn't? As far as he could tell he hadn't treated Amadyne any differently than he had before. Well, maybe that's not quite true, he definitely noticed her more, but not so much that anybody else would have noticed.

Oak continued to eat, not noticing Mara's teasing or Rohan's reddening face.

Fortunately, they were interrupted by Galvor.

"Hiya team."

They looked up at with pleasure. Galvor was like a shiny new penny. He was always bright and welcoming. Somehow he managed to make everybody smile when he spoke. Maybe it was his deeply accented voice that tilted and turned with each syllable, or maybe it was because he never took himself seriously.

Mara said that lessons with him were both amazing and infuriating. He was an incredibly talented Bio-Mover but couldn't stop himself from making jokes and playing pranks on his younger pupil. She grimaced, "I'm all up for a good joke, but if he turns one more chair leg into..." she turned red, "into something it shouldn't be, I might, I might just need to tell him it isn't that impressive."

"Takash is lookin' for ya. I think he's a bit jumpy about it as well. He told me to come get you right away."

They looked at one another. What could it possibly be? They were due to start the days lesson soon anyway.

"C'mon then!" quipped Galvor, turning to leave.

They scrambled to their feet, dumped their leftover gruel in the bins and jogged after Galvor.

When they arrived, they were surprised to see that Amadyne was already standing there looking smug. Clearly she knew what was going on and didn't feel like sharing the information.

"Good, you're here," started Takash. His voice clear and level, but Rohan thought he could hear a slight strain.

"Take a seat," he waved at a row of tables and chairs that stood in front of him.

They rushed to their chairs, scraping the metal legs on the floor in their rush to be seated.

"You may be wondering why I cut your lunch short. The simple answer is that we have work to do. Over the past few months we have been training you to be members of the Faithful. We have been training you to use your abilities, to make good decisions and most importantly, to work as a team." He looked at them closely as he said this, as though daring them to disagree. When nobody moved, he nodded and continued.

"We have decided that you are ready to take on small missions."

Mara squeaked excitedly as he said this, barely able to contain her excitement.

Takash levelled her with a blank look, silencing the room once again.

"As such, all other training will be temporarily suspended. From now until the mission date, you will be doing all your training with me. Is that understood?"

They nodded eagerly.

Rohan was excited, this is exactly what he had been hoping for. He was tired of the constant training, heck he'd been training for years and never been on a mission. He was also relieved to take a break from Odger. Even though he could see the improvement in his control, he did not enjoy the company of the grubby Steeler. This was a chance to put everything they had been training for into practice.

"Good," nodded Takash approvingly. "Your mission will take place in six days from now. It is a very simple mission." He looked at each of them as though warning them not to make it complicated. "Whilst officially it is classed as an Urban Retrieval mission, most call it a smash-n-grab. The purpose of the mission is to take back surplus medical supplies and drugs for redistribution to the people of Central. These supplies are kept underground in an old shipping container based here," he pointed to a large map spread out in front of him. Rohan strained his neck to see better. The map was of the city.

"We expect there to be multiple defences. There will be at least two guards, two checkpoints and the container will be locked." He looked at Rohan. "That won't be a problem will it?"

Rohan gulped. He was getting better, but he was nowhere near Odger's level yet. "No Sir," he lied, hoping he could figure something out.

"The people that we are taking this back from are dangerous people. They will not hesitate to hurt or even kill you."

He didn't have to quieten them this time. The air was sucked out of the room with this simple statement. This was real. This wasn't a training run anymore and the consequences could be devastating.

"These people have beaten, robbed, and killed others to build their supply. We do not need to feel sympathy for them." Takash emphasised his last point making it clear that he expected them to use force if necessary. "This particular group, or gang, is known as the Sun Bringers. Their MO is to burn their victims' homes and businesses, often with them still inside." He paused, letting that sink in for a moment.

Rohan was familiar with the Sun Bringers. They recruited a lot of the unwanted from Shackle St. He knew exactly how ruthless they were and the length they would go to in order to extort people.

Next to him, he saw Oak stiffen. He knew that Oak harboured a lot of resentment towards the gangs and rightly so. They had destroyed his home and family. Mara was also looking at him, her eyes betraying her concern.

Takash looked at Oak noticing his discomfort. "It that a problem son?"

Oak seemed to snap out of a trance. "No Sir."

"Make sure it isn't," snapped Takash, returning his gaze to the map.

Unlike the rest of them Amadyne seemed to be relaxed about the whole idea. As excited as Rohan was for the mission, he was still nervous. How could she look so calm?

"The plan is to enter here," Takash continued pointing to a cross street half a mile from their target. "On the right-hand side of the road there is a collapsed grate. It leads directly into these tunnels." He traced his finger along a narrow line on the map.

"Once inside, follow this path in order to get to the container. If you make a wrong turn you could be lost in those tunnels for a long time. Here" he stabbed the map "is the first checkpoint.

This shouldn't be a problem. It a minor one, usually a junior scout making sure you have the brand."

"The what?" asked Oak, interrupting Takash.

"The brand," answered Rohan instead. "It's something the Sun Bringers use to identify themselves. They usually burn it into their skin." He remembered one of the timed-out unwanted showing theirs off. They had almost bumped into each other in the market one morning as Rohan scouted for food. While they weren't friends, there was always a connection between the people who grew up in Shackle St. He had seen it burned deeply into his wrist.

"From memory," Rohan continued, "it looks like a triangle with teeth."

"That's about right," grunted Takash. He picked up a marker from the table and holding the cap between his teeth he drew a triangle with spikes on the two long edges.

"This is it. Don't worry about it too much. We can easily draw it on, and make it look real."

Rohan nodded, pleased that he had been able to contribute.

"The second checkpoint is a little more difficult. I mentioned that we expected at least two guards. These guards are usually more experienced members of the Sun Bringers and are unlikely to let us through voluntarily. You're going to have to find a way past them." He looked up from the map to make sure they were following. "Next, you have to reach the container. Our intel tells us that it's not manned, but we expect there to be some physical defences in place. This includes trip wires, stakes and probably some form of tar or something. Remember, we aren't dealing with a sophisticated fighting force, we are dealing with a bunch of arrogant psychopaths."

Rohan nodded. He knew the Sun Bringers were ruthless, but Takash was right, they operated with brutality, not finesse.

"Once you crack into the container you need to take as many of the bottles, syringes, and bandages as you possibly can. As this is a smash-and-grab mission, we don't expect you to bring back truckloads of supplies, but we do expect you to fill these," Takash held up a big black backpack that was almost the size of Mara.

Mara nearly choked when she saw it, Oak merely nodded in understanding.

"The toughest part of the mission is getting out. Making it in is easy."

Easy? Rohan thought. It sounded insane at the very least. "Can't we just come back the way we went in."

Takash looked at him, "Exactly. The biggest challenge is that there is one way in and one way out. There are other tunnels you can take, but they'll only lead you further into Sun Bringer territory. Your best chance of success is to get in and out as quickly as possible. Utilise the power of surprise. Hit them hard, hit them fast and get out." He paused for a moment to let that sink in.

"Once clear of the tunnels, you will meet the other members of the Faithful. They will take the backpacks from you to distribute at a later date. Get back here as soon as possible."

The silence in the room grew as they ran the plan over in their minds. Rohan thought that it sounded a little vague. It was like trying to complete a painting with only one colour. Sure, it could be done, but it was going to look a little messy.

"Will you be leading us?" asked Mara uneasily.

"No, Amadyne will be leading you in this mission,"

Amadyne stepped forward proudly. Rohan grimaced. This is how she knew what was going on.

"Amadyne has shown herself to be a leader and with her experience at the Clinic, we believe she will provide exemplary service to the Faithful."

Mara looked sideways at Rohan, trying to gauge his reaction. He nodded slowly in response, and nodded once more at Amadyne, trying to portray his confidence in her. While he was a little surprised, he couldn't fault their decision. If he'd been in Takash's shoes, he would have made the same choice.

"Any questions?" asked Takash as he rolled up the map tied it with a piece of thin twine.

"I didn't think so. Let's get back to the training floor. We have a lot of work to do."

The next few days were filled with role play after role play. They practised their first meeting with the scout, they practised getting past the guards and they practised breaking into the container. Takash had even found an old container to practise on.

As Rohan examined the door, his first thought was to rip it clean off its hinges but after explaining his plan to Takash, he was quickly dissuaded.

"Do you want to tell everyone you're there?" asked Takash exasperatedly. "You might as well ring a bell and announce your arrival."

Rohan had to admit that he was right. He hadn't developed enough control to move anything quietly. Instead Takash insisted Rohan try and pick the lock and avoid alerting the entire gang.

Rohan wasn't the only one getting cold water poured on his ideas. When discussing ways to get past the guards Amadyne suggested silencing them permanently.

"It would be easy. They wouldn't even know what hit them" she insisted as they sat around one of the tables.

Oak nodded in agreement.

Normally this would have surprised Rohan, but since they started planning the mission, Oak had been acting strangely. It was painfully obvious that his issues with the gangs were going to impair his judgement.

Fortunately, Mara was on Rohan's side.

"Don't you think leaving bodies lying around might attract attention?"

Both Amadyne and Oak seemed disappointed with this observation, and only relented when Rohan suggested they disable the guards instead. Mara could bind them using vines and Oak could bop them on the head.

"Bop them?" laughed Mara after he'd explained his idea. "That's the word you're going with?"

"How else would you describe it?" asked Rohan sheepishly. "You hold them and Oak," he demonstrated by pumping his fist quickly in a kind of tapping motion, "he bops them."

"Ok, ok," laughed Mara.

Amadyne remained surly and if anything was more herself than usual. She walked amongst the cell, critiquing every move they made and commenting on how it could be done better.

Rohan could appreciate that she was stressed, this being her first command, but grew frustrated when she told him how to mould the key.

"You bloody do it then," he told her after her yet another comment.

"Just trying to make sure we're perfect," she responded haughtily.

The truth was that Rohan was running out of time. He'd been trying to make the stupid key for days. The closest he had gotten was a lumpy bit of steel that looked more like a potato than a key. In desperation, he went looking for Odger.

"It takes years," explained Odger as he fondled the lock Rohan had brought in his long slender fingers. His nails were, like always, long, yellow and caked in dirt. His long nose peered over the lock as he examined it.

"And this is the lock you are trying to open?" he asked narrowing his eyes.

"Um, no, not that one."

"One like it then?"

"Ah, I'm not sure. I haven't seen it yet."

Odger rolled his eyes, "Then why are you trying to open this lock? Even if you can make a key to open this one," he held up the brass lock, "it won't open anything else."

Of course it won't thought Rohan realising his mistake. He had just embarrassed himself again.

"Why don't you just soften the metal and force it into the lock, then harden it and turn. Like this."

Odger took the lock and using the piece of wire he kept in his pocket, forced it into the keyhole. The softened metal squeezed and moved into the gaps inside the lock until it was completely filled. Odger then squeezed the metal left on the outside, pinching it into a flat shape. He flexed his fingers and turned the makeshift key. It moved easily, as though designed to fit. Rohan watched as the lock popped open with Odger grinning happily.

"It's been a while since I did that," crooned Odger, his face shining with joy. Rohan could almost see his fingers twitching as he looked for more locks to pick.

Then, as though Odger remembered where he was, he almost threw the lock back at Rohan. "I trust this is for some sort of mission?"

"Ah, yeah."

"Good, good," muttered Odger. "Don't let me catch you unlocking doors for fun now. Nasty business that is." Rohan could have sworn he saw his teacher wink at him, but Odger turned and left before he could decide if that is what had happened.

Oak threw himself into the practice like a maniac. He took on any suggestion Takash, Amadyne or anyone gave him. He practiced smashing through concrete barriers, carrying concrete slabs and throwing chunks of rock across the training ground. He worked with a cool frenzy as though he could prepare for any situation that might arise. Both Mara and Rohan watched him with concern. This was not the Oak that they knew. Normally he was more reluctant to show off his full strength. Amadyne seemed to be the only one that appreciated his attitude. Even Takash looked concerned when Oak immediately agreed to try some of Amadyne's more aggressive suggestions.

Finally the day arrived.

Instead of their usual red leathers, they were dressed in an array of mismatched rags, designed to match those worn by the Sun Bringers. In the days before leaving Rohan had advised his cellmates to stop showering. Cleanliness wasn't a virtue valued by the Sun Bringers and would easily identify them as outsiders. Also, he added half seriously, it wouldn't hurt if they smelled a bit more. As one of the unwanted at Shackle Street, he hadn't noticed the smell, but he had noticed when someone was perfumed, or even clean. It could be a dead giveaway during their mission. As a result, his cell mates now resembled a filthy collection of misfits. Even Takash wrinkled his nose as he rose to address them.

"We have a job to do today. Nothing more, nothing less. As members of the Faithful, we expect and demand nothing but success. Don't be afraid to use your abilities, don't be afraid to fight back, and don't be afraid to take a risk. You are the Faithful. Do your duty."

With that he nodded and walked away.

Rohan wondered whether he wanted to look back, or if he really was as dispassionate as he pretended to be.

They had arranged to meet at the tunnel entrance as light started to fall. Amadyne had decided, and rightly so thought Rohan, that travelling together would look suspicious. As such, they left the Clinic separately, each determined to make the mission a success.

As Rohan arrived at the tunnel entrance, he could see Mara learning against the wall hidden in the shadows. Amadyne and

Oak were scheduled to arrive soon after. Unfortunately, Oak was conspicuous in any situation, so leaving him to wait at any point had not been an option. He would be the last to arrive, signalling the start of the mission.

Amadyne arrived shortly after, her distinctive stride giving away her presence even before Rohan saw her.

They waited in the shadows watching as the sun descended below the buildings. It felt like an eternity watching the tunnels and waiting for Oak to arrive. Finally as the last rays fell he appeared. Rohan could immediately sense that something was wrong. He was walking too fast and even at a distance, Rohan could see that his body was covered in a waxy sheen.

Rohan looked at Amadyne, and before she could stop him, he stepped in front of his friend.

"Oak," Rohan hissed, trying to keep his voice down. "What's going on, are you ok?"

Oak looked down, but it was like he didn't even see him.

"Oak," Rohan hissed, "Come on man, what's wrong?"

Oak stared at him through red eyes, nodding his head as though listening to some imaginary beat.

"Oak" Rohan hissed again, but to no avail.

He looked at Mara and Amadyne pleadingly. Something was seriously wrong, but before he could do anything, Oak leaned forward and smashed his fist into the concrete wall that connected the steel grate to the entrance of the tunnels. The grate rung loudly as it fell to the floor, its hinges still attached to the concrete wall that no longer supported it.

This was not the plan. They were supposed to creep into the tunnel, using Rohan's abilities to sneak inside.

Amadyne swore but rushed past Rohan and entered the tunnel with Mara following close behind.

"What was that?" hissed Amadyne, her eyes flashing in the darkness.

"I don't know," whispered Rohan, "There's something wrong with Oak."

They turned to look at him as Mara patted the giant's hand gently.

"Fix it then!" she hissed and started to move further into the tunnel. Rohan looked at Mara and shrugged. Mara, unable to believe what was happening grabbed Oak by the arm and started to lead him towards the first scout.

"Why aren't we stopping?" Mara hissed as she caught up with Rohan.

"I don't know," he whispered back.

"Shhhhhh," a voice came from the darkness in front of them. It was Amadyne. She walked back towards them, her eyes blazing.

"We're on a mission, or have you forgotten," she demanded to know in hushed tones.

"We haven't forgotten," Rohan snapped back, "but something is wrong with Oak. We shouldn't be doing this. We have to go back."

Amadyne looked at him as though he was crazy.

"We are not turning back. This is our mission, and we will complete it. Didn't you hear Takash? It's our duty as members of the Faithful."

Rohan wanted to argue, but he could see, through the moonlight that streamed in through the stormwater drains that she would not be moved.

He looked at Oak and Mara in despair, then turned to follow Amadyne.

As they made their way down the tunnel, Rohan could see a single light shining. It grew brighter and brighter as they grew closer. Finally he could see the dim outline of a person seated on the ground, leaning against the tunnel wall.

"Halt," came a voice from the same direction. "Who goes there?"

He saw the figure jump to their feet as they crept forward.

"It's just us," shouted Amadyne with confidence. Her voice echoing down the tunnel.

"Who's us?" the figure asked they waved the light in front of them.

Rohan caught his first glimpse of the scout. He was older than Rohan expected, probably 19 or 20. Rohan wondered whether he'd been a part of Shackle St too.

Amadyne waved casually, as though she belonged in the tunnels. "We're Sun Bringers, like you. We've just been out collecting some of the payments." She held up one of the backpacks. They had stuffed it with paper and rocks to make it look full. If he looked inside it, they could be in trouble.

"Where from?"

They had been expecting this question. Takash had warned them that they might be asked.

"Up top, between Davey and Long St. You know the gardens with the red walls there? The old lady that lives there." Amadyne answered swiftly.

The scout looked relieved. "Oh, ok then." He clearly had no idea if Amadyne was telling the truth or not, but the answer seemed to pacify him. He sat back down and lowered the light. "Can't be too careful. It's worth more than my life to let the wrong persons in."

Amadyne nodded in agreement and led them past their first obstacle.

Rohan watched the scout as he passed. This was wrong. That scout was too old, and too experienced to be placed out there. That was junior members' work. Rohan looked at his arm where they had drawn the Sun Bringers brand. It wasn't a perfect replication, but in the dark it should have passed. Rohan found it unnerving that they hadn't been asked to produce the brand. He looked at the scout closely and found a pair of pale blue eyes watching him return. Rohan hastily turned away, now more convinced than ever before that they should turn back.

"Amadyne," he hissed, trying to get her attention. "Amadyne."

She looked back but ignored him, preferring to continue to the second check point.

Rohan glanced at Oak. He was not doing well either. His movements were robotic, and his pupils were dilated. It was unnerving. Mara looked worried as she walked beside him. Neither had seen him like this before. It was as though he was a shell, operating purely on instinct.

As they approached the second checkpoint, Rohan could see two guards standing at attention. This was what he expected. These guards were well equipped and by their stance Rohan could see that they were well trained. They weren't trained in the same way they were at the Grey, but their methods, brutal as they were, were effective. In order to train, the Sun Bringers often pitted their newest members against one another. Promotion was often a result of winning, while losing diminished your standing. No matter how poor a fighter you were, you learnt to survive by any means necessary. This meant employing every dirty trick in the book. It also paid to injure your opponents, permanently if possible. This stopped them coming after you and prevented others from challenging you. Rohan eyed the guards in their path he could see that they had earned their promotions the hard way.

As Amadyne approached the guards, neither moved to clear the WAY, nor did they ask who was approaching.

"Let me past you idiots," snapped Amadyne doing her best impersonation of a gang member. She was nothing if not confident thought Rohan, while doing his best to look in a hurry.

They ignored her but looked over her shoulder at the lumbering Oak.

"What's wrong wif im?" one of them asked, his voice ringing out across the tunnels.

Amadyne turned and looked at Oak, "Got jumped by some of them snuff chewers," she answered, impersonating his accent slightly. This was impressive, she hadn't copied it completely, but just enough to make it sound like her own.

"He looks big enough that e' coulda' handled em," the guard responded thoughtfully.

"Nah, he's a puppy this one. All muscles, but as simple as a tree stump."

Mara glared at Amadyne's back, but Oak didn't move or make a sound.

"Hmm, yeah, we get a few of those," the guard mused.

"Now let me past," tried Amadyne again.

The guard raised a large knife. It was the same kind of knife Rohan had seen the gangs use before. It was a long piece of metal, taken from an old street sign. It had been ground to a sharp edge on one side and flattened into a kind of handle on its far end.

"Not yet pretty," he sneered, pursing his lips, and blowing a kiss at Amadyne. "First we gotta make sure you aren't some of them Darkhoods."

Darkhoods were one of the gangs in competition with the Sun Bringers. While dangerous, they were relatively small compared to the Sun Bringers. It seemed odd that they were being checked for rival gang marks thought Rohan.

The guards that Rohan had privately named Big Mouth and Mute pushed past Amadyne and Rohan, focusing their attention on Oak and Mara. They circled them like hyenas looking for a feast. As Big Mouth leaned forward and sniffed Mara's hair, he saw Oak twitch.

"Hmmm, I like this one," Big Mouth said loudly as Mute nodded. "You can have the other one if you like."

He reached forward and grabbed Mara by the waist, pulling him close to her, his face inches from hers. "Wouldn't you like it, a big man to look after you."

Rohan screamed inside, but Mara remained cool and collected. She lifted a hand resting it on Big Mouth shoulder and pulled him closer still. She leaned in close and whispered in his ear. "You should know by now, women don't need a man to look after them." With that she slammed her knee into his groin and watched him fall to the ground.

Rohan was impressed, but not surprised. Mara definitely knew how to look after herself.

Mute jumped into action. He ran at Mara, knife raised above his head. But before Mara could disarm him, Oak had seized him and slammed his head into the side of the tunnel. It made a sickening crack that echoed down the tunnel.

"Noooo," screamed Amadyne quietly, the sound barely escaping her lips as she fought to contain herself.

Mute fell to the ground, leaving a red smear on the concrete behind him.

"What have you done?" she hissed angrily, her eyes red with fury.

Oak looked at her impassively and blinked.

"No, no, no," she muttered pacing between the curved walls. "This was not supposed to happen."

She looked at the members of her team, and then down the tunnel. They could see the container now, it was only a hundred yards away.

She looked at Oak and made a decision. Walking over to Big Mouth, who was still writhing in agony she slammed her fist into his temple, knocking him out cold.

"Run." It was the only word she needed to say.

Amadyne sprinted towards the container with Rohan chasing close behind. He didn't even have time to check if the others were following. As they ran down the tunnel it dipped lower and lower until it opened up into a vast cavern, lined with balconies and pathways.

The container, about the size of a small room, stood to one side, standing out amongst the piles of cardboard boxes, steel bins and plastic bags. The bins were rusted and dented from hauling rock and stone out of the lower tunnels. They stood discarded in the cavern along with the other trash. Rohan looked at the place with disgust. Takash would never have allowed the Clinic to operate like this. There was no order, or evidence of care. It was a chaotic jumble of storage and trash.

"Open the lock," demanded Amadyne looking around nervously.

Rohan shook his head, trying to clear his mind as he moved towards the doors of the container. It was just like they had practised. Across the handles of the doors hung a bulky steel chain, linked together with a brass lock. Relieved, Rohan pulled the ball of steel out of his pocket.

With Odger's advice, he knew how to crack the lock. It was going to be easier than he thought.

He reached for the lock and watched in disbelief as the chains slid off and cascaded to the floor. It hadn't even been closed.

Amadyne turned to him amazed. He looked at her blankly. Something was not right. Oak and Mara had caught up and were also staring at the chains that now lay on the dusty ground.

That's when they heard it. It started with a single laugh echoing across the cavernous ceiling. A high-pitched squeal that seemed to permeate their skin with its filth. It was joined by another, then another until a chorus of laughter enveloped them from every side.

Rohan spun around, trying to find the source. At first, his eyes couldn't penetrate the darkness, but eventually he saw it. A lone flame lighting up the cavern, sharing its warm glow with its surroundings. Then, like the laughter, it was joined by another, then another and then another until they could see their tormentors.

They were surrounded by an army. There were dozens of faces looking down on them.

Rohan felt his heart sink and watched as Amadyne, and Mara's shoulders fell at the same time. It had all been a trap. It had felt wrong from the moment they arrived and now he knew why. The wrong scout, the cocky guards, and the open lock. It was all too easy.

Rohan swung the door of the container open. As he expected, it was empty, the coated steel glowing slightly as the light of the flames peered inside.

He didn't know what was going to happen next. But he did know that it wasn't going to be pleasant. In the distance he could hear the shuffling of feet and the sound of gravel being crunched as boots made their way towards them.

Rohan turned to look at Oak. This must have felt like history repeating to him. The fires, the approaching army, the feeling of helplessness. Unlike the rest of them Oak stood resolutely. His shoulders squared and his chin tilted up in defiance. Rohan admired him. He was standing tall in the face of danger.

The Sun Bringers came closer, bringing their torches with them. Rohan could see that they were also dragging chains behind them. They were covered in black soot and clanged as they bounced off the hard floor. As they approached they unclipped the knives that hung on their belts, laughing as they waved them at their prisoners. Between all the gang members coming toward them he spotted a tuft of long blonde hair. It was Asha. It seems like she had thrived in the gangs and was now leading one of the units. Rohan didn't know what to think. They were never close but nor had they wanted to kill each other. At that same moment she recognised him, disbelief spreading across her face. As quickly as that realisation crossed her face, it disappeared, replaced with grim determination. She and Rohan both knew the cost of disappointing the Sun Bringers and it was not a price she was willing to pay.

Rohan looked away, his heart still beating loudly in his chest. He turned to Oak, hoping to draw courage from his friend, but this time something was different. The giant was smiling. Not the smile of a person greeting an old friend, but the smile of a person that has lost their mind. It stretched from ear to ear and forced his lips apart into a toothy grin. Even the approaching Sun Bringers were disturbed by his smile; it was as unnatural as it was unnerving.

Then Oak did something so crazy it saved their lives.

Still smiling, he raised his hand. Encasing his fists were huge chunks of concrete. He had taken the cement from the floor around them and used it to transform himself into a human wrecking machine. He smiled again and charged at the lights that surrounded them.

At first Rohan could only watch. Oak had truly gone insane. There was no possible way they could defeat all the Sun Bringers around them. But suddenly, that didn't matter anymore. All that mattered was helping his friend. All that mattered was being there with Oak.

Rohan screamed at the top of his lungs and rushed to join Oak in the fight. Oak was swinging his fists of fury like a man possessed. Not able to distinguish between friend, foe or even furniture, Oak pounded his first into anything that came near. The result was devastating. Not only were the Sun Bringers running for cover, but the very floor upon which they were walking rippled with the power of Oak's movements. It was raw and unbridled destruction.

As Rohan ran at the Sun Bringers he called a large piece of steel pipe that had been lying on the floor, perhaps 20 feet away. It sprang towards him as though called by its master. Without knowing how he did it, Rohan transformed the pipe into a smooth solid staff that shone easily in the firelight. He caught it with one hand, astounded at his own actions, but focused on the fight ahead. Without thinking further, he swung the staff at the nearest Sun Bringer. It smashed through the torch they lifted to protect themselves and collided with force into his skull. In the same smooth motion he moved into his battle sequence. All those years training at the Grey and the Clinic came to the fore. He moved like liquid silk weaving his way between the Sun Bringers defences, striking hard and often. The tip of his staff now coated in blood as he tore through their best attempts to block his rampage.

Meanwhile Mara and Amadyne stood in shock as Rohan and Oak charged the enemy line. This was not part of the plan and certainly wasn't part of any of the tactics they had tested at the Clinic. Mara reacted first, recognising the opportunity that presented itself. The lack of plants and timber in the tunnels didn't stop her. Even without the aid of her abilities, she was a force to be reckoned with. Like Rohan she charged the line, picking up a discarded knife as her weapon.

Together they pushed the Sun Bringers back, scattering them like a deck of cards. The Sun Bringers ran from side to side trying to avoid Oak's blows and the blur that was Rohan and Mara. They were panicking. They had never fought an enemy like this before. Not an enemy that could call on the elements and make the ground shake with their movements.

Amadyne quickly joined in. She had removed the small glass ball that she always kept in her pocket and was using it to devastating effect. She swung her arms over her head, directing the shiny marble into the body of those Sun Bringers who had not yet entered the fray. They dove as the ball pierced flesh and bone and returned to her a glistening red.

As they crossed the cavern, Rohan thought he could see a path out. He started to work his way towards it, cracking skulls as he stepped forward. It was about that time that he felt the ground beneath them shake once more. He looked back at his friend. It wasn't Oak this time; he was busy fighting three Sun Bringers that had managed to get close.

What was it?

Then it dawned on Rohan. "Get down!!!!" he screamed. "Get down!!"

Somehow Mara and Amadyne heard him above the commotion. Their training had taught them to trust one another completely and they instantly fell to the floor.

Oak on the other hand continued his rampage. He was wild with blood lust and rage. He screamed as he continued to swing his giant fists, blood and spittle covering his face and dripping from his chin. He looked at Rohan with eyes as black at night and smashed his hands into the floor once more. The concrete beneath him rippling and exploded at its edges.

"Noooo," screamed Rohan, his voice unheard by the giant. Rohan had understood what nobody else had. Beneath them ran a series of tunnels, all crossing over one another forming a catacomb. Though they had stood unused and empty for over a hundred years, they were not used to this kind of activity. The shake that Rohan had felt earlier wasn't the aftershock of Oak's attack, it was the first of the tunnels below collapsing.

Rohan realised that after one collapsed, the rest were likely to follow. They needed to stop what they were doing and get out.

Rohan ran towards Oak "Stop! Stop!" He waved his hands at his giant friend, but it was like trying to call a bird out of the sky. The bird couldn't see him from so far down, nor did it care to listen.

He looked around in desperation, more and more Sun Bringers were streaming into the cavern. They had been attracted by the noise and were now shoring up their defences. Rohan looked helplessly at Oak. He needed to stop him, or he might kill them all. Wishing it didn't have to be him, Rohan turned towards his friend, twirling his staff as he did so.

Oak eyed him with suspicion. Rohan could tell he was having difficulty separating friend from enemy. Right now, Rohan didn't know which one he was, but knew he had to stop Oak from shaking the ground. He quickly decided that his best chance of success was to approach him while distracted. A focused Oak would dispose of him as easily as swatting a fly. He waited until Oak was forced backwards by two Sun Bringers waving torches. Oak growled in anger and raised his hands over his head once more. He was no longer intent on hurting people and was now focused on pure destruction. He smashed his fists into the ground once again causing the Sun Bringers to fall to their feet. Rohan moved quickly to close the gap between him and the Giant. Bounding across a concrete slab that had forced itself out of the ground, Rohan leapt into the air and swung. Oak turned slowly, too late to stop Rohan's staff from striking him in the side of the head.

Mara screamed.

Rohan had pulled his strike at the last moment but feared he had gone too far. He watched as his friend's eyes turned blank and he tumbled headfirst to the floor. The Sun Bringers in front of him looked up at Rohan is astonishment. One moment they were about to be swept aside, the next they were saved by their own enemy.

Then he felt it again, only this time the ground didn't stop shaking. He hadn't made it in time.

Rohan watched as whole sections of the floor began to fall away. The Sun Bringers in front of him understood what was happening and immediately ran for the edges. The place they'd been fighting only moments before disappearing before their eyes. It didn't fall in one easy movement, but rather fell in pieces, disappearing into the cavity like paint flaking off a ceiling. Rohan could see Amadyne scrambling as the floor beneath her began to slip. She sprung across the cracks that appeared, lunging from concrete block to concrete block in an attempt to reach the edge of the cavern.

Mara was more fortunate; she had found herself on the far end of the tunnels, closer to the exit and away from the collapsing tunnels. Rohan looked at his feet to the unconscious Oak. At any moment they might fall into the abyss. He reached down and grasped Oak's hand, dragging him slowly towards Mara. The ground lurched beneath them, slipping slowly, like a tree falling in the forest.

Rohan dragged Oak over the rough floor, desperate to move them both. Tears streamed from his face as he strained to save his friend. The floor was slipping faster, and Rohan could feel himself losing control. Mara screamed, her voice awash with anguish as she saw her friends disappearing in front of her. Then Rohan saw it.

To his right was one of the steel bins that had had littered the space. It had been partially flattened on one side, but it suited Rohan's needs perfectly.

"Come." The bin shot towards him, stopping only inches from his feet. Rohan looked at Oak and he made his decision. He tipped the bin onto its side, pushing it up against the still body of his friend. and heaved Oak inside. It wasn't easy, and Rohan had to roll Oak, forcing his legs up as he struggled to fit him in.

Rohan stared at the bin, hoping that this would work. He took a deep breathe to settle his nerves and with an almighty effort he pushed the container. He'd never tried to push anything this big before. Odger had been focused on making sure Rohan had control before he attempted to push objects. Rohan could see why. Even though he had pictured the direction of his push in his mind, the bin struck off at an angle, quickly covering the collapsing floor, but smashing into the tunnel walls to the side rather than shooting up the tunnel. It was enough, Oak was clear of the collapsing floor. Rohan realised why pushing an object was so difficult. It was like trying to kick a ball. If you hit it perfectly in the middle, it would fly with accuracy in a straight line, but hit it slightly to one side, or mistime your kick and it would deviate instantly. No wonder Odger wanted him to focus on control.

Rohan turned back to the scene unfolding before him. Most of the Sun Bringers had made it to the edge of the cavern, but Amadyne was still struggling. The ground beneath her had fallen further than anywhere else. It was a miracle that she was still on her feet. Rohan watched as she sprinted across the edges of the cavern, looking for a way up. Every time she got close, one of the Sun Bringers would force her back. They threw knives and torches at her, preventing her from climbing the walls to safety. Normally she would have made short work of them, but her glass marble was nowhere in sight. She must have lost it when the ground collapsed. He could hear her screaming at them, but her voice was lost in the commotion. Rohan made an instant decision. Without waiting to see if Oak was ok, he sprinted around the cavern, staying close to the walls. As he did so, the last of the tunnels seemed to collapse, falling with an almighty thud, and throwing a shower of dust and debris into the air. Rohan shielded his eyes as he ran towards Amadyne.

"Amadyne," he yelled, trying to find her through the dust. "Amadyne."

"Rohan?" he heard a voice yell to him. He could feel the panic in her voice. It was strained and raspy, as though she had been yelling for hours. As the dust began to clear, Rohan could see why. The ground in front of him had opened up and created a scar in the earth. It was the depth of four tunnels and as wide as one. It had pushed her into a corner with no way out. It was no surprise that she had been scrambling to climb the walls.

She screamed at him, "Rohan!! Help!!!"

He watched as she jogged along the other side of the scar, looking for anywhere she might be able to cross. He knew she was searching in vain. To his right he could hear the Sun

Bringers screaming. What had been a simple trap had been turned on its head by Oak's explosiveness. A number of them lay dead, strewn amongst the collapsed tunnels and the rest of them were crowded into the balconies that surrounded the cavern below. Rohan watched as they started to climb down the walls, hollering loudly. The looked like scorpions descending on their victim, watching, and waiting to strike.

Amadyne saw them too.

Rohan was too far away to help. He couldn't reach her in time. He thought about moving the steel that reinforced the concrete to build a bridge, but quickly dismissed the idea. Any movement could collapse the ground on which she stood. Then he saw it, the container, perched precariously in the corner above Amadyne's head. It was just long enough to cover the scar.

"Amadyne!" he screamed, waving his arms at her, and pointing to the container above her head. She looked at him and understood instantly. Running to one side she gave Rohan the thumbs up.

Rohan took a deep breath and looked at the container. "Come."

Although Odger had never been able to measure the width of Rohan's range, even he would have been surprised to see the large steel box slide from its precarious landing. As Rohan called it towards him it slid along the rough concrete floor, scratching its underbelly with a piercing squeal. He didn't have to move it far. Within moments it started to fall, at first slowly, as though peering over the edge, then with a sudden rush. It tumbled forward ringing like a giant bell. Its edges crumpling like paper as they slammed into the remnants of the concrete tunnels below.

"Oh no," thought Rohan. It was rolling the wrong way. He tried to push it to one side, but it had too much momentum. As it crashed into the floor at the same level as Amadyne it lurched and spun, flinging itself into the scar.

For one hopeful moment, Rohan held his breath.

It stuck.

"Run Amadyne, run!!!" he screamed at her. He could see the container slipping already.

Amadyne didn't need to be told twice.

Like a sprinter at the gun she bolted towards the scar and with an almighty leap, landed perfectly on the corrugated shell.

Perhaps it was the extra weight, or perhaps it was unlucky, but immediately the container began to shift, twisting as it fell.

He tried to hold the container, using every bit of control Odger had instilled in him, but it was incredibly heavy and still carrying some of the momentum from the fall. He felt his control being wrenched away from him like the night snatching away the day. Then, for one brief moment, a single heartbeat, it stopped. It was enough. Amadyne regained her footing and leapt, hands outstretched towards Rohan. The container slipped, continuing its inevitable journey downwards.

Rohan leaned forward and with a satisfying smack grasped Amadyne's wrist.

Rohan hauled her out of the scar as the container reached the bottom of the cavern below. Her face was covered in blood, dust, and tears. She had been certain that her time had come. They paused for the briefest of moments, drinking in the breath they thought had been their last. Rohan watched as the Sun Bringers trapped on the other side of the scar screamed in frustration. Their big plan had turned into a giant mess. It would set them back years.

As Rohan turned away from the scene, he caught a brief flash of long blonde hair standing on one of the upper ledges. It was Asha. Her face was caked in a grimy mixture of dust and blood and there was a long red gash down her right arm. She stared at him, both angry and confused. He was glad that she'd survived but hoped they wouldn't meet again. He glanced at Amadyne and started to run back towards up the tunnel towards the exit. Somehow Mara had managed to revive Oak and although he seemed groggy and confused, he was able to limp alongside. As they reached the grate to the surface Rohan helped Mara and Oak exit, only to feel a hand on his shoulder.

He stepped back to face Amadyne.

She looked at him, her eyes glistening like the first rain of spring. She seemed to be searching for something, maybe the right words, maybe no words. Instead she stepped forward and hugged him. Her hold was strong and intense, but at the same time soft and delicate. They both needed it, more than they would ever care to admit.

Slowly Amadyne withdrew, the tunnel around them silent as Oak and Mara waited outside. She smiled and stepped through the grate.

Chapter 22

"What the hell happened?" demanded Takash as they sat in front of him.

In the days following their first mission, Rohan realised how fleeting fame was. Before setting off for the tunnels, he was enjoying a brief moment in the spotlight. Ever since returning, that perception had shifted. It was clear that the entire Clinic viewed them as failures.

He eyed them in turn, finally resting on Oak.

"And what happened to you. According to this story of yours," he waved his hand across the table, "you were more of a menace than a nuisance. It's a miracle you didn't kill yourself and your team."

Oak dropped his head, his shaggy hair sinking between his knees.

"I don't even remember what happened," he whispered to the floor. "It's all my fault."

"No it's not," snapped Mara, rubbing his back. "I'm sick of you saying that. Ever since we got back, all you've done is blame yourself. None of us knew it was a trap. None of us could have predicted that."

"You don't get it," Oak snapped back. Rohan looked up surprised. Oak didn't snap at Mara often.

"It was my fault. I...I was angry. I was so angry. All I could think about was hurting them, hurting them for what they did to me, to my family."

This was not the Oak any of them knew.

"I couldn't calm down, I couldn't sleep, hell I couldn't even think." He lowered his head further. Rohan thought he might topple out of his chair if he slunk any further.

"So, before the mission…" he paused, looking at Mara. "I took some snuff. I thought it would relax me," he explained. "I guess it was mixed with some pretty hectic stuff, because I don't remember anything after leaving the Clinic."

Mara looked at him shocked. It was as though her vision of who Oak was had been destroyed in that moment. The room fell silent as they watched Mara wrestle with the new information. Though Mara and Oak's relationship was strong, Rohan could see Mara's heart breaking. He had kept this from her. To her it was a betrayal of everything they held dear; he had destroyed her trust. Standing slowly Mara looked at the anguished figure before her and slapped him with all her might. She stalked from the room, leaving Oak to trail after her, desperate to explain.

"Hmph," Takash grunted, ignoring the undertone of the interaction. "A rookie mistake. You need a clear mind for this type of work."

He turned to Amadyne, "Did you have any idea about this?"

She shook her head, remaining silent as Takash watched her. This was a new Amadyne. Ever since the mission, she had lost her confidence. Rohan knew that, like Oak, she blamed herself. They had all noticed Oak acting strangely, but it was Amadyne's decision to move forward, even after Rohan had begged her to stop. Instead of approaching each activity like she had already mastered it, she was tentative and uncertain. Rohan didn't like the new Amadyne. Although he hadn't entirely liked the old one either, he much preferred it to this simpering shell. He knew she was tough and could easily out move any of them. He wanted to see that woman come back stronger, but looking at her, he couldn't tell if she could, or even wanted to.

Takash looked disappointed.

"It wasn't Amadyne's fault sir," Rohan found himself saying. "It wasn't her fault Oak went crazy. That was unexpected. Amadyne drove the mission and made sure we made it to the supply container."

"So you knew something was wrong right from the very start and you still pushed ahead with the mission?"

Amadyne groaned and lowered her head further.

"That's not what I…" Rohan interjected before Takash silenced him with a single look. This revelation angered him more than any other and Rohan could see him struggling to control his temper.

Finally he spoke again, albeit through gritted teeth.

"Amadyne, you were the designated leader on this mission, and you failed in that responsibility. You failed to support your team, and let arrogance and pride override your decision making. I believe that in time you will become a good leader, but right now, you are not ready to assume that responsibility."

Amadyne nodded, unable to disagree with Takash.

"And you," he turned on Rohan, "these people are supposed to be your family. It doesn't matter if you are scared about upsetting them or hurting their feelings. Sometimes you need to speak up louder, you need to hold them accountable. A real friend will tell you the truth, not just what they want to hear. You are equally as responsible for this mess."

That hurt more than anything else Takash could have said. Rohan had never had a family before, and the idea of hurting the first one he'd ever had pierced his heart like a dagger.

Takash sighed, as though disappointed.

"This is also my fault. I placed too much expectation on you and didn't provide enough support. I should have been there with you, to lead you through your first mission. My demands were too high, and I put this on you too early. For that I am sorry."

Rohan looked at him surprised. That was the last thing he expected him to say. Takash had rightfully ripped into them for turning what should have been a simple smash-and-grab into a giant mess-up. An apology from him was almost a relief.

Takash continued, "There is a major mission that we, as the Faithful will be undertaking shortly. I had hoped to bring you along. But after what happened, it is clear that you are not ready. When we leave, you will stay behind."

Rohan didn't even have the heart to protest.

For the next few weeks all that anybody could talk about was the upcoming offensive. Although the mission objectives were supposed to be secret, rumours ran through the Clinic like wildfire.

What they did know was that the offensive was designed to reclaim farmland and harvesting machinery from the North. A few years ago, the North had overrun this part of Central and taken control of the fertile land. For the North, it was an opportunity to cement their dominance over the weaker region. For Central, it was the heart of their food production. The vegetables and grains that could be grown in this area could feed nearly a quarter of the population. This would enable the region to feed the sick, the elderly and the unwanted. No longer would these people be left to fend for themselves. They could actually start to rebuild their society. On a more selfish note, the area had previously supplied the Grey, including the Clinic, with most of their food supply. Veterans of the Clinic spoke fondly of the variety of vegetables they used to receive, as opposed to the consistent, but dull diet they lived with now.

Rohan and Amadyne listened to these rumours glumly, knowing they weren't going to be a part of any action.

Ever since their failed mission, Rohan and Amadyne had been spending a lot of time together. Not only were they excluded from any mission briefings, but Oak and Mara were spending a lot of time arguing, and nobody wanted to be around them. Mara couldn't believe how irresponsible Oak had been and was furious with him for endangering their lives. Oak on the other hand was doing everything he could to win her back. He scoured the vegetable gardens for wildflowers, bringing these to her each day and leaving small gifts on her bunk each night. He even tried giving her some of his daily rations, until she unceremoniously dumped them over his head.

Amadyne, Rohan discovered, was a lot easier to like once she had been stripped of her arrogance and sneering comments. Although Rohan missed her confidence, it was clear that she noticed a lot more than he gave her credit for. She commented on Oak and Mara's relationship, explaining that Mara wasn't really angry at Oak for endangering them, but rather that he hadn't come to her. Rohan looked at her in surprise. She had always seemed somewhat annoyed at their closeness.

Rohan also discovered a previously hidden sense of humour. Although he had glimpsed it on occasion, like when Oak broke their newspaper structure and the time he'd tricked Takash, he hadn't realised that she could be so irreverent. She was a particularly good mimic and had a knack for copying Galvor's accented speech. All in all it made social isolation a lot more pleasant than he could have imagined. Still, it was hard not to feel left out when everybody was excitedly talking about their roles in the offensive.

"What do you think they're talking about today?" Rohan asked Mara as they watched the other members of the Faithful convening in the Cutting Room. It was the only place where they could all be housed, and as such it was used as the meeting point to discuss the offensive. Apart from some of the newest initiates and the retired Faithful, only Rohan, Oak, Mara and Amadyne were exempt from these meetings. Oak had even suggested dressing in disguise to try and sneak in. Rohan and Amadyne looked at each other and burst into fits of laughter. The idea of disguising Oak as anything was laughable. Amadyne's suggestion that they covered him in feathers and send him in as a chicken brought on a new fit of laughter. Even Mara broke into a smile. She had still not forgiven Oak and the idea of tarring him like a chicken appealed to her.

"They are probably discussing strategy," replied Mara, making a point not to look at Oak. "From what I can gather, they are expecting a lot of resistance. The farms aren't just important to Central. For the North, it helps keeps us vulnerable, while making their own lives a lot easier. Not only that, but it's a psychological statement for them as well. By taking the farms, it essentially said 'We can take whatever we want' to the people of Central. I think Edith wants Takash to take them back to show them, and us, that Central is not a second-rate region. We will fight back."

"How crazy do you think it's going to be?" asked Rohan before continuing, "I mean, imagine all those Movers fighting in one battle. It's going to be epic."

"Yeah, but the North has Movers of their own," responded Amadyne. "It's not like it's going to be a cake walk or anything."

"How do you know the North has Movers?" asked Rohan surprised. He'd been so focused on Central, that he hadn't really thought about the soldiers of the other regions.

"I.. I just assumed they did," stammered Amadyne turning red.

"Of course they do," snapped Mara. "Amadyne's right. Besides, you've heard the rumours haven't you?"

Rohan looked at her confused.

Mara lowered her voice to a whisper. "You know, the black ribbon in the Cutting Room."

"What, the one at the other side?"

"No, the other black ribbon," responded Mara sarcastically, "of course that ribbon. Don't you know why nobody talks about it, or why it was such a big deal that you made it so far?"

"Um, not really. I just assumed it was because it was my first try."

"Well, that was partly it, but it was more because they hoped that somebody else might make it to the other side. Nobody has come close in years."

"Yeah, but what's that got to do with the black ribbon?"

Mara sighed, frustrated by Rohan's repeated interruptions.

"Well, do you remember how I told you that the ribbon was put there by a Controller?"

Rohan nodded slowly.

"Well, that controller was called Valdis. Now Valdis, was a bit like you and Amadyne," she gestured with a single thumb at the unusually quiet Amadyne. "He was super smart and a really good Mover. Actually, he was better than you. He was one of the best Movers the Clinic has ever seen. He must have had dual abilities as well, but it was more his control that was amazing. The rumour is that that he could throw a pin through a brick wall and call it back through the same hole."

Rohan's eyes widened. Getting anything to move in a single direction was hard enough, let alone with such precision.

"He wasn't that good," mumbled Amadyne to nobody in particular. Rohan thought he detected a hint of jealousy in her voice. It was good to see at least a little bit of the old Amadyne coming back.

"Anyway, he is the only one to have run the wires successfully," Mara continued.

"And then?" asked Oak, completely engaged in the story.

Mara glared at him but continued, "well, like I said, Valdis was amazing. They would have competitions between all the Faithful, and he would always win. Eventually, he started to think he was better than everybody."

"It sounds like he was," grinned Rohan.

This time both Amadyne and Mara glared at him.

"As I was saying," continued Mara, giving Rohan an unimpressed look, "Valdis started to think he was better than everyone else, and began petitioning to be the leader of the Faithful. The problem was that nobody really trusted him."

This time Oak interrupted her, "It sounds like he was the best. Why wouldn't he be the leader?"

"Because, although he was a great Mover, he wasn't a great leader. He was arrogant and bad things would happen when he was around."

Mara leaned in further, drawing her audience closer.

"Every time he went on a mission, somebody would get hurt."

Rohan looked at Oak nervously, thankful that he couldn't remember Rohan stuffing him into a bin and shooting him across the cavern.

"Usually it wasn't one of the Faithful, but someone from one of the regions who would end up getting killed, or seriously injured."

Rohan was surprised. On their own mission they had seriously hurt some people, and nobody had batted an eyelid.

"I know that happens all the time, but it was usually a guard that could have been knocked out, or a rookie that was running away scared. At first people thought it was a coincidence, but it kept happening. Then it got worse. People from the Faithful started dying. They would turn up dead ages away from the battleground and not beaten or bashed but killed with a single action."

She mimicked a blade cutting across her throat.

"Nobody could ever prove anything but going on a mission with Valdis made people nervous. So, when he was rejected from being leader, nobody knew what was going to happen. At first, nothing did; he went about his training as per normal, took part in missions and was, by all accounts, a loyal member of the Faithful. But after a while, strange things started happening again. Some of the Clinic's remote stations were attacked, stores went missing and a lot of missions started to go wrong. It seemed like the North was always a step ahead. Turns out, it was Valdis's doing. After he was rejected by the Clinic, he went to the North and asked to join. They agreed, as long as he provided intel for them. So, he gave up all the secrets of the Clinic, sacrificed a lot of the Faithful and almost crippled Central. Then, when people here finally figured out what was going on, he disappeared."

"He disappeared?" asked Rohan.

"Well, not so much disappeared, as went to join the North. He even took a few of his friends with him. He saw them as being more ruthless and giving him a better life. I guess his friends saw it the same way."

"I kinda get it," offered Amadyne her voice scratchy as she tried to whisper. "I mean, if you were offered the chance to go North, wouldn't you take it?"

Mara, Oak, and Rohan looked at her incredulously.

"I'm not saying I would but think about it. You get more food, a house and medicine. I don't blame people for wanting to go."

"Yeah, but then you would have to be a Northerner," laughed Rohan easing the tension slightly. "I don't think I could ever do that. The North has treated Central and the other regions like second class citizens for too long. Joining them would be like giving up."

Amadyne looked a little affronted but didn't push it any further.

"Anyway, that's how I know the North has Movers. I know we're special, but I am certain that we are not unique."

Chapter 23

While the rest of the Clinic was engrossed in preparation for the for the offensive, for Rohan and the others, life returned to normal. Morning classes with Odger resumed and afternoon classes with Takash continued to like they had before. However, there were a few discernible differences, the first being that Odger was throwing bigger and more painful objects at Rohan. As Rohan successfully managed to control three metal balls, Odger pelted him with tin cups, spoons and even rocks; whatever was closest. Although Rohan managed to block these out and focus on the balls, they still left bruises and occasionally cuts.

Alternatively, in Takash's classes, Rohan found himself taking on a greater leadership role. Mara and Oak were too mad at one another to collaborate on their own and Amadyne was still reeling from their mission. Rohan was surprised to find that he enjoyed the responsibility. He found that he pushed himself harder than before, trying to become an example to his team. For a while this worked well, with each cellmate taking on the role assigned, but soon it became tedious. Mara and Oak did anything they could do to spite one another. They refused to work together and, when forced to, would find a way to make the other look bad. It was infuriating. Rohan was most upset at Oak. Oak was supposed to be his best friend, but instead was making life difficult for him. When he confronted him about this, Oak looked surprised and ashamed.

"I'm really sorry Rohan. I didn't think anybody else could tell."

Rohan looked at him stunned. "I think a blind man in a cave could tell."

Oak looked down at him. "I mean, I didn't think our fighting was affecting others. It's just that…..I'm trying so hard," his voice cracked as the emotion poured out of him. "I tried so hard to explain myself, but Mara won't listen. I know I messed up, I know I did, but why can't she understand that I didn't do it to hurt her?"

Rohan looked at his friend as the tears ran down his face.

"I just want things to go back to the way they were. I miss her. I miss holding her. I miss…I miss being with her."

Rohan didn't know what to say.

"I…I'm sorry Rohan. I'll try and do better. I promise."

Rohan put his hand on his friend's shoulder, then hugged him. It wasn't much, but it was the only thing he could think to do. Oak hugged him back, his cheeks, now wet with tears resting on the top of Rohan's head.

"Thanks man."

Rohan shrugged awkwardly and grinned at his friend. "If I can help….?" He let the question hang, as Oak nodded his thanks.

It wasn't an easy time for any of them. Other than getting to know Amadyne a little better, the only thing Rohan really enjoyed was his evening runs. He realised how much a part of his life it had become when he missed a night. He felt incomplete, like his day wasn't done. It was freeing to be able to travel in any direction and know that nobody could follow him. When life at the Clinic started to take over, whether that be Odger's classes, Takash's training, or Oak and Mara's fighting, it was a relief to take that time for himself and let his mind wander.

He assumed that Amadyne felt the same sense of freedom that he did. As if drawn to the place, Rohan found himself seeking out the small courtyard where he had seen her practising. He tried to stay away, but something tugged at his heartstrings, aching to see her in action once more. Unfortunately for Rohan, he never caught her in motion, but every so often he caught a glimpse of her through the buildings, or down an empty street. She was definitely still heading out of the Grey, hoping to find the same freedom that Rohan had. In these moments, he had thought about calling out and letting her know that he was there, but something held him back. He realised that he valued his solitude and assumed that she did as well. So he remained quiet and enjoyed the knowledge that they each shared a secret.

As the date of the offensive grew nearer, stress levels heightened across the Clinic. Nobody was running the wires, the Cutting Room was silent during meals and the training yard was busy all the time. As a result, Rohan's cell was condemned to the classroom.

"This stinks" moaned Rohan as they trudged up the stairs towards Za'Niyah's trust room. They had spent the last few days reading ancient battle tactics and theories about moving abilities. While Rohan could see the value, he would have preferred to be practising these theories as opposed to reading about them. It was frustrating to be pushed to the side.

"I know we could be doing something," exclaimed Amadyne as she pushed the door to the room open. "I mean, we are literally doing nothing to help right now."

"We're staying out of the way," responded Mara glumly.

Oak didn't say a word. He just slumped into his chair sighing loudly.

"It wasn't even our fault," continued Mara. "Most of us did the right thing. If someone," she glanced at Oak, "hadn't acted like a complete idiot, we would be on the mission right now."

Oak sighed again. Rohan felt sorry for him. Mara hadn't let up since the meeting with Takash and it was getting old and repetitive.

"At least it will all be over soon," he offered, looking for a silver lining.

"Yeah, and that will be soooo much better," replied Mara sarcastically. "The rest of the Faithful are going to go out on this amazing mission and will forever be remembered as the ones who took the farms back. When they ask what we were doing during this historic event we can say 'we stayed home'. It's hardly the story of heroes is it?"

Nobody knew what else to say, so they sat in silence until Za'Niyah arrived.

"Good afternoon all," she announced through bleary eyes. "Takash is caught up in preparations for the offensive and has asked me to step in instead."

"Does that mean we're finished reading," asked Rohan hopefully.

Surprisingly Za'Niyah nodded.

"Today we have a different role. As you will be staying behind when we leave tonight, you will be required to lock up."

"Lock up?" asked Amadyne surprised.

"Of course," responded Za'Niyah equally surprised. "You didn't think that we left the Grey completely unprotected when we went out did you? No, the Grey is too important to leave unattended. It might be ok for you and the few other remaining members of the Faithful, but we need to consider the recruits in the Grey that don't know what's going on. We need to protect them and ensure their safety."

Confused, they followed Za'Niyah back down the steps and into the training yard. It was eerily silent, as those that would normally be in training were seated in yet another briefing.

"If you look around," Za'Niyah announced, "you will see that there are only two entrances to the Grey: one into the Grey itself, and one into the Clinic. If anything happens, we need you to activate the blockades."

"Blockades?" asked Oak, as they looked around. As far as Rohan could tell, there weren't any gates attached to the buildings.

"Yes, blockades," repeated Za'Niyah. "If you look closely at these buildings to the left and right of the gate, you will see that they are not in the same level of repair as those around them."

Rohan had noticed that before but assumed that it was a strategic decision to leave them in disrepair; they weren't needed, so why waste the energy repairing them.

"Although they mightn't look like much, these building are some of the most important at the Grey. Come, I'll show you."

Za'Niyah motioned for them to follow her into the building on the left-hand side. As they entered Rohan could see that like the Cutting Room, the building had been gutted. There were no ceilings or floors, in fact it was a giant shell. Unlike the Cutting Room, this building had been filled. At first Rohan thought it was pure garbage. He spotted concrete blocks, timber trusses, steel girders, dead trees and plastic drums filled with water. It was a mishmash of materials. It extended the entire height of the building and almost its entire width. The place in which they stood was the only clear area in the entire structure.

"Brilliant," whispered Mara in awe.

"Brilliant?" thought Rohan. This was insane, how could this help them?

Mara, sensing Rohan's confusion smiled in the darkness. "Don't you get it? It's like when Takash made us move all the trash in the compound."

"Huh?" Rohan's voice echoed the thoughts of the others.

"Think about it. If you were going to attack a gate what would you do?"

Rohan thought about it.

"If the gates were steel, I'd probably just move them, or target the hinges." He shrugged, "either way, they wouldn't last long."

"Exactly. It wouldn't be an issue. Now, what if the gates were made of…let's say cement. What would you do then?"

"Ahhh, not much I guess," he hesitated, feeling as though he was walking into a trap.

"Ding, ding, ding. Correct again. You would be useless, but Oak here, could easily do the job."

"Yeah…"

Mara sighed. Clearly trying to lead them to the answer was not working.

"So instead of making the blockade out of one material that any Mover could break down, they made it out of lots of different materials. To get in they would need multiple Movers, with multiple ranges and multiple abilities. I guess they could do it eventually, but it would take a long time."

Finally Rohan understood. It was brilliant.

Za'Niyah was grinning broadly now. "Excellent Mara. You have understood perfectly."

"But how do you get back in?" asked Amadyne, her brow furrowing.

Za'Niyah's face darkened. "We don't. If we need to blow the blockades, it means those on the outside have to stay there. It's a sacrifice that we are willing to make."

The group hushed at this statement. Up until now they had only been feeling sorry for themselves. They had only thought about their selfish desire to be part of the offensive. They hadn't considered the danger, and the possibility that some of them may not return.

It was with a sombre tone that Amadyne asked the obvious question.

"How do we do it?"

Za'Niyah pointed to a series of wires that ran up the inside of the walls.

"These wires are attached to a series of explosives that will knock out this main wall," she patted the structure next to her. "To trigger that explosion, all you need to do is pull that lever." She pointed to a chrome handle that stood alone in the corner of the room.

"From the moment you pull the handle, you will have 10 seconds to get clear. If you don't, the wall will collapse on you."

Rohan took a deep breath. This was a big responsibility.

"Fortunately," Za'Niyah continued, "it is unlikely that you will ever need to trigger that explosion. Even if the mission does go bad, Odger has been tasked with the responsibility of blowing the gate."

"Odger?" Rohan almost laughed. "You can't be serious? Odger is, at the very least, unreliable."

Za'Niyah raised an eyebrow. "Odger has proven himself, in more ways than one, to be a loyal member of the Faithful and as such he should have your respect. Additionally, I believe he is your teacher. Although I admit his methods are...questionable, it is clear that your moving abilities have developed under his tutelage. If I were you, I would reconsider my attitude."

Rohan looked at her surprised. It was clear that many of the other Faithful saw Odger the same way that he did. Entrusting him with an important mission seemed like a bad idea, but Za'Niyah was not opening the subject up for debate. He gulped and nodded his head instead.

"Good. The only reason that I am showing you this, is as a back-up. If the worst does occur, and it won't, you need to be prepared."

Over the course of the afternoon Za'Niyah showed them around the walls and defences of the Grey. It was much more protected than Rohan could have ever imagined. It seemed as though it could withstand a full-scale attack. The walls were thick and like the blockade they were made from thousands of objects, all designed to create confusion amongst enemy Movers. It was an incredible series of defences that Rohan had never noticed. Rohan could tell that the rest of his cellmates were equally impressed, although Amadyne seemed more concerned than anything else. She asked Za'Niyah a lot of questions about defence tactics, the likelihood of an enemy breaking through their defences and the best ways to defend once they made it inside. The old Amadyne was definitely coming back. She wanted to be the leader of everything, and even though they were being left behind, she had found an opportunity to win back her credibility. Rohan admired her for it.

Chapter 24

As night fell, the Clinic was quiet. Rohan lay in his bunk wishing for the sounds of activity. He never realised how ingrained the daily sounds to the Clinic had become. He missed the creaking of doors, the sound of bootsteps on the hard floors and the inevitable laugher that flowed from around the compound. Somebody was always doing something, and it added life to the old hospital.

"Rohan, you still awake?" He heard Oak ask through the darkness.

"No," replied Rohan smiling despite himself.

"Ah, good," responded Oak, "because if you were, it would mean that you were nervous. And I don't like it when you are nervous."

"I'm not nervous, I'm unnerved. There's a difference."

"Really? What's the difference then?"

"Well, if I was nervous, it would be because I think something might happen. But I'm unnerved, which means something is, or isn't happening, and that's making me nervous."

"That's very complicated."

"Yes, yes it is," Rohan grinned. It was a stupid conversation, but just what he needed right now.

"Have you slept at all?"

"Nah, I've closed my eyes, but I can't fall asleep either. Like you I am … unnerved."

Rohan sighed. Sitting here in the dark was not accomplishing anything. He wasn't sleepy, and he knew he wouldn't sleep until everyone was back.

"You know," he started conspiratorially, "since there is nobody here…there is nobody to enforce curfew."

"What about Odger?"

"Pfft, we could hear him coming even if he did get up. That bracelet around his ankle should be warning enough."

Without further hesitation, Rohan threw his legs over the edge of his bunk and jumped out. "I'm going out. Wanna come?"

Oak was already pulling on his pants.

Five minutes later they were breathing in the cool air of the night.

"I don't think I've ever seen the Clinic this late at night," Rohan observed as they made their way to the training yard. "It's kinda creepy. I think it's the whole abandoned hospital thing." As they reached the courtyard, Rohan looked around. Everything was lit in a dull silver glow as the moon beamed down upon them. The rock and cement that made up most of the compound glistened in the moonlight as the cool air left a layer of dew upon their hard surfaces.

"It's so quiet," observed Oak casting his eyes at the entrance to the Clinic. "And so dark." It was true. Without the lights of the missing Faithful, the Clinic felt like a shell, alone and abandoned. Fortunately, Rohan could see the presence of light creeping over the walls of the Clinic, coming from the rest of the Grey beyond.

"Hey, did you wanna check out the rest of the Grey for a moment?" Neither of them had been back to the other side since they graduated to the Clinic. Although it was never home, it was a place they had both grown fond of.

Oak replied with a grin and started back up the stairs towards the top of the Clinic.

Although the Clinic and the rest of the Grey were separated, there were access points where you could cross between them. Takash used them on a daily basis as he balanced his role between breaking new recruits and working with the Faithful.

As they reached the roof of the Clinic, Rohan looked down. From here he could see into both sides of the wall and well into the city. Oak was right, it was dark, but also beautiful. From here

Rohan could see the streets he was so familiar with and marvel as they meandered through the city. It was surreal seeing it from this height on such a cool crisp night. Unlike the Clinic, the Grey still showed signs of life. There was the occasional flicker of light, or movement of shadows across closed curtains. It was all part of their daily routine.

Rohan was so lost in thought, he almost forgot that Oak was there with him.

"What do you think that is?" asked Oak as he looked back toward the Clinic.

"What?" asked Rohan, searching in the direction Oak was pointing.

"Just watch."

Rohan stared into the space Oak was pointing but couldn't see a thing. All he could see was the shape of the buildings and the glow of the moon above. Then he saw it.

"Yeah, what was that?" he asked out loud.

In that brief moment he had seen a light shine bright against the building projecting the image of a person. They waited in silence, searching for it once more. This time it flashed again but much closer. Although it was still a long way away the shadows grew long and painted a clear picture of what was coming.

"Oak" Rohan started cautiously "Go wake Odger. Tell him someone's coming. I'm going to go and check it out."

Without waiting for a response he started to run across the roof of the Clinic, landing easily upon the concrete ledges that separated it from the Grey. He moved like a cat, placing each foot down with perfection, as though drawing the ground to him. He was aiming to make it to the far side of the wall, so that he could head into the city on the other side. Running at full speed he crossed the roofline above the training ground and reached the point where the Clinic connected to the wall and then spread into the city beyond. Without breaking stride he lept. Those watching may have thought a bird had passed overhead, or a cloud had temporarily blocked the shimmer of the moon. It was a smooth transition from one side to the next. That's not to say that anybody could have made this single leap, in fact, nobody had attempted it before; they hadn't needed to.

As Rohan ran towards the approaching figures, his mind raced as fast as his feet carried him. Who were these midnight intruders, and what did they want? Rohan's first thought was that it was the Sun Bringers looking for revenge. They had certainly caused enough devastation and death to anger them, so it was a distinct possibility. As he grew closer, he dismissed the idea. The Sun Bringers were dangerous, but they survived more through implied threat and perception than through outright warfare. No, if this had been the Sun Bringers, they would have come bearing torches and trying to burn the Faithful out of the Grey. This had to be someone else.

Rohan skipped along the hard edges of the dilapidated buildings, careful not to kick any loose gravel or rock that might give away his position. Finally he stopped, his heart beating so loudly he was scared that the intruders might hear. He was close enough to hear their voices, even if it was a muffled conversation. He watched them approach, getting closer and closer, moving with purpose and confidence.

That was the first indication to Rohan that these people were no ordinary citizens. They were too organised and too disciplined to be any local force. It was clear they had training and knew how to move undetected. It had been pure luck that Oak had noticed their light. Rohan assumed that they were making their way to the Clinic utilising a map of sorts. They had to be. It wasn't as though the Faithful promoted the location of their headquarters. Rohan had lived in the city for his entire life and not known it existed. The use of the single flash of light was one of necessity. As they inched their way through the dark streets, the moonlight would be hidden from them, leaving them stranded with little to guide their way. They had no other option, and the risk was small. Fortunately for Rohan, he'd been able to convince Oak to come for a midnight stroll.

Finally they turned the corner and stepped into the moonlight. Rohan swore as they revealed themselves.

Standing below him, not more than fifty feet away was an advance party of soldiers dressed in distinctive black. Even in the soft moonlight their buttons shone, and the steel from their blades glinted. They were Northerners.

"What are they doing here?" Rohan hissed to himself. "They are supposed to be at the farms. No, no, no!"

He watched them, not daring to move as they reviewed the map and continued their march towards the Grey.

He hoped desperately that Oak had found Odger.

He waited until the last of the soldiers passed beneath him and then sprinted back along the rooftops, ensuring that his silhouette was not visible against the faintly lit sky.

As he arrived back at the Clinic, he was relieved to find not just Oak and Odger standing on the rooftop, but Amadyne and Mara as well.

"It's soldiers from the North," he exclaimed through rasping breaths. "There is an advance party, but I'm certain that there's a bigger force following behind."

"Bah," sneered Odger, his eyes looking around shiftily. "Why would they be coming here? If anything they should be at the farms."

"I dunno," said Rohan, his voice still coming in pants, "but they seemed to know where they were going. It won't be long until they get here."

They looked at Odger, his yellow eyes glowing in the darkness.

Rohan saw it in that moment. Behind his sour attitude, his mocking tone and his general untidiness, Odger possessed a cunning mind, and it was running at full speed.

He snapped into action before Rohan could catch his breath.

"Oak, get down to that training yard and start blocking the gateway with the walls from the training cells. Mara, alert the Grey. Hopefully, we don't need them to fight, but we need them to be aware that we are under attack. Once you're done there come back and help Oak with the wall. "

He glanced at them, "We need to protect the Grey at all costs. The recruits in there are too fresh and are not equipped to deal with professional soldiers. Rohan and Amadyne, round up anyone left in the Clinic. Get everybody up and in action as soon as possible. We are going to need all the help we can get before this night is through."

"And what are you going to do?" asked Rohan, still unsure of Odger's actions.

"I'm going to try and contact the rest of the Faithful. They need to know what's going on here. Then I'll activate the blockades. Oak, I need you to hold the gate until I get there. Can you do that?"

Oak nodded.

They stood looking at him, astonished at the transformation.

"GO!" demanded Odger, turning towards the Grey.

Rohan couldn't find a reason to argue with Odger. He still didn't trust the rat-faced man, but his plan seemed to make sense. So he sprinted, Amadyne at his side, towards the Cutting Room. Down and down they ran, jumping over the steps and crashing into the walls of the staircase. Rohan reached the mess area first and yanked the steel triangle off the wall. Even though they all referred to it as a bell, in reality it was a steel rod that had been bent into a triangular shape. He spun and ran towards the barracks, ringing the bell as loud as he could. Behind him, Amadyne started banging on doors forcing anybody left to tumble drearily out of their rooms.

Rohan left her behind. He would wake them, Amadyne could explain what was going on. He ran down the hallways yelling and hollering, making as much noise as humanly possible. The

Clinic, which had been so quiet only minutes before, was suddenly a flurry of activity. Those few remaining members of the Faithful snapped into action as Amadyne explained the situation. This is what they had been training for. All those hours of practice weren't for nothing. They ran towards the Cutting Room to await Odger's orders.

In the training yard Oak was tearing bricks and stone from the cell walls to block the entrance to the Clinic. He was quickly joined by some of the other members of the Faithful. Together they pulled the training yard apart, blocking the gateway in a haphazard mess.

As Rohan re-joined Amadyne and pushed the last few stragglers towards the Cutting Room, they heard a huge explosion, follow almost immediately by a huge crash. Odger must have blown the first blockade. Rohan hoped that he would be able to blow the gate at the Clinic soon. That explosion would have warned the intruders that they were onto them.

As they organised people in the Cutting Room, Odger couldn't be found. Rohan found himself walking in front of them, explaining the situation and comforting some of the newest additions to the Clinic. Looking at the people gathered there, he could see the fear in their eyes. Even though some of them were experienced Movers, he found himself taking charge.

"Alright," he yelled, giving up on Odger arriving in time. "Some of you may be wondering what is happening, some of you may have already figured it out. Let me clarify the situation for you. We are under attack."

He paused letting his words sink in.

"All we know right now, is that soldiers of the North are making their way here. We spotted an advance party heading this way, but we expect a larger force to follow. We need you to protect the Clinic, and those in the Grey."

"But what can we do?" asked an elderly Mover, one that Rohan had barely spoken to before.

"All I can ask is that you do what you can. There is a reason you are all here. Whether you've been here for a long time," he looked at the grey-haired Mover, "or only a few weeks, you are a member of the Faithful. Right now, we need you on the top of the walls. We need to know what is coming, and if the time comes we will need you to fight and defend your home."

The members of the Faithful nodded at him, and like a well-oiled machine quickly they made their way to the stairs determined to do their bit.

From the training yard, Rohan could hear Oak bellowing. He ran to see what the commotion was about. As he arrived, he could see Oak throwing rocks into the gateway, the cell walls coming apart in chunks as he pushed them towards their intended target. His face was sweating with the effort. Mara had returned from the Grey and was assisting where she could. She had quickly realised that rock alone wouldn't be enough to stop the Northerners getting in, so she used her abilities to grow the plants and roots that had covered the tops of the training cell walls. She forced them to grow between the rocks, creating a honeycomb effect that pulled the rock and stone together to form a much stronger wall.

"What's going on?" yelled Rohan over the noise of the brick cracking and smashing.

"They're here!" Oak yelled back. "They are trying to pull down the wall. We have a bit of a head start, but it's not going to take them long."

As Rohan glanced at the gate, he could see holes starting to appear.

They had arrived much sooner than he had thought. Those people on the wall were going to have to fight.

"Amadyne, Amadyne." He yelled out her name, but received no response.

Where had she gone? He could really use her on the walls right now. Her glass marbles would help hold the soldiers back. And where the hell was Odger? He should have been back by now.

Rohan made a decision and ran to the walls himself. As he ran, he spotted Odger shuffling quickly across the yard. About bloody time! That blockade needed to come down now. They were running out of time.

As Rohan reached the top of the wall, his worst fears were confirmed. The soldiers he had seen were indeed an advance party, but now they were joined by a much larger force. There must have been 200 soldiers down there. There was no way that Oak and Mara's temporary wall could last long. As Rohan looked around he found what he was looking for. Along the edges of the wall where there had once been concrete ledges, the thousand steel spikes that had reinforced the structure remained. They had been left there deliberately, designed to prevent outsiders from scaling the walls and entering the Clinic. It looked like a garden of death and rust. It was perfect for Rohan's requirements. He ran towards them, and plucked the rusted stems like flowers, snapping them with ease. He was surprised it came so easily. He'd found himself doing more and more things that were not in the realms of a traditional Steeler. He flashed back to the tunnels when he'd transformed the piece of pipe into a monochrome staff. It was only a small change, but it was a skill normally associated with a Bio-Mover.

As he looked at the advancing army below he gathered up his steel bolts and started to fire them into the crowd below. He knew he didn't need to be perfectly accurate, so threw handfuls of the jagged steel stalks into the air and watched them fall. As they fell, he pushed them with all his might, converting them from falling debris into deadly arrows. He watched as they sprayed the enemy soldiers below. Some of the bolts struck the ground at their feet, sending sparks flying into the darkness, whilst others hammered into the thick black mesh that covered their chests.

They scattered like dust in the wind, unsure where the attack had come from. Inspired, the other Movers on the wall started to hurl objects over the sea of steel spikes and send them crashing below. Bricks and rocks were the easiest and most readily available material. Like Oak, a number of them had the ability to move blocks, and did so, sending down a hailstorm. Rohan found himself being squeezed out of the battle as the other Movers pounded the enemy from above. Instead he took another handful of the spikes and started to pinpoint the leaders of the Northern company below. With each attempt his accuracy improved until he was hitting his target consistently. He leapt from ledge to ledge, balancing on the very edges of the building, working to find a clear shot.

Below, Rohan could see the enemy reforming. They had been so focused on bringing down the gate, they hadn't prepared for the resistance from above. That was changing now. These were experienced and professional soldiers and it didn't take long for them to regroup. They stepped back from the walls, rendering their attacks useless, and instead started to fire their own projectiles at the wall.

The edges of the building exploded around them. In a reversal of fortune, they were showered with metal spikes, brick, and cement.

"Get back!" Rohan screamed as he saw one of the new Movers knocked to the floor with a metal stake through his left eye. He ran along the edge of the building, disregarding his own safety, pushing his own forces back behind cover. What the hell was Odger doing? That blockade should have been down by now.

Suddenly it all made sense. Odger wasn't going to blow the blockade at all, in fact he was probably doing the opposite. Rohan thought about all the times he had made disparaging remarks about the Faithful. Hell, he didn't even want to be there. Rohan thought about the bracelet on his ankle. The Faithful had kept him like a prisoner for years. This was the perfect revenge. In desperation Rohan searched for one of the retired members of the Faithful, someone he could rely on. He spotted the perfect candidate, hunkered behind an intact section of wall.

"Hey I'm Rohan." The idea of introducing himself in the midst of a battle seemed crazy, but he needed this man to trust him.

"Yeah, I know," growled the old-timer. "I was there when you ran the wires. Good effort that. They call me Helmut." He knocked his bald patchy head with his knuckles.

Rohan nearly laughed.

"I'm gonna go blow the blockade, but I need you to cover me. Do you think you can do that?"

"Son, I've been on more missions than you've had breakfasts. I might be old, but I can still create havoc. You get to where you're going. We'll take care of those Northerners below."

Rohan nodded reassured and ducked out from cover. He sprinted towards the stairs that led back to the training yard and catapulted himself downwards.

As he broke back out into the open he could see Oak and Mara still working feverishly on their wall. Oak had slowed to a snail pace, the effort of moving so many bricks taking its toll. Mara on the other hand seemed to revel in the chaos. She darted from one side to the other, placing her hands on her growing plants. They had certainly developed since Rohan saw them last. Instead of a myriad of weeds, the rocks were now encased in strong tree roots that didn't simply hold the rocks in place but strangled them and forced them into position. Her hair was matted in sweat and her face was covered in a mixture of mud and blood, combining to form a brownish gunk.

He wished he could stop and help, but he needed to get that blockade down, he needed to stop Odger. He rushed towards the building and thrust open the door.

He was greeted with a familiar darkness, the light of the moon failing to enter the space. He waited, allowing his eyes to adjust.

It felt like an eternity. Every second he wasted might mean the death of somebody outside.

He felt along the wall, his hands outstretched, looking for the lever that would blow the wall and release the blockade. After a few moments he found it. It was cold to the touch and scratched as his hand gripped the rough metal.

Relieved he yanked on the lever and waited.

Nothing.

He tried again, yanking it up and down, desperate for it to work.

Rohan realised in horror that the lever had already been pulled.

"Noooo!" he screamed, panic threatening to overtake him. What was happening? Why wasn't this working? Za'Niyah had made it look so easy. She told them that the lever was connected to the explosives. It was supposed to be easy!

Suddenly Rohan heard a soft groan. He spun, looking for its source. His eyes had adjusted to the darkness now, and he could see, propped up against the far wall, a small weedy body.

"Odger?"

What followed could only be described as a gurgle, as the blood escaped from Odger's lungs and dribbled out of his mouth.

"Odger?" Rohan looked at him confused. Only moments ago he had been convinced that he was the enemy.

Odger couldn't speak. Rohan looked down to see the front of his yellow robes glistening as the blood seeped from a huge wound in the middle of his chest. Rohan strangled a cry. As much as he'd hated his teacher, he'd never wanted to see this. He'd never wanted to see anybody like this. He crouched down next to the rat-faced man only to realise that he was kneeling in a pool of his blood. He knew in that moment that Odger would never make it out of the room. Odger coughed again, blood spraying Rohan in the face. He wiped it away, not even caring. He held his mentor, embracing him as the light in his eyes began to flicker. Odger, using the last of his strength raised his hand and pointed to a section above the lever.

"The wires." The words were barely audible as his hand fell and his head dropped one last time. Rohan watched as the life disappeared from his body, leaving behind its crippled host. Rohan lowered him to the floor, gently placing his head upon the smooth concrete. He took a moment to stare at the man that had shaped him into the Mover he was. Any feelings Rohan had for him were gone, replaced with a coldness that seemed to permeate his entire body. As he looked down at Odger he stared at the wound in his chest. Somehow, and Rohan didn't know how, but it stirred something in him. It seemed familiar.

He closed his eyes, his mind racing. In the space of thirty seconds Rohan's world had been turned upside down. Something was wrong, and if it wasn't Odger, then who had betrayed them?

Walking slowly over to the lever Rohan traced his hand along the wall, unsure what he was looking for. Odger had said 'the wires' but what did that mean? Then he found it, the wires had been cut. He held the frayed edge in his hands and realised that not only had the wires been cut, but a large section had been completely removed. Who could have done such a thing? He looked around into the darkness but found no answer. All that was left was Odger's lifeless body. Rohan grasped the edge of the wire and looked up to find its closest connection. He focused his attention on the thin copper needles that protruded from their plastic casing, wishing them to grow, but to no avail. The wires were too thin, and they faded away as soon as they stretched. In frustration he pounded his fist against the wall. The concrete wall flaked gently, as his hands scratched its surface.

He walked towards the open door that led back into the training yard. It was almost clear now. Oak and the other Faithful had stripped it of its bones, leaving nothing but a memory of what it was supposed to be. Rohan looked up at the walls. He could see others fighting there, but he could also see that they were being bombarded with rock, stone, and glass. Surely they couldn't last much longer.

With Odger dead and a traitor in their midst, Rohan didn't know what to do next. Then, as though in slow motion he watched as Oak's wall started to fall. He saw bolts of steel slice their way between the rocks and pierce the flesh of those on the other side. He saw two of the Faithful fall in one foul swoop. The rocks that Oak had placed in the gap started to crumble as the pressure of the Movers on the other side pushed them to the side. Still encased by the roots Mara had grown, they simply fell away falling in a shower of gravel and dust.

Rohan knew that defeat was inevitable, but he also knew that he could never abandon his family.

He raced over to the training yard joining Oak and Mara as they battled in earnest to hold back the masses beyond. As Rohan ran towards them, he snapped off some of the metal rods that once held the cell walls up. As he had on the wall, and on his last mission, he shaped them according to his will. They bent quickly into two large hooks, the inside and outside edges shaped into razor sharp blades. At the base the steel curled to fit his hand, leaving the steel pattern as a grip.

"I'm going over!" he yelled at Oak, not stopping to say more.

Oak looked at him in amazement, then nodded.

"Cover him," he bellowed to the Faithful around him, rousing them once more. Rohan didn't wait to see if they were listening; instead, he ran straight up the rapidly disintegrating wall.

Rock, steel, and brick flew past Rohan as he reached the top of the makeshift structure. Behind him, the Movers were giving him everything they had. Their projectiles landed amongst the Northern Soldiers, creating a momentary diversion. As Rohan surveyed the scene below, it was clear the soldiers were on the verge of breaking through. Rohan felt a moment of pity for them. These were the weaker soldiers, fodder for the front line. They were there to take anything the Faithful could throw at them, leaving the experienced soldiers to mop up the mess. Rohan summed up the situation in a fraction of a second, never stopping and never standing still. To do so would have been suicide. Instead he sprinted along the concrete slab that sat atop the pile and launched himself into the crowd of soldiers below. Seconds later, the wall behind him exploded. Oak had clearly decided that hiding behind a failing wall was no longer a viable option. So, instead of piling rocks together, he used his ability to throw them apart exploding the fragile structure in a single push. Behind Rohan the remaining Faithful rallied, brandishing weapons of all types and sizes. Oak brandished giant slabs of concrete as a makeshift shield, and Mara had transformed one of the roots into a fearsome staff edged with spikes at each end. Rohan himself landed amongst the shocked soldiers of the North.

As he landed, he rolled onto the black bitumen that coloured the city streets. He felt his muscles scream at the impact, but instead of curling up in pain they recoiled like a spring pushing him into action. The blades in his hands slammed into the road, sending sparks into the air. In an effort to regain control he swung his hooks into the closest thing he could find. It was the black leathered leg of a Northern Soldier. He heard a voice cry out, but it felt far away, as though it belonged to a memory. The inside of the hook sliced through sinew and flesh as its razor-sharp edge continued on its arc. Rohan rolled to his feet, spinning instantly as the soldiers closed in. With a swift backhand he caught the throat of a stunned soldier. That look never left her face as she fell to the ground, eyes wide in shock. The soldiers of the North hadn't even had time to pull the blades out of their resting place as Rohan ran amok, his blades whirring as he cut a path through their ranks. Their abilities were of little use as Rohan unleashed his fury, his speed preventing them from disabling him. Rohan moved with the precision of a diving hawk, never use two strokes when one would do, never looking back to witness his own carnage.

He forced his way forward, step by bloody step, puncturing bodies and slicing skin with each stroke of his hooked weapons.

The blood in Rohan's eyes and hair was so thick he didn't even realise he had reached the main force until they closed ranks and pushed him back. This broke him out of his trance almost immediately. He had to keep reminding himself that these were professional soldiers and at a whim they could destroy everything he knew. He eyed the long line of soldiers that stood, blades poised and screamed in frustration. His blood lust up, and his thirst for revenge stronger than ever. They had attacked his home, they had killed Odger, and they had nearly destroyed his family. He felt the need to fight.

He turned back towards the Clinic, recognising for the first time the support that had followed him beyond the gate. He looked to see Oak fighting two soldiers and Mara pulling her spiked staff out of the body of another. He had pushed so far forward he had left his enemy as his rear. He had broken the first rule of battle strategy. Don't let your guard down. Thankfully, the rest of the Faithful had been there to support him. He snarled at the line of soldiers and instead turned his focus towards protecting the few Faithful that remained.

As Oak swung his giant fists, exposing his back, Rohan saw a soldier rise up to strike him. Without thinking Rohan threw one of his hooked blades. It caught the soldier in the side of his head, sticking instantly. He tumbled to the ground, his blade slicing Oak's ear as he fell. Oak looked around surprised, but grinned when he saw Rohan.

"It seems that you've learned to fight."

"I had a good teacher," Rohan yelled as he launched himself back into the fray. It seemed as though Oak and the remaining of the Faithful had overcome the scouting party and were now putting down the stragglers. Rohan assisted where he could, gutting and slicing those that still stood.

Finally he stopped. There was nobody left. The members of the Faithful stood apart, exhausted and bloody. Rohan moved closer to Oak and Mara, eyeing the soldiers as they stood resolutely at the edge of the battlefield. It was clear they were waiting for something. Rohan eyed them suspiciously. The victory was within grasp; all they had to do was kill a few rookie Movers and some of the elderly veterans. What was stopping them?

A silence fell over the two opposing forces. After the orchestra of battle, the stillness was unnerving and filled with static. Rohan glanced at their faces, looking for some clue.

Then, he heard it. The sound of boots crunching in the gravel behind him.

Chapter 25

Rohan didn't even need to turn. In his heart he knew who it was. He recognised the familiar footsteps.

It was Amadyne.

He turned to see her striding between the soldiers stepping over the rock and bodies that littered the ground.

She walked with her head held high and her shoulders pulled back, her eyes focused on the wall of Northern soldiers in front.

The soldiers defending the gate stood motionless, too shaken to move. Amadyne was one of their own. They had been there when she came to the Grey and when she progressed to the Clinic. They had seen her run the wires. Hell, they had sat in the Cutting Room and eaten a hundred meals beside her.

In Amadyne's hands she held the wires that had been ripped from the walls of the blockade. They all recognised them, comprehension dawning on the faces of those still awaiting the explosion. For Rohan it all started to make sense. Odger hadn't been trying to destroy the Clinic; he'd been trying to save it. To prevent him from blowing the blockade, Amadyne had killed him and ripped the wires from the walls. Rohan thought back to that moment with Odger. The hole in his chest was consistent with the wounds Amadyne inflicted with her glass marble. Rohan knew he had seen it before, on their first mission.

As Amadyne passed Rohan she looked at him, her eyes lingering over his bloodied figure. In that moment Rohan knew he should feel rage or anger, but instead he only felt pity. Her face wasn't the face of a victor. It was the face of a person trapped in a life they didn't want.

Her chin dropped, just a fraction as she looked at him, her eyes glistening. Rohan wasn't sure if it was her way of apologising, or if she just couldn't bear to look at him. Whatever it was, it broke him inside. He had grown close to Amadyne, thinking of her as more than a cellmate. He wasn't entirely sure how he felt about her but knew that a part of him broke as she looked away.

She continued walking, moving towards the rows of soldiers only metres in front of them. As she approached a tall woman stepped forward, saluting her in a formal fashion. Amadyne nodded in acknowledgment.

"Welcome back" Rohan heard the woman say, "Your father, Commander Valdis is expecting you."

The air in his lungs turned to lead and he felt his heart hit the bloodied ground beneath him.

Amadyne was never on their side.

The moment before he'd felt pity, as though she had been tricked into betraying them. He'd felt, especially over the last few days, that they'd grown closer, and that there was a part of her that never wanted this. That hope was now a pile of ash, burnt and blackened.

The crashing realisation that she'd betrayed them not once, but twice stung deeply. Their failure in the tunnels made more sense. He understood her desire to move forward when they'd begged her to stop. It was her chance to hand over three Movers to the North. She could have walked out of the tunnels once she revealed herself as the daughter of Valdis. Only, it had gone wrong when Oak went crazy.

Rohan stood stunned, watching as Amadyne disappeared beyond the wall of approaching soldiers.

If it hadn't been for Oak, Rohan might never have moved.

"Rohan...Rohan!" Oak yelled, breaking the spell. "We have to retreat. We have to protect the Grey."

Rohan nodded numbly, his feet moving while his mind remained still.

They pulled back through the gate leaving the soldiers in black to advance purposefully forward.

"What do we do now?" asked Oak as they entered the Clinic once more. He looked around but was met with a stony response. Even Mara seemed to be out of ideas.

"We try and hold out," replied Rohan with more confidence than he felt. They had lost, he knew that, but perhaps Odger did get a message to the rest of the Faithful. If they could hold out, and for long enough, maybe they could survive.

"Hold out? Hold out for what?" demanded one of the remaining Faithful angrily. "There's nothing left. Look around us!" He waved his hand at the decimated training yard, that was now nothing more than an empty car park.

"We hold out for hope," replied Rohan softly. "I know it looks bad. But we have to believe that there is still some possibility for survival, otherwise we might as well walk out there and give ourselves up." He looked at those standing in front of him. "I don't know about you, but I have no interest in joining the North. I am Central, and I will defend it while I can."

He turned and started to walk up the stairs to the wall. "We still have the advantage. We know the Clinic, and we have the high ground. Join me......or join them." He glanced at the advancing army and then continued up the stairs.

As he had before, Rohan snapped the metal spikes that covered the walls and held them in his hand. Behind him, the rest of the Faithful trudged up the stairs, looking mournfully over the wall.

"We need to let them in," Rohan announced to the shocked faces of those around him.

"We don't have the strength to keep them out, but what we do have are these walls. By keeping them in, we can prevent them from running through the rest of the city. We can also protect the passageways to the Grey. We need to protect the recruits. So when they get inside, I want us to get in behind them, and block their exit. Can you do that?"

They nodded, relieved to have a plan.

"Good."

"Oak, I need you to destroy the pathways into the Grey. It doesn't matter how you do it, just get it done."

Oak nodded and left immediately.

"You two," he pointed at two of the junior members of the Faithful. "We need ropes to scale down these walls. Find what you can. The rest of you," he grinned, "let's not make their entry into the Clinic too easy. We still have the high ground, and we can still inflict some damage. Let's make sure they earn every step."

With that he turned and fired the metal bolts into the soldiers below, collecting shoulders, legs, and chests in the spray.

The remaining members of the Faithful cheered and using their own abilities started to pelt the soldiers below with everything at their disposal. The battle had turned a full circle, and once more Rohan was defending the walls, but this time there was nobody coming to save them.

The soldiers of the North held rank with such discipline that Rohan couldn't help but be impressed. They moved forward in perfect unison, deflecting many of the attacks from above. Rohan's own hailstorm of metal bolts was pushed to the side like a swift wind through a wheat field. Although Rohan had believed they could thin their numbers from the walls, the reality was a different story. They marched through the gate quicker than he could have ever imagined. Oak and the two Faithful rookies had only just returned when the last of them crossed beneath them.

"Over the edge," screamed Rohan, knowing that at any moment they could make their way to the top of the walls and finish what they had started. He grabbed the ropes and tied them to the rails that ran along the wall and threw the slack over the edge.

"Get going. Oak, with me, Mara, organise them below."

As fighter after fighter leapt over the wall, Rohan raced to the staircase that led to the training yard. He focused his mind and tore the rails out of the walls, forcing them into the corridors, blocking the path to the top.

"Oak, collapse those walls!"

He didn't need to be told twice. Oak stretched out his arms, and with a giant clap the walls crumbled down, brick and cement falling onto the rails Rohan had just placed there.

"It won't hold them long, but hopefully we can get off the ledge before they get here. Already they could hear yelling below as the Movers of the North worked to clear the debris.

Rohan looked back towards the ropes. Everyone was down except for him and Oak.

"GO! I'll catch up."

Oak hurled himself off the edge, his hulking frame stretching the rope to its breaking point. Rohan took an extra moment to view the scene below. Mara had organised the Faithful below into two rows. The soldiers hadn't yet realised that they were blocked in, but that was about to change. He could see them looking back in confusion as others were still trying to access the staircase. He was about to leap off the wall when he spotted something in the distance.

Through the gap in the buildings he could see shafts of light pouring through. At first he thought it was the sun rising, but quickly dismissed the idea. Then he realised, Odger had made contact. It was the rest of the Faithful. They were on their way!!

Rohan scaled down the wall easily and landed with a soft thump.

"They're coming," he yelled triumphantly. "Takash and the rest of them, they're on their way!"

They looked around, as though expecting them to break through the line of buildings at any moment.

"All we need to do is hold until they get here."

The other members of the Faithful seemed to grow in front of Rohan's eyes. The knowledge that Takash was coming was enough to brighten anyone's spirits. There was a reason he was so respected. He was their leader, even more so than Edith thought Rohan.

Oh no. Edith. He had completely forgotten about her. When they had been waking the recruits he had deliberately avoided going to her room. He'd assumed that she would be better off safe in her room rather than fighting on the front line. He cursed at himself. They'd abandoned her inside the Clinic.

He didn't have the time to think about it now; all he could focus on was holding the line and keeping the soldiers from the North inside until reinforcements arrived. Subconsciously he glanced over his shoulder. He hoped they wouldn't be too long.

Fortunately for Rohan and the other survivors, the Northerners were too busy exploring the Grey to fully comprehend the situation. They were going from room to room, methodically searching for any remaining Movers. Door after door they were met with silence. Rohan only hoped that it would be a while before they found the steel door that led to Edith's rooms.

It was then that that someone inside finally understood the significance of the guard at the gate. They had broken through Rohan and Oaks blockade and were now standing on the walls. Like Rohan, they spotted a row of light moving quickly towards them. Even the dullest of soldiers could see that something was coming. Suddenly, the cool and collected activities of the soldiers became aggressive and erratic. They started to knock down walls and doors desperately searching for someone. Rohan guessed it was Edith. If their plan had been to knock Central to its knees, killing the leader of their resistance was a great way to do it. Rohan cursed himself again. How could he have forgotten about her. She meant everything to the people here and Rohan didn't know if the Grey could survive without her.

The Northern soldiers seemed to focus their attention on two areas. The first, the search for Edith; the second, getting out of the Clinic. Though they were a sizeable force, they were no match for the Faithful Army that was on its way. Rohan guessed that this was no more than a single unit of Northern soldiers. They charged at the gate desperate to break through and back into the streets beyond. From there they could disappear into the night.

Rohan wasn't having it. As they approached he fired steel bolts at them once more, bouncing them off the bitumen floor beneath them. They sprang up, slamming into the legs and feet of the soldiers in front of him. It wasn't a winning strategy, but it might be enough to stall them. Surprisingly, Mara seemed to be the most adept at stalling their foes. She grew entire roots out of the ground, and as they twisted and bent into shape they grew thorns that cut with surgical precision. This pushed those inside the walls back further. Oak did Oak things. He was picking up all the rock and brick he had thrown earlier and hurtled them back into the Clinic. Rohan thought that by the time they were done, he might have rebuilt the training yard.

On the other side, they used their abilities to break down the defences with supreme efficiency. They operated as a single unit, tearing at Mara's roots, and deflecting many of Rohan's bolts. Rohan knew that their time was short. They had superior forces, resources, and abilities. As he launched yet another volley of steel he could feel himself flagging. He had been running on adrenaline all night and it was starting to show. To his left and right his fellow fighters were also slowing, some, like Oak, barely able to raise their arms any further. While he didn't doubt their spirit, eventually their bodies would fail.

He watched bleakly as even Mara fell to her knees, her energy reserves spent. He knew the time had come. As if in slow motion they broke through the last of the roots blocking their way and with an exuberant cheer they launched themselves at the survivors. Rohan pushed himself to the front of the group and held his hooked blades up in readiness. He was the last one standing, and he would fight until his last breath.

As Rohan glared at the advancing soldiers he saw a moment of hesitation cross the faces of those leading the charge. He watched in abject curiosity as their courage seemed to melt in front of his very eyes. Instead of attacking him, they scattered like leaves on a blustery day. Rohan turned in time to see Takash leap past him followed by hundreds of other Movers all charging towards the Clinic.

Revitalised, Rohan joined them whooping excitedly as they carved their way through the soldiers, ripping them to shreds like a dog with a paper doll. As he looked around he could see the Faithful taking back the Clinic, ruthlessly evicting the North from their home, and taking back what was theirs. He almost cried in relief. He watched as Takash directed his forces calmly before wandering over to where Rohan and the rest of the survivors stood.

"Anything we need to know son?" asked Takash, his eyes still glancing over the remains of the training yard.

"Yes," wheezed Rohan. As soon as he has stopped, his body had gone into involuntary shut down. He was more exhausted than he thought.

"Edith. She's still in her room. We didn't get her out."

Takash didn't even bother to respond. He started sprinting towards Edith's rooms, pushing past enemies and allies alike. Rohan, summoning his final reserves chased after him. If Edith died, this would all be for nothing.

As they approached the door, Takash didn't even slow down. He pummelled into it, blowing it off its hinges. The door spun away and crashed into the furniture that lined the room. Inside, Rohan could see two soldiers in black. Behind them, Edith seemed to be wandering around, as though unaware of the danger she was in. Rohan didn't know was happening. Why wasn't she screaming, or at least trying to defend herself? The larger of the two soldiers stared at Takash and smiled, his toothy grin revealing a sinister motive. He motioned to his compatriot, and before Rohan or Takash could do anything, he raised his sword and slammed it into Edith's body.

Chapter 26

Rohan gasped as the first soldier grinned in satisfaction.

But it wasn't Edith death that shocked him, in fact, it was the opposite. Edith didn't appear to have been affected by at all. Rather she continued shuffling about as though nothing had happened.

Takash responded immediately. Moving forward he slammed his fist into the stunned face of the soldier and wrenched the sword from his grasp. With a swift movement he killed him, then approached the white-faced soldier behind.

The soldier stood, knowing that something was not right, but having no comprehension. Takash looked at him darkly and slammed the blade into his chest, piercing his heart in one precise thrust. The look on his face turned from one of confusion into a blank stare. He slid off the sword and crumpled to the ground.

Takash threw down the blade in disgust and walked back to the first body, checking for a pulse. Once satisfied the man was dead he stood and surveyed the scene. The light of the morning was beginning to break over the walls of the Grey and Rohan could see the weariness that had settled upon Takash's face. He took no joy in his actions but seemed resigned to their necessity.

Meanwhile Edith continued to wander about, speaking to nobody in particular. But as the room flooded with light, Rohan saw what he had never seen before. The beams of light travelled softly through the old woman, washing out her presence like water on paint. Her very being was corporeal and seemed to disappear in the light.

Rohan looked at Takash in wonder. What the hell was going on?!

Takash spoke without turning to face him. "We'll need to discuss this, but right now you need sleep, and I need to take back the Grey."

Rohan didn't think he would ever sleep again. His mind was wide awake, searching desperately for an answer to what had just happened. After the battle and Amadyne's betrayal he didn't think anything could surprise him, but this was a whole new level. He watched as Takash marched out of the room, leaving to take charge once more.

Rohan didn't know how he managed to stay in control. It seemed as though Rohan's first impression of him was accurate; he was a rock. Alternatively Rohan wanted to vomit. He heaved his body forward and made his way into the light, shielding his eyes as he exited Edith's dark chambers. The only thing he knew for certain was that he needed to find his friends and make sure they were ok.

After checking the makeshift hospital and the Cutting Room he finally found them in the barracks, Mara nestled in Oak's arms as they slept peacefully. It seemed that the night they'd experienced had overcome the distance between them. He considered going to find Takash, but instead lay down and let exhaustion take hold.

The following days were a chaotic mixture of stories and repairs. Takash revealed that the Faithful were already on their way home when Odger's message arrived. They had arrived at the farms to find the fields deserted. Knowing how important they were to the North's dominance over Central, Takash had immediately sensed that something was wrong. As a result, he left a small force to secure the fields and reset course for home. As they raced towards the Clinic, there were more and more signs that something was afoot. The streets were empty and the usual sounds that filled the night were replaced with an eerie silence. Although they pushed as hard as humanly possible to get there, they had been all but certain that their efforts were in vain.

As far as Rohan was concerned, their arrival couldn't have come at a better time. They were able to defeat the North, save the recruits in the Grey and send a message to the other regions. Central was not their plaything.

However, the battle left its scars. Many of the veteran Movers that stayed behind had been killed. These were people who had given their lives for the Faithful and had served Central for a number of years. More than that, they were the friends and family of people in the Clinic. It was with grief and anguish that these heroes were buried.

As Rohan watched the burials, he buried his face in his hands. He hadn't known many of them well, but they had saved his life and the lives of hundreds of others. As he watched Odger get lowered into the ground, his heart broke. Although he had despised the man in person, he had almost single handedly saved the Clinic. Rohan wouldn't miss the sneering comments and his sadistic training methods, but he would miss what Odger represented: loyalty.

Through the haze of grief, the Clinic began to repair itself. The cells were rebuilt, the buildings were repaired, and the blood was washed from the concrete floors. The remaining members of the Faithful lent on each other for support, sharing in their loss. And although the wounds remained, life quickly started to return to normal. For Rohan, Oak, and Mara this means chores, training, and classes.

"I can't believe she was a traitor" exclaimed Oak as they sat down in the Cutting Room "And when that lady said her father was Valdis" Oak put his fingers to his temple pretended to have a brain explosion.

Rohan looked at him glumly. "She definitely fooled me."

"She fooled all of us" Mara corrected him.

Amadyne's betrayal had hit them hard. While others had known her, she'd been a part of their cell. They felt responsible for her.

"Did I ever tell you that I caught her out in the city once?" Rohan asked.

Mara's eyes almost bulged out of their sockets. "WHAT!!"

Rohan lifted his hands defensively. "Woah, I didn't know at the time. I thought she was out clearing her head like me. Why would I suspect she was leaving messages for the North?"

Mara shook her head in disbelief "How did we miss it? The stories about her dad, her attitude, and now her mysterious trips out of the Clinic. We should have spotted something."

Oak shook his head. "We saw what she wanted us to see, most of the time…"

Rohan looked at him surprised. "Most of the time?"

"Well" Oak explained. "Amadyne never fit in with the Faithful. She'd been here for years but didn't have any friends or anything. I think she drove people away deliberately as a way of protecting herself. But there were a few moments, like that time in Za'Niyah's class, or in the training yard when she seemed like a proper person. It was only for a moment, but I think that was the real Amadyne."

"Maybe" Mara offered half-heartedly, unconvinced by Oak's reasoning.

Rohan wasn't sure what to believe. He'd felt there was more to Amadyne, but after her betrayal he couldn't be sure. All he knew was that people had died because of her.

They sat in silence, none of them knowing what to say next. It was only when Takash approached that they snapped out of their stupor.

"Rohan, with me." It wasn't a question.

Mara and Oak looked at each other confused.

Rohan shrugged, and then followed. He'd been waiting for this conversation but wasn't sure if he wanted it to happen or not.

"I suppose you're wondering what happened that night?" Takash asked Rohan as they stood once again in Edith's rooms.

He continued without waiting for an answer.

"What I am going to tell you cannot leave this here. It is too important. It is the reason I killed those two Northern Soldiers, and the reason we had been living safely in the Grey."

Rohan waited, noting the "had" in Takash's words.

Takash took a deep breath before continuing.

"Edith as you know her…is not real." He paused, letting his words sink in. "What you saw, was a recording, a hologram captured long ago."

"A hologram?"

"It's like a video but played from multiple projectors. When you put them together, it looks like a solid image. If you look you can see the projectors here" He pointed to the ceiling.

Rohan looked up, and for the first time noticed the small black boxes hidden amongst the rafters.

If you play them in a dark room, they can look real. That's why you never saw Edith in the Clinic or in the Pen."

He looked at Rohan expectantly and was rewarded with the obvious question.

"But why?"

Takash smiled grimly. "What you may not realise is that in its inception, the Faithful was fragile. When we were young and inexperienced it was only Edith that held us together. If she had died, we would have crumbled. Our enemies knew this, and targeted her, sending Movers, soldiers, and spies to kill her. Fortunately, she was smarter than both them and us. She knew that even in death she could protect us. She insisted we find a way to record her as a way to keeping her alive in the minds of our enemies. This allowed her to remain the target while we grew comfortable in our positions within the Faithful. Before

Edith passed we recorded hundreds of scenarios. We played these to every recruit to reinforce the belief that Edith was still alive and in charge."

Rohan thought back to his own meetings with Edith and realised with astonishment that Takash was telling the truth. Edith had never spoken directly to Rohan. She'd always used general terms, and never come close to touching him. He felt a little embarrassed that a recorded hologram had played such a big part in his growth as Mover.

"But it seemed so real," he protested to Takash.

For once Takash laughed. "That's the point. We needed people to believe that she was the leader."

"But don't you get sick of lying to everyone, and pretending to take orders?"

Takash sighed.

"Yes, every day I wish we didn't have to maintain the lie. But then I think of the lives that have been saved through this deception. What do you think would have happened if the North hadn't been so focused on killing her? Do you think you would you standing here today?"

Rohan considered this, and slowly shook his head. No, they would have killed every last member of the Faithful that night. It was only their search for Edith that distracted them from the massacre.

Takash eyed him seriously.

"That's why I killed those two soldiers, to maintain the lie."

Rohan could only nod slowly. He didn't know how to process what he'd been told. All he could to was stare glumly at Takash.

Before leaving Takash swore him to secrecy, warning him that he couldn't tell anyone what he'd learnt. Rohan understood why, but every part of him ached to tell Oak and Mara.

As he returned to the Cutting Room, he discovered that his friends had already left. They'd likely gone to meet with their mentors and would be gone all afternoon. They hadn't yet found a replacement for Odger, so Rohan sat and watched as the Faithful went about their daily lives.

He watched as they carried out their chores never knowing they were being led by a ghost.

As the weeks passed Rohan found himself watching the leaders of the Grey. Though they publicly praised the effort of those rebuilding the walls and reengaging the defences, he could see that they were distracted. This was especially evident in Galvor and Za'Niyah. He could see the lines in their faces tightening as the days wore on. Alternatively Takash remained as stoic as ever, his temperament as consistent as the rising sun.

When he raised these observations with Oak and Mara, he was relieved to hear that they had noticed the same thing.

"Galvor doesn't even smile anymore," commented Mara as they sat down to eat in the Cutting Room. "It's weird, when we have our classes, he delivers them like he's reading from a book. There's no laughing or fun anymore, it's all serious."

"How about Takash?" he asked Oak.

Oak shrugged, "About the same…although he does skip a lot of classes. I think they must be meeting with Edith a lot."

Rohan's stomach lurched. He hadn't been able to tell them what happened that night. Instead he nodded in agreement and turned the conversation towards some of the more mundane elements of life at the Clinic.

Oak had just finished telling a story about dropping a concrete slab on his toe when they were interrupted by Za'Niyah.

"Takash would like to see you in the upper classrooms."

She, like Galvor looked tired. Her eyes were bloodshot and her normally neat appearance looked slightly dishevelled, like she'd been sleeping in her clothes.

Rohan looked at the others surprised. The last time they had been called to the classrooms by Takash they had been given a mission.

They knew better than to ask questions, so quickly put away their food trays and followed Za'Niyah up the stairs.

When they arrived, they found both Takash and Galvor waiting for them, stern looks on their faces.

"Za'Niyah could you please close the door?" Takash requested as they took their seats. "We don't want to risk any…eavesdroppers."

Rohan could see the strain on the faces of Takash and Galvor. It appeared that their observations were not unfounded. The leaders of the Faithful were dealing with something big, and for some reason, they were going to be a part of it.

Takash sighed. It was clear that he had resigned himself to some sort of decision but was not happy about it.

"As you know," he started, "the Faithful were betrayed by a sleeper agent of the North, one of your team members. This led to the attack on the Grey and the death of some the greatest Movers we have ever seen. This includes your mentor," he looked at Rohan, "and one of the bravest men who had ever served. What you may not have understood, were the full ramifications of this act. When Amadyne betrayed us, she gave away our numbers and our weaknesses. As you saw, the Grey is vulnerable, and with this knowledge, we could be easily overcome.

Rohan glanced at Mara and Oak, trying to gauge their thoughts.

"Now that they've seen our defences, it will be easy for them to attack again. What we faced last time was only a small strike force. Next time they will send a larger army to dispose of us once and for all."

Takash paused, letting these words sink in. This was why they looked defeated. They understood that winning the battle had only delayed the inevitable.

"Can't we simply move?" asked Mara meekly. "Then we could rebuild."

"We could," answered Takash, "but in doing so we would leave behind the only defences we have. We could easily be caught out in the open, giving us no chance at all. At this time, we don't think it's a viable option."

"What makes you think the North is going to attack again anyway?" asked Rohan. "Won't they try and take the farms back first?"

"If food were a vital resource for them, that would be the logical assumption." Takash agreed, "However, we don't believe they need the little they provide. They only ever took the farms as a strategy for controlling us. With another attack expected, and our defences already stretched thin, we have recalled our Movers and abandoned the farms."

"So what then? We sit here and wait for them to attack?"

"No," interrupted Za'Niyah, her voice firmer than Rohan had heard it before.

"For the past few weeks we have been discussing the purpose of the North's attack on the Grey. At first we thought it was merely opportunistic, a chance to catch us with our guard down. But as we learnt more, we realised that it was a calculated strategy."

Rohan leaned forward.

"As Takash mentioned, the North does not rely on Central for its food. Central's real value to the North is the labour they provide to feed their mines."

"Slaves," corrected Rohan as visions of his parents flooded his mind.

"Correct," Za'Niyah continued. "However, it appears that this arrangement is coming to an end."

Rohan looked at her surprised.

"We know that Amadyne had been passing information about the Faithful for a long time. This meant they could have attacked at any time. This prompted as to ask, what changed? And why were they attacking now?

Galvor nodded in agreement.

"We've since discovered that their largest mine is drying up. This means no more iron, or coal, which could cripple their region, and change the power balance. Unfortunately for us, they found a new site. All they need are the bodies to dig it out."

"That still doesn't explain why they attacked us" exclaimed Mara.

"Without the Faithful, there would be nothing to stop them from rounding the people of Central up like cattle." answered Takash sternly.

Rohan didn't know how to respond. It was little wonder they'd been so stressed.

Takash looked at Galvor and Za'Niyah before nodding.

"That's why we need you."

Rohan shifted uncomfortably in his seat. He did not like where this was going.

"The North has never had to rely on Central for food because they were able to trade with the other regions. Now that their mine is dying, we believe it's likely they're taking it by force. This is good news for us. It means that at least one of the other regions has a reason to dislike the North."

Rohan, Oak, and Mara looked at each other nervously.

"On our own, we are not strong enough to push the North back. We don't have the army, the food, or the weapons. However, if we could create an alliance, we may be able to mount a sufficient force to trouble them."

"So, what are we supposed to do?" asked Oak his eyes staring intently at Takash.

He sighed again.

"Unfortunately, the senior leaders of the Faithful…," he glanced at Galvor and Za'Niyah, "…are well known to the North. Now that they know our position, we would be followed the moment we set foot outside the Grey. Fortunately, you three are still new. They don't know who you are yet, or what you can do. This means you still have the freedom to move about without being watched."

Comprehension dawned on Rohan.

"So, you want us, three new Movers, to cross Central, walk into the other regions and convince them to lend us their army?" Although Rohan said this with as much sarcasm as he could muster, the question remained relevant.

For the third time Takash sighed.

"Yes."

End